GRIDIRON GIRL

IRON VALLEY SERIES

TAMARA GIRARDI

wisewolfbooks.com

 WISE WOLF BOOKS 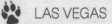 LAS VEGAS

WISE WOLF
BOOKS

This is a work of fiction. All of the characters, organizations, publications, and events portrayed in this novel are either products of the author's imagination or are used fictitiously.

GRIDIRON GIRL. Copyright © 2022 by Tamara Girardi.
All rights reserved.
For information, address Wolfpack Publishing,
5130 S. Fort Apache Road, 215-380 Las Vegas, NV 89148

wisewolfbooks.com

Cover design by Wise Wolf Books

ISBN 978-1-953944-65-8 (paperback) 978-1-953944-18-4 (hardcover)
978-1-953944-62-7 (ebook)
LCCN: 2021948226

First Edition: March 2022

GRIDIRON GIRL

IRON VALLEY SERIES

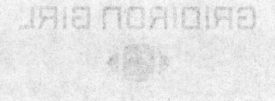

To Domenick, Michael, and David—the quarterback
brothers who inspired this story

I'D RATHER REGRET THE RISKS THAT
DIDN'T WORK OUT THAN
THE CHANCES I DIDN'T TAKE AT ALL.
—SIMONE BILES

CHAPTER ONE

IF YOU DON'T LOVE WHAT YOU DO, YOU WON'T DO IT WITH MUCH CONVICTION OR PASSION.

—MIA HAMM

THE MOMENT WAS PERFECT. SOFT OFF ALLY'S FINGER- tips, the ball floated toward me. No spin. I dug my toes into the sand and exploded upward. My palm crashed against the ball, forcing it down. Hard. Right to the sideline, where two shirtless beach boys scrambled to prevent it from hitting the sand.

Point and match.

Ally hugged me, screaming and jumping at the same time. The guys groaned and rolled onto their backs; sand stuck to their torsos like granulated shirts. We'd spent weeks challenging the self-declared volleyball prodigies and the same amount of time losing to them. Classic poetic justice, we defeated them as the sun set on our last beach day. And on our own terms—a well-placed spike by us, not a mistake by them. But as my best friend celebrated with a high-pitched screech in my ear, I couldn't muster an excitement to rival hers.

"Good game," the guys conceded, shaking our hands. Then one of them added, "Hey, Julia. You hit pretty hard. For a girl."

Heat exploded inside me, but I managed a tight smile. The words *for a girl* should never be added to any sentence. "You too," I said.

His eyebrows crinkled in confusion.

Ally chatted with them about the highs and lows. I tried to join her. My mind ran through the possibilities: "You were so close on that last play," or "You played us really tough," or "Better luck next time." I couldn't commit to any of them though. For starters, there wouldn't be a next time, a realization that lifted my spirits and then deflated them again. I'd be leaving the beach for home. Beach volleyball might be done, but gym volleyball had my name on it.

Unfortunately.

A worthy distraction, fifty yards away in the surf, Owen Malone stood tall above the calm waves, a dark figure against the setting sun and sparkling sea. From this distance, I couldn't smell the ruggedness of his cologne mixed with salt water and sand, but I'd nuzzled his skin enough in the past few weeks to have the scent of his muscled body memorized. The two glorious dimples on his tanned face were also out of view. What was it about dimples anyway? In biology, our teacher had told us dimples were defective muscles in the face as if that could distract us from their absolute adorableness. Temptation tugged at me, and I considered tackling him into the depths of the water to breathe in everything about him.

"You could at least pretend not to drool over my brother when I'm a foot away," Ally said.

Twin brother, to be precise, which made her even more sensitive. I swear. For her sake, I looked away. Until she bent down to dust sand off her legs. With perfect form, Owen threw a football to his stepfather, who caught it with ease. On the erratic pass that followed, he dove sideways to grab it and splashed into the Gulf. He jumped up, shaking the water from his hair and holding the football above his head to signal a victorious catch before he flung it to his little brother, David. David—or Davie, as I liked to call him—caught the pass, and Owen lifted him onto his shoulders to celebrate. His stepdad joined them, patting Owen on the back. His tanned, toned back.

Ally snapped her fingers an inch from my nose.

"Sorry, what?"

She shook her head. "Never mind."

We collapsed onto our blanket and cracked open icy Gatorades from the cooler. The orange liquid chilled a trail down my throat.

"Delicious," Ally mumbled between sips.

"Mm," I agreed.

The sun rolled down the sky, glowing bolder and larger as it neared the horizon. The last sunset in how long? When would I be back to the beach? Everyone, especially my parents, expected me to earn a scholarship to play college volleyball next year, and I'd need to spend the summer after my senior year working to save for books and spending money. Not lounging on the beach with my best friend and boyfriend.

Unfortunately.

At the water's edge, Owen clapped his stepfather's back in a one-armed hug, ruffled Davie's wet hair, and jogged toward us shirtless, his own hair curling at the ends. With water droplets across his chest and shoulders. And the orange, purple, and pink hues of the sunset behind him. I might have let out a tiny groan at the sight.

"Give me a break," Ally mumbled, then called to her brother, "Towel off over there, away from our stuff."

Owen fell onto the blanket beside me, tickling my neck with his wet nose.

"Remind me not to chug Gatorade with you two around," Ally said. "I'm gonna be sick."

Without taking his gaze from mine, Owen responded, "Then you better look away because I'm about to kiss my girlfriend."

"Is that right?" I whispered.

Owen's lips were wet and salty, and they moved over mine with a soft rhythm perfected over six months together. I traced my hand along the back of his arm, the tightness of his triceps impossible to resist. When we broke apart, I rested my forehead against his for a long moment. He sighed and smiled before repositioning himself behind me on the blanket.

"Someday, I'm gonna get you alone," he whispered into my hair.

"Someday, I'm gonna let you," I teased right back.

I leaned into him while we bid the sun adieu in silence. My pulse quickened with anticipation as the golden edge kissed the surface of the Gulf and tucked itself in for the night. The three of us sat in silence, appreciating the breeze on our faces and the colorful view.

"I can't believe vacation's over," Ally finally said.

"Me either." The last four weeks with my best friend, my boyfriend, and their family sparkled in my memory. Lazy afternoons pressed against Owen in a hammock tied between two palm trees. Early morning walks in the surf with Ally before the heat of the day gripped the coast. Roasting marshmallows at beach bonfires, and devouring spicy fries, seafood, and all the deliciousness we could find on St. Pete Beach.

And it was all over.

"My sister's looking smug, so can I assume you girls won?" Owen said.

I kissed his cheek. "We did indeed."

"Nice job."

"I don't want to brag," Ally said in a voice that declared she was totally bragging, "but no team in the conference will be able to touch us this year."

"The season hasn't even started yet," Owen countered. "You don't want to be too confident. You never know what'll happen."

Owen spoke from experience. The top receiver on our football team, he mourned the recent loss of the team's quarterback, Chucky Bass, to a torn ACL. A season with potential had come crashing down in one moment. An entire legacy was at stake. For a decade, one of my three brothers had quarterbacked the playoff-bound Iron Valley Vikings. The results—like the many end tables, bookshelves, and windowsills in my house covered with trophies—were telling. The Vikings won the conference seven of the ten years. Each of my brothers had been named an All-American and gone on to play college ball, along with about half of their teammates.

"I get that nobody can replace Bass, but has anyone stepped up to show any promise at summer workouts?"

Owen shook his head. "Not even close. Apparently, our options are to throw more picks than receptions, go Wild Cat every play, or completely reinvent the game of football."

"Is the cat thing bad?" Ally asked.

Owen and I exchanged a look. We tried not to make fun of her cluelessness. Not every girl grew up being quizzed about *Xs* and *Os* on the back of restaurant placemats, spending rainy afternoons in a basement film room, and playing backyard football on a field painted with their family's name.

Three quarterback brothers. What could I say?

"What?" Ally protested. "I know the first and the third things are bad. Give me some credit."

I wrapped my arms around Owen's neck. "Something will work out. You still have camp."

He didn't look convinced.

"This is depressing," Ally said. "And I'm hungry. Let's go eat."

She suggested our favorite waterfront dive with delicious chicken wings and spicy fries. Walking down the beach, Ally rambled about how amazing our volleyball season would be.

Beside us, the color of the water darkened with the sky. It was Owen's senior year too. After two years of catching the well-placed passes of my brother Jake, he'd become accustomed to success. Knowing success and then losing it was much harder than never knowing it at all. At least, that's how it felt for me, and I was only a fan of the team—not a player. My brothers sacrificed parties, girls, grades, and just about everything high school offered to build a legacy on the turf. A legacy that, in a matter of months, might be altered forever.

While expectations for the football team were low, on the volleyball court they were high yet attainable. The six starters—including me at outside hitter and Ally at setter—moved around the court in a perfect rhythm of passes, sets, and spikes. We knew each other. Anticipated each other's decisions.

Maybe that's why volleyball felt too easy. Too safe. Despite knowing how the team counted on me, faking something that wasn't in my heart was so not my style.

CHAPTER TWO

PROCRASTINATION IS ONE OF THE MOST COMMON AND DEADLIEST OF DISEASES, AND ITS TOLL ON SUCCESS AND HAPPINESS IS HEAVY.
—WAYNE GRETZKY

I NEEDED TO TELL ALLY—THE LIKELY CAPTAIN OF OUR state championship–contending volleyball team—that volleyball didn't feel the same. But she'd tell me to suck it up and play.

That it was a slump.

It didn't feel like a slump.

After a shopping spree with her to celebrate my eighteenth birthday, I vowed I'd break the news over a cupcake. Let the sugar soften her up a bit.

Ally pulled her Honda into the driveway of our brick colonial, which stood silent. Empty. These days I was essentially an only child. I'd never admit it to them, but I desperately wanted all my brothers to be home again—fighting with me over time in the bathroom, attempting to swindle me into doing their chores, making our mother laugh.

She didn't laugh nearly as much around me.

Juan was the quarterback coach of his alma mater, Braddock College, a small, Christian school about an hour away. Jorge would be starting as a fifth-year senior at a school in Jacksonville, Florida—that is, if he managed to stop chasing girls enough to actually go to class. And Jake was a red-shirt freshman at Western Pennsylvania State. Although Juan and Jake were close by, football commanded their time. I wondered if they were as disinterested about their upcoming practices that week as I was about mine.

Probably not.

Maybe my parents would drive down to Western Penn so we could have my birthday dinner with Jake tonight. Even if he wasn't free, he would clear his schedule for me. Unless that schedule included football. In our family, football came first.

"It's your birthday, Jules," Ally said. "Smile."

She bounced toward the house like Tigger as I trailed behind resembling Eeyore. Until I crossed the threshold and a chorus of "Surprise!" erupted. There at the front of a thick crowd of family and friends stood Juan and Jake. Juan held a tablet with Jorge's smiling face standing on a Florida beach. I laughed and cried, throwing myself into Jake's arms.

"I can't believe you're here!"

Juan hugged us both, lifting the screen above our heads, so Jorge could virtually join the embrace from nine hundred miles away.

"I missed you guys."

"We missed you too, Little J," Juan said.

When we separated, cameras from all angles snapped photos, and we stood in a line, smiling for each one of them. The Medina quarterbacks and their baby sister. Their arms were like shields protecting me from every fear that had plagued me in the last few days.

After the photo op, they huddled in a corner, chatting about practices, plays, and competitors while I greeted the rest of my guests, my *abuelita* first.

"How's the political campaign going?" I asked when I hugged her. She'd spent the summer knocking on doors to earn votes for the Iron Valley School District Board—her first attempt at politics, or as she would describe it, giving back to the community that gave so much to her.

She waved the question away and kissed my cheek. "Fine. I love the education, and the people know this. They will love me back in November."

"I'm sure they will." As if there was any other choice with Ita.

"That young man of yours, *mi cielo*," Abuelita said. "He is looking handsome today in that white linen shirt."

I laughed. "It's a polo, Ita."

"It's lovely. Is his *abuelo* single? A widower perhaps? I don't recall knocking on his door."

"Abuelita!" But my pretend outrage didn't slow my grandmother. She fanned herself on her way to Owen, looped her arm in his, and whispered in his ear. I wasn't convinced I wanted to know what she was saying. I might've only had one living grandparent, but she had more sass and personality than all of my friends' grandparents combined.

While she chatted up my boyfriend, who happened to be nearly sixty years her junior, I thanked my aunts, uncles, cousins, neighbors, teammates, and friends for coming.

At the tail end of the pleasantries, I felt an arm around my waist. "Happy birthday, babe," Owen whispered in my ear over the shouts and laughter.

I gave him a peck on the lips. "I thought Abuelita had you cornered. Wasn't sure I could compete."

"Abuelita loves me," he said.

"She does indeed. Especially in that white polo."

Owen smoothed the front of his shirt and popped his collar. Despite his silliness, he looked good. "And what do you think of it?"

I offered him a flirty shrug as if the tingling throughout my body every time he was close didn't exist.

"Uh-huh." He brushed his fingertips against my palm. "Well, I have no problem saying you look good in that dress."

"You did pick it out," I said, and a sudden image of what it might be like to let him take it off had my heart beating as hard as if I'd sprinted the bleachers.

"Looking good, birthday girl," said Chase Creel, Iron Valley's kicker and the youngest son of our overbearing school board president.

Owen draped an arm over my shoulder. "Back it up, Kicker Creel."

The rest of the guys laughed, and Jake slipped between me and Owen, pushing my boyfriend's arm away. "Maybe you should back it up, Casanova. That's my baby sister."

The teasing and the laughter continued as my parents ushered everyone outside to our pavilion where the food waited and considering their audience—a group of high school athletes—the ushering didn't take much effort. The football and volleyball teams dove in, piling slices of cheese quesadillas with homemade guacamole and salsa onto their plates alongside plantains and spicy chicken.

Dad tended to the lechón, a Puerto Rican tradition. The whole pig roasted on a spit over an outdoor oven my late *abuelo* had built for occasions like these. As my friends and family swiped food from the tables, pride overwhelmed me. Eating at my house was a celebration even when it wasn't someone's birthday. Dad's parents had immigrated from Puerto Rico and Mexico and met here. Mom's parents were American with Italian ancestry.

The food in our house...it was good.

With three boys and a girl with a boy's appetite, my parents cooked in bulk. And in stages. The football and volleyball teams abandoned the food tables with a few morsels left, but my mother and aunt scooped additional trays of warm quesadillas from under the table and swapped out the old for the new. Then they added fresh, homemade margherita pizzas. The boys didn't notice. They were too busy watching Dad and Juan carve the pig. A series of shouts told me they'd beheaded Porky. Before long, the boys were back at the table, looking for seconds.

"You should cater our practices, Mr. and Mrs. Medina," Chase said.

"My days catering for the football team are over," my mom said, pride in her voice. "The volleyball team is my sole focus now."

"Then I'll be at more games this year." Chase laughed in that charming way some teenage boys seem to have with older women. Although my mother had enough practice with my brothers' friends over the years to identify the tactic, she still ate up every word.

"Who wants to lose?" Jake yelled, and the guys scrambled onto the field behind our house with a bag of footballs. Ally followed suit, grabbing a few volleyballs and leading the team to the sand court my parents installed when I was ten. I felt a greater urge to jog onto the field than the court. Dread settled on me like a weight that was strong enough to push my feet inches into the ground. Instead of joining in,

I found my way to the tree swing and watched everyone else.

The sounds of my childhood filled the open space—arguments about whether the ball was in or the receiver was out, cheering over touchdowns and spikes. Even the adults joined in. My mom and aunts jumped on the volleyball court, and my father and uncles drafted teams for a football tournament. My brothers, of course, played quarterback, but my father threatened anyone there with instant mortality if they tackled one of his college-playing/coaching sons. When Juan's team eliminated Jake's from the tournament, he came to sit with me.

"You good, Little J?" he asked.

"Eh," I shrugged. No use lying to him.

"Talk."

I told him about volleyball. While I couldn't bring myself to tell Ally any of it, with Jake, the words tumbled out.

"You could be burned out," Jake suggested, still stuffing his face. "It happens a lot. I see some of the guys coming in like this. All they ever wanted was to play college ball. Now they're division one and they don't feel it anymore."

Maybe that's what it was. But did the passion ever come back? That competitive drive had fueled me for so long that I wasn't sure who I was without it.

"It's only a couple months," he said, but a couple months felt like forever. And then there was still college if I continued on this path to a scholarship.

"I don't think I can do it."

"You mean...you want to quit?"

Quit was an ugly word in the Medina household. Winners never quit, and Medinas were winners. Period.

"Jules?"

"Maybe..."

Jake whistled. "That's big. You sure about this?"

If I followed my gut, yes. If I let my head contribute an opinion, things became muddled.

"Have you talked to Mom and Dad?"

"No," I said emphatically.

He snorted. "Can you wait until I leave to break the news to Mama Coach?"

"I was hoping you'd tell her for me," I teased. Telling my mother, who happened to be the head coach of my volleyball team, invoked enough fear in me that I considered playing simply to avoid the conversation.

"As Abuelita would say, *para nada*!" My brother laughed.

So much for solidarity among the Medina kids.

"And here I was thinking you could break the news to Ally too. She's always been a little sweet on you."

He puffed out his chest. "Who hasn't been?"

I pushed him, and he almost fell off the swing. "Can we focus on me, Narcissus? What if I shouldn't leave the team? What if I regret it?"

"Why play if your heart's not in it?" he said quietly. "Life's too short. You need to spend it doing what you're passionate about."

He was right. Of course. My brother, the zen master. Juan was the leader, Jorge the clown, but Jake was the thinker.

Me? I was the *girl*.

"You sticking around?" I asked, hopeful.

He scowled, but his demeanor was playful. "I'm not leaving you alone with that receiver. I see the way he looks at you."

"He's my boyfriend, Jake. He's supposed to look at me like that."

Jake made a "yuck" sound complete with trembles of physical disgust. "You're my sister, Julia. Nobody's supposed to look at you like that. I still can't believe Mom and Dad let you spend a month with him at the beach."

"I was with Ally too. And their family."

Jake's expression read a simple word: *bullshit*. I didn't blame him. Truth was I couldn't believe my parents had let me go either. But my brothers spent the summer living on campus and my parents were both traveling for work conferences, so staying with Ally's family seemed natural. And pretty awesome.

"How are things with you and Lover Boy?"

"Owen. His name is Owen."

"I know his name," Jake said.

"You liked him just fine when he boosted your stats last year."

"Please. I boosted his stats."

Jake's laugh told me I had executed the proper *bullshit* expression myself. "Fine. Great receiver. Not good enough for my baby sister."

Not that anyone ever could be in my brothers' eyes. But in mine, Owen fit me like the perfect pair of Spandex. The looks and physical stuff were there for sure, but Owen saw me as more than the tomboy I was. He didn't mind my athletic shorts instead of heels. He never judged my huge appetite. If anything, taking down a burger and fries with a side of wings impressed Owen.

I could be myself around him, and that was a beautiful thing.

I rested my head on Jake's shoulder and listened to tales of his summer practices, formations he loved and plays he hated, what he thought of his coaches, and on and on. I could listen to my brothers talk football for hours, which was good because that's mostly what they did. Like a pink sponge in a blue sea, I soaked it all in.

CHAPTER THREE

🏈

EMBRACE THE OPPORTUNITY, NO MATTER WHAT IT IS.
LOOK AT EVERYTHING IN A POSITIVE LIGHT.
—JULIE ERTZ

GUESTS TRICKLED AWAY, LEAVING A PILE OF UNOPENED
presents and a lineup of football players reminiscing about their days together on the gridiron. Ally had roped the volleyball team into some craft project that she generously excused me from since it was my birthday. I joined the guys around the firepit. Most of them had been Jake's teammates, but none had played with our oldest brother, Juan. He initiated the family tradition of slinging touchdowns as the first Medina quarterback, and most of the guys at my party, like me, had been kids watching Juan on Friday nights in awe. That awe, exaggerated by the firelight, manifested on their faces as he shared the stories I'd heard so many times before.

But I still listened to every word. When Juan finished a tale of a playoff game reminiscent of the first Eli Manning New York Giants Super Bowl win with wild catches and chaotic plays in the last drive, everyone looked equal parts inspired and eager to play.

"One more game?" Kicker Creel asked.

He tossed a football to Juan, but the ball was too high for my brother to catch it from his seat around the fire. Everyone booed, and Jake yelled, "Clearly not a Medina!"

The guys organized themselves into two teams while I switched on the spots that weren't as bright as Friday night lights but still did the trick. By the time they stopped fighting over who belonged where, Juan had to head back to campus to break down the doors of his players' dorms and check for drugs, drinks, and girls.

"C'mon, man," Jake shouted.

"Curfew," Juan said. Considering he coached at a Christian college, 'nuff said. He kissed my cheek and headed into the house to collect a package of food, clean laundry, and cash, no doubt, from our parents and Abuelita.

"That's it then, guys," Owen said.

Jake stretched his shoulder. "It's cool. Steady QB time."

I snagged the ball from Jake. "No way. You've been throwing all night. Dad will kill you if you overwork your arm. I'm in."

Chase, who was set to be on my team, raised his hand. "Anyone up for a trade?"

I threw the ball and hit him in his gut, which triggered a cacophony of laughter and jeering from the other guys.

"I'll take that trade," Owen said and pushed a hunched-over Chase from my team to Jake's. "You can throw me touchdowns anytime, babe." He kissed me, and Jake emphatically covered his eyes.

"My sister, dude."

The kiss wasn't romantic but territorial in some weird manly way. I supposed I should have been grateful Owen didn't pee on me.

Jake changed the subject by yelling at me for injuring his players. "We get first ball as a penalty."

"Not a chance," I yelled back, and we huddled up. My team consisted of Owen; a linebacker the team affectionately called Square since he was super serious off the field and resembled the shape of, well, a square; and a running back everyone called "D" although I had no idea what that stood for. Not a bad team for backyard ball.

Jake's team included him, the kicker, a lineman who had the kind of inflexibility that could benefit from an unlimited membership to Yogis R Us, and a tight end. We *so* had this.

Jake whispered to his team with his back to me, but he could have been shouting. I knew him *and* his tendencies. For instance, he'd hate losing a receiver like Owen for a kicker like Chase. Good kickers could make or break close games for organized football teams. Everyone knew that, but in backyard football, if someone kicked the ball it was usually out of anger, not strategy.

Otherwise, Jake liked trick plays. Lots of them.

Square deferred to his offensive teammates when we took the ball first. Owen suggested a quick pass. From five yards out.

"Owen, I can throw the ball farther than five yards," I said.

"I know, babe, but I don't want you to get hit."

We weren't even playing tackle.

We lined up. Square snapped the ball to me. Jake jumped up and down, waving his hands in my face at the line of scrimmage. Jake's team covered my guys tight, so I pump faked and ran, securing three yards before my brother dropped me.

He knocked me down playfully, but Owen snatched him up. "What the hell?"

"It's fine," I said, trying to defuse the tension.

"Yeah, she's fine, Romeo," Jake said. He pushed his shoulder into Owen's and trotted back to his huddle.

"You okay?" Owen asked.

I slapped the ball and nodded. I was *fine*. Perhaps I should convey a lesson on the differences between real live girls and china dolls.

"D, go ten yards and then come back to me," I said, getting my head back in the game. "Owen, run a quick slant. Square, I'll fake a handoff to you, then get open a few yards down field."

Jake ran his mouth, but I didn't hear the taunts. Like Juan taught me when I was a kid, I read the matchups in front of me. My receiver against Jake's kicker. My running back against Jake's lineman. Either way, I liked my odds. Owen was the first to break free, but Chase actually kept up with him.

D, on the other hand, beat the lineman with room to spare. So much room, I felt butterflies when I set my feet. I couldn't mess this up. Focusing on the Iron Valley Football logo on D's T-shirt, I let the rest of the field fade away. The ball rolled off my fingers like a whip, zipping through the air and right into D's chest. He bobbled it but salvaged the catch and ran for a touchdown. I smacked Jake's butt, the Medina family way of saying you got owned, and ran to D to celebrate.

He rubbed his chest and coughed. "You knocked the wind out of me, Medina."

"Shut up." I had no interest in taking any more *for-a-girl* crap.

"No. Really." He nodded at me with respect in his eyes.

Heat filled my cheeks. "Don't get soft on me, D."

But *I* felt a little soft inside. Respect. For *my* pass. My strength. My accuracy. I kind of wanted to hug him.

With Square on our team, we crushed Jake's offense and got the ball back quickly.

"I have a lineman and a kicker!" Jake said, pounding the ball into the ground. "They'd rather swat or kick the ball than catch it."

"Then run it," I called over my shoulder on my way back to the huddle, not exactly blaming him. I wouldn't want his team either. On the third play of that drive, I threw the ball ten yards to Owen for a touchdown. For my team, the motions clicked, and the score climbed.

"One more drive," Mom called from the back porch. "It's getting late."

Volleyball camp was starting in two days, and Mom was all about training your body for a necessary "upcoming sleep pattern shift". Which meant she wanted me in bed. Soon. The laughter and adrenaline from the backyard game seeped out of me as if my mother extended an imaginary needle across the field and popped my idealistic bubble. Jake caught my eye, but before he could go all brotherly on me, I tossed him the ball. "You gonna let this end in a shutout?"

He shook his head with a smirk. "Who let you play?"

We huddled up. "It'll be a trick play," I whispered.

"He doesn't have the personnel to trick anyone," Owen said with a laugh.

True story, but I knew he'd try anyway. "Watch for the hook and lateral. It's his signature backyard play."

At the line, I danced in my brother's face. One of his least favorites. The chicken dance. Complete with the annoying tune.

We covered Kicker Creel well, so with nowhere else to go, Jake dumped the ball to his lineman who moved like a tank down the field. I pretended to follow but didn't fully commit. No way my brother would leave the final play of a game to a lineman. Sure enough, the lineman pulled up and lateraled the ball to my brother. For a lineman, the throw wasn't bad. I mean, if a tank threw a football, it would probably look like that. Jake moved his body in position to cradle the ball, but I stepped in the passing lane, snatched the ball out of the air, and took it to the house.

Jake collapsed on the grass and groaned while we cheered. "My little sister destroyed my reputation."

"Don't flatter yourself," I said, dropping my elbow into his chest and pushing a huff of air from his lungs. "You didn't have much of a reputation to begin with."

CHAPTER FOUR

SETBACKS HAVE AN UPSIDE; THEY FUEL NEW DREAMS.
—DARA TORRES

LATER THAT NIGHT, SHOWERED AND READY TO CATCH
up on summer television Ally and I had been too busy to watch in
Florida, I propped up my pillow to find a folded piece of notebook
paper with my name scribbled on it. I knew the handwriting instantly.
I hugged it to my chest and jumped off the bed. I couldn't believe
he'd managed to sneak it there!

Every night we were in Florida, Owen had slipped a torn sheet
exactly like this one under my pillow. Inside was always a simple line
about the day—what he'd loved the most. The first note had had me
giddy and awake the whole night. It had said, *Showing you around
my second home, the place I've been coming to since I was a kid, was
my favorite thing about today.* The moment I'd read it, I wanted to
rush across the hall into the room he shared with Davie and hug him
on the spot. Instead, I reminded myself of the walk we'd taken that
afternoon, our fingers intertwined, him introducing me to the other
families staying at the condo. How he'd wrapped his arms around me
and held me to his chest as we watched the calm Gulf waves slap at
the shore. The palm trees, water, and sunshine had made my stomach

flutter, but despite all of the beauty, what really made me feel as if I might fly away in the breeze at any moment was the realization I'd be there for four weeks.

With Owen.

Finding that note under my pillow our first night increased my expectations for the trip even more, and day after day, it delivered.

The next morning, I'd pulled Owen into the hallway while everyone else was sitting down to breakfast and kissed him without a word. He couldn't stop grinning at me over his blueberry stuffed pancakes. Maybe it had been my morning encouragement, but that night, a second note found its way under my pillow. This one read, *Snuggling in the hammock with you.* Every night, the notes appeared. Every morning, I kissed Owen thank you.

Being back home, I never expected them to keep coming, but somehow, he'd done it. I unfolded the paper.

Catching a touchdown pass from you.

Come to think of it, that might have been my favorite part of the day. Or close to it. After the catch, I'd run to the end zone and jumped into Owen's arms. He'd lifted me, and we spun around, celebrating. I'd thrown a lot of backyard touchdowns over the years, but never to my boyfriend. For a moment, it was just us on the field. I kind of liked it that way.

****

TO MAINTAIN TRADITION, OR AT LEAST SOME VERSION of it, I woke up the next morning and texted Owen a virtual kiss, complete with fireworks animating the screen.

I imagined him lying in his unmade bed with tousled hair, hearing the beep, and picking up the phone from his bedside table. Our beach vacation taught me he would be sleeping shirtless. A fluttering yearning flared inside me at the thought.

My phone beeped with a good morning text from him.

I replied: *Good morning to you.*

Then I extended my arms and legs to opposite corners of my queen-sized bed to stretch the stiffness of sleep away. I read his note from last night one more time, feeling a silly grin spread across my face.

With my phone nearby in case Owen texted back, I searched the kitchen for breakfast operations. Frozen egg-and-sausage sandwiches. Frozen waffles. Frozen pancakes. An unwelcome frosty theme. At the beach, Owen and Ally's mom had spoiled us with extravagant breakfasts—eggs and bacon, ham-and-cheese omelets, blueberry-stuffed French toast, chocolate pancakes. Envisioning that decadent deliciousness that *so* wouldn't be on my plate that morning—ugh, torture. If Mom or Abuelita were there, they'd make something equally satisfying. Even Dad had some cooking skills. The whole process daunted me, especially for the benefit of one person.

They'd gone to mass, which they generously let me sleep through on my last day of summer, and would be at the diner by now, enjoying delicious pancakes, bacon, fried potatoes—I needed to stop.

Surrendering, I tossed the box of waffles onto the counter and plugged in the toaster as the doorbell rang. I was tempted to ignore it, especially in my short shorts and cami, but Abuelita's campaign team dropped off signs, flyers, and other materials day and night. Wrapped in a jacket my dad had left on a hook in the kitchen, I opened the door, expecting someone delivering a stack of Ita's latest paraphernalia. Instead, I found Owen.

He stepped inside and kissed my cheek. I took initiative and instead kissed him on the lips, just as I did so many times in that hallway of the condo. "I loved the note."

"Clearly," he whispered. He lowered his lips to mine in one more soft brush. "I brought breakfast."

He carried a brown paper bag, wet with grease at the corners, to the kitchen and unloaded it. I recognized the tan Styrofoam boxes immediately.

"Is that from—"

"The diner? Yep." He tossed a fried potato into his mouth, which made mine water.

"How'd you know I wasn't at mass?"

"Ally's there. She saw your parents and texted me."

The scent of fried potatoes mingling with bacon and sausage was sublime. "I knew I picked a good best friend."

Owen held a box out of my reach. "And a good boyfriend."

I kissed him again. "That goes without saying."

"Still," he grinned, "I don't mind you saying it."

I reached for the box.

"Right. For you: chocolate chip pancakes, fried potatoes, one extra-crispy slice of bacon, and one sausage link—not patty."

"You make me sound so high maintenance," I said and bit into the sausage. The juice exploded in my mouth. So. Good.

"You know what you like, and you have good taste." He playfully gestured to himself. "Obviously."

I threw a potato at him. He dodged it and pulled me close so quickly Dad's jacket slipped from my shoulders. Owen peeked downward at my revealing pj's.

"What happened to the baggy T-shirts and shorts?"

"When I'm at home and not in the company of my boyfriend and his family, this is what I sleep in."

"Really?" he said, lowering his lips to my neck.

"Mm-hmm," I mumbled as his kiss moved to my shoulder and then finally back to my lips. I was pretty sure I tasted like sausage, but in boy terms, that was like gold, right? His mouth was soft and delicious, with a tease of salt from the potatoes. With my parents being out, I expected him to deepen the kiss, to wrap his arms around me and push my back against the fridge out of sheer, undeniable passion like they did in movies. *Something.* Apparently, the comforting aroma of our breakfast provided a stronger temptation.

"I have big plans for today," Owen said, retrieving the milk from the fridge I should have been pressed against at that very moment.

"Do those plans involve more kissing?"

"Most definitely."

Then I supposed a break for sustenance was fair. We climbed onto the barstools and shuffled around the boxes, plasticware, and napkins until we were satisfied with the mounds of food before us. I slathered my pancakes with butter and syrup while Owen did the same with his French toast, and we dug in.

"This is delicious."

Owen winked at me. "You're not the only one with good taste."

"So tell me about these big plans," I said, forking a stack of pancake into my mouth.

He shook his head. "It's a surprise."

****

AN HOUR LATER, WITH FULL BELLIES, WEARING ATH-
letic gear and packing a cooler of drinks and snacks, Owen and I rode
in his father's old pickup to the surprise destination. He opened his
mouth to say something but stopped. Then did so two more times.

"Owen...?"

He sighed. "Here's the thing. Being back at home has been an
adjustment. My dad's on my case as usual, but it's more than that.
I got used to you always being around." He looked sideways at me
with blushing cheeks. "I liked it."

I reached across the bench seat and squeezed his hand. "Me too."

He merged onto the highway. "Is that what's been bothering you?"

The sweetness of his words pulled at my chest. "You noticed
something's been bothering me?"

"Of course I noticed, Jules. It was a big reason for today. In Florida, we could sneak away to one of the hotels or cabanas on the beach
anytime."

"By 'sneak', you mean pretending to belong at the biggest hotel
on the beach only to get caught and sent away in shame?"

We both laughed at the memory.

"It was good while it lasted," Owen said with a grin.

Most things are.

"With practices starting tomorrow and being away from you, I
thought we needed some time," he looked sideways at me, "alone."

Owen turned down the driveway that led to our community play-
ground. He parked the truck and shut down the engine before leaning
across the seat to tuck my hair behind my ears and trace my neck
and chin with his magical fingers. "Today's about us," he whispered.
"Our last day of summer. Let's enjoy it."

He climbed out of the truck. I hopped down from the passenger
side and rounded the back where he stood holding a volleyball in one
hand and a football in the other.

I grabbed the football and headed for a shaded grassy area. Owen jogged into position about ten yards away.

"I can throw farther than that," I teased, and he responded by backpedaling eighty yards.

He cupped his hands around his mouth and yelled, "Is this good?"

We walked toward each other until only about twenty yards separated us. "Don't be obnoxious," I warned. "It's not attractive."

He tugged his shirt over his head. He knew my absolute weakness: his bare, sculpted torso. "You sure about that?"

Not. At. All.

I shot the ball into his chest, and air whooshed from his lungs. He threw it back over the distance with ease, and we went on like that for a few minutes before I asked, "So what's going on with your dad?"

"The usual. I'm not practicing hard enough. I'm not focused enough. I'm not living his dreams enough."

I caught the ball and dropped back a step before returning it to him. "Sorry."

He spun the ball in his hands. "I try not to let it bother me, but sometimes, I don't know what he wants me to do. I have no control over whether we have a good quarterback or not, but somehow he doesn't accept that."

As a receiver, Owen relied on a strong quarterback. Without one, he couldn't perform up to his full potential. He couldn't attract scouts. While the football team had a gaping hole, the volleyball team was solid, partially because of me.

The thought of playing volleyball didn't excite me like it used to, but could I...not play?

No. I couldn't quit.

I'd play.

And what? Not like it. Dread it?

Hate it?

For what? A scholarship to play it for four more years. What sense did that make? And why did high school sports always have to be about a scholarship anyway? Why couldn't they be about learning teamwork, building skills, exercising, and staying healthy?

Or—*gasp*—having fun?

I sighed.

If I quit, I'd be the one to create the void. How could I do that to my teammates? To Ally?

Owen pressed the ball between his arm and his side. "Jules? What is it?"

His face wrinkled in concern, but I couldn't tell him. I wasn't sure I even had the strength to go through with quitting. If I did, what would he think of me? How would he react to me putting his sister in the same situation he's in?

I shook my head. "Nothing. I'm fine."

He studied me, not looking convinced. "It's hot out here. Want a drink?"

"Sure. That'd be great."

He tossed the ball to me underhand. "I'll run to the car—"

"No," I interrupted. "I'll come with you."

He looped his fingers in mine and kissed the back of my hand. His phone buzzed in his pocket, and a look at the screen had him sighing and completely unaware of it. The reaction only came from the calls of one person—his dad.

CHAPTER FIVE

NOBODY EVER SAID, "WORK BALL!" THEY SAY, "PLAY BALL!" TO ME, THAT MEANS HAVING FUN.
—WILLIE STARGELL

OWEN LISTENED FOR A SECOND, LOOKED MY WAY, AND held up a finger signaling I should give him a minute.

I nodded, feeling a twinge self-conscious since Mr. Malone did not like me. Okay, that wasn't entirely true. He didn't know me, but he definitely didn't like me dating his son. Mr. Malone envisioned his son as the quarterback. Owen had played the position in middle school, but when he graduated to the varsity squad, the position was taken. By Jake. From that point on, Mr. Malone's detested anyone with the last name Medina. Owen had moved to receiver and never looked back, which if you asked me, Mr. Malone should've thanked my brother for. Owen was a standout receiver. His routes were crisp and accurate enough to terrorize defenses, and if the ball was placed anywhere near him, he'd catch it. Every. Time. Truly beautiful to watch. His highlight reel was bound to impress colleges, and he had a much better chance of being recruited at receiver than he ever would have been at quarterback.

"Dad, I've been catching today."

Silence.

"At the park. I played yesterday too."

Silence.

"With a bunch of the guys."

Owen glanced at me, and I got the sensation that I didn't want to hear what his father was saying. And that it was probably about me. I headed for the truck and reached my hand into the cooler's icy water to grab a bottle. By the time Owen joined me, the drink was half gone.

"Everything good?"

He nodded.

I didn't believe him. "Look, if you need to get home..."

"No," Owen said. "Today's about us."

With one call, his father had siphoned the playfulness from the outing and reminded me that while his mom and stepfather supported our relationship, Owen (and Ally, for that matter) was back to living with his father.

Yet another reason to miss the beach.

Owen stared into the distance. For a minute. Then two.

"Do you want to talk about it?"

He sipped his water a few times before speaking. "He wants me to try out for quarterback."

"Really?" I hoped my tone didn't reveal I thought the idea was awful.

"He thinks it's my time or whatever." Owen raised his hands in surrender. "Nothing against Jake. I loved playing with your brother."

I'm not sure I'd go that far, but they had respected each other on the field.

"Is that what you want?"

Owen didn't even hesitate. "No. Moving to receiver was the best thing I ever did."

We agreed on that. "Did you tell your dad?"

Owen sighed. "Can we not talk about this—about serious stuff today?"

"Absolutely," I said, but I didn't want to be done talking about it. I wanted Owen to know that he was a kick-ass receiver, and he shouldn't feel pressured to be something he wasn't by anyone—even his father. Leaning against the truck with his shoulders slumped and his head down, Owen looked shorter than usual—vulnerable, even.

"Hey," I said, wrapping my arms around his neck.

He lowered his face to my shoulder. "I don't know what to do."

"You said you wanted to play receiver, so that's what you do. Put your energy into that."

He didn't respond.

"I have confidence in you."

"You have confidence I can tell my dad no?" By the sound of his voice, I'd half expected to see tears on his cheeks, but he recovered that look of intensity he so often showed the world, communicating at the same time that the conversation about his dad was over.

Maybe he didn't want to talk about it. Maybe he didn't want a solution. Maybe, though, for him...I'd find one.

"It's wicked hot," I said, willing to let the discussion pass. For now. "Wanna go back to my house to swim?"

"What if I told you we could swim right here?"

I exaggeratedly searched the parking lot. "Here? Is this when you tell me you're really Harry Potter and you can conjure me a swimming pool with a simple spell?"

He pumped his open bottle through the air, sending a stream of ice-cold water onto my cheek and down my front. In the heat, it felt amazing. I returned the favor. Twice.

"Okay, okay. I surrender. So do you want to swim or what?"

"I didn't bring my suit."

His eyes twinkled. In a husky whisper, he said, "Where's your sense of adventure?"

****

TO REACH THE SWIMMING HOLE, WE HAD TO CROSS the creek and walk down the other side. The water flowed quickly under the shade of the trees, sporadic sunbeams sparkling on the surface. Random rocks provided natural zigzagging pathways. Some were easier to navigate than others. Ahead of me, hopping along the protruding stones, Owen accentuated the view. His thin athletic shirt revealed the outline of his shoulders, and with each jump, it shifted upward.

"You're awfully quiet back there," Owen said.

"I'm admiring your ass."

His foot slipped on the next stone, and he nearly fell into the water. When he regained his balance, he turned to me, laughing.

I shrugged. "Not what you expected me to say?"

"Julia, I've learned not to expect with you. I'm almost always wrong."

Points for spontaneity.

He winked. "How about you go ahead and offer me the chance to admire you?"

"Give up my view? Not a chance, buster."

He nodded and hopped to the next rock, but the path ended there. The jump from his rock to the other bank stretched too far.

"Wait a sec." Owen demonstrated the kind of maneuver you see in a game of highly competitive Twister to retrieve a nearby stone, improving the view yet again. He tossed the stone expertly into the water a few feet away, tested it with his own weight, and leapt to the bank on the other side of the creek. I followed suit, my momentum taking me right into his arms. Instead of letting him stop me though, I pushed until his back was pressed against the hillside behind him.

"You know," I said with a soft peck on his lips, "I can get across on my own."

"I do know," he said kissing me back. "You're quite capable, but sometimes you could pretend to need me. To stroke my ego."

He scooped me up, wrapping my legs around him, and pressed me against the trunk of a nearby tree. He slid his tongue over my bottom lip, sending a warm shiver down my spine. His hands tangled in my hair, or maybe those were stray branches. I didn't care. All that mattered was getting twisted up with Owen Malone. He pressed his lips hard against my own, and I opened my mouth to welcome them.

After a few breathless minutes, he leaned his forehead against mine and sighed. "So, swimming?"

I laughed. "That's what you said."

He squeezed my hand and pulled me closer to him as we walked along the wet soil several minutes in silence.

"So," Owen said, "are you going to tell me what's been bothering you?"

I walked and debated. Owen had confided in me about his dad and football, and I did want to talk to someone. My dread for the season had started like a tiny sprout in Abuelita's garden, but over the last few weeks, that sprout became a yard full of weeds. Massive. Uncontrolled.

Unstoppable.

"I'm dreading getting up for practice in the morning. And it's only the first day." Speaking the words aloud made me twenty pounds lighter. I stopped short of admitting I considered quitting.

"I don't know what to say. I thought you loved volleyball."

"I did. But I don't know. I guess it changed."

"What changed?"

Good question. Since the morning I woke up at the beach and didn't feel the urge to rush to the sand court, I'd asked myself that same thing. When Ally finally got me out onto the beach, I'd miss a dig or a serve, and instead of being angry and wanting to push harder on the next one, I felt...fine.

"I'm not sure. One day, I didn't want it as badly."

He squeezed my hand. "Have you told Ally?"

"No." I turned to gauge his reaction.

He looked me in the eyes and said, "I won't say anything, but you should talk to her."

I resumed walking. "I know."

Volleyball spoke to Ally's soul, and she wanted everyone else to feel the same. Admitting I didn't—to her, to my mom—not sure I was ready for that.

We rounded a bend, and the swimming hole came into view. While the sun peeked through the trees, the area boasted a surprising amount of privacy—from the road on one side and the edge of the high school's property on the other. Owen kicked off his shoes and stripped down to his boxers before doing a cannon ball into the water.

After a few seconds, he shot upward and shook the excess water from his hair like he'd done so many times on vacation.

"It's perfect," he said. "You coming in?"

I looked back toward the park and ahead toward the school. Nobody was coming. Owen watched from the water as I peeled my sweaty tank top over my head, revealing my teal bra, and slipped off my shorts. The bold, colorful pattern of my underwear could pass at first glance as a bathing suit. Maybe. Oh well. I climbed the hillside to reach the tire swing and hopped aboard. I swung out over the water but wanted a better feel before I jumped. When the swing's trajectory brought it back to the bank, I launched myself again, this time plopping into the creek next to Owen. The water cooled but didn't chill me. Owen was right. It was perfect.

He slipped his arm around my waist and pulled me to the surface. He pushed my wet hair from my face. "I wasn't sure you'd actually go through with it."

I ran my finger along his chin to his lips. "And here I thought I'd taught you to expect the unexpected."

CHAPTER SIX

*TRUE CHAMPIONS AREN'T ALWAYS THE ONES THAT
WIN BUT THOSE WITH THE MOST GUTS.
—MIA HAMM*

THE MORNING SUNLIGHT FOUGHT ITS WAY THROUGH
the small windows that lined the ceiling and reflected in bright, elongated squares on the gym floor. My shoes squeaked across the fresh wax. I'd never understand why the maintenance crew waxed the floor right before volleyball season. Clearly, they never tried to dive or sprawl on a floor that ripped your skin apart with every inch.

Mom disappeared into her office while I unpacked the balls and warmed up my arm by throwing and spiking against the wall. Other players filtered in. Underclassmen moved around the gym in hesitation, but the returning varsity players laughed and teased each other. Balls bounced off every surface, echoing in the enclosed space. Repetition of the words "mine" or "got it" or "heads up" surrounded me. It used to feel like home. Today it felt more like a song I knew every single word to but the melody felt played out.

We ran drills in the morning and scrimmaged in the afternoon. The starting six crushed the JV, causing particular strife for a sophomore named Melanie, but she kept taking it. Our middle hitter, Sam, spiked

Ally's set right at her. Melanie dove, shooting the black-and-purple paneled ball back to me. I squatted and soared upward, widening my fingers and pressing them over the plane of the net. The ball smacked against the wall of my hands and dropped to the shiny hardwood between two junior varsity girls who sprawled a second too late.

My teammates erupted in cheers, stomping their feet in our signature rhythm. As Ally took the ball back to the serving line, the JV team repositioned themselves for more. Ally's jump serve landed in the middle of the court again, with girls diving too late for it to matter. More stomping and cheering occurred on our side.

"Water break," shouted our assistant coach, Steve, while Mom pepped the JV with a speech about how it was their place to challenge us, to make us better. I remembered being on that court, listening to those words, and believing my sole responsibility was to push the varsity. I felt used and useless at the same time. Shouldn't the varsity push themselves? Aim to deliver the ball to the exact inch of the court it belongs? Chugging my water, I promised myself that's what I would do. If volleyball didn't interest me like it once did, I would figure out a way to spark my love for the game with small, silent challenges of my own.

I tossed my water back into the corner of the gym and took my position on the court. Play ensued, and I aimed with every touch of the ball. The first set was high outside giving me ample time to get into position. I made my approach, jumped, and as my body piked, I swung, connecting with the top of the ball and snapping my wrist downward. *Line,* I thought, and the ball landed within six inches from the white out of bounds line.

Nobody was even close to defending it. One for one.

The next set was a quick shot. *Power cross court,* I thought. The ball went where I wanted it to. Melanie dove again, and the ball slapped off her forearms into the bleachers. Two for two. I spiked the ball. Tipped it. Passed it. Set it. Each time, I aimed, and my success rates were high. Thirty-two accurate, and five missed balls. Melanie attempted to play more of the points than any of the other JV girls. The girl *had* something.

Ally hugged me after practice. "You were on today, Julia."

"Definitely," Sam said. "I thought that ball I tipped off the block

43

was hitting the floor for sure. Nice dig."

"Thanks," I said.

Mom called us to the bleachers for our daily review. With the cart of game balls at her side, she praised random players for digs, sets, spikes, and serves. And for award-worthy moments off the court. With each praise, she tossed a ball. If you got one, then no after-practice chores. The worst chore was loosening the net and lifting the poles from the floor and hauling them across the gym to the disorganized storage closet.

Sophomore year, a girl broke her ankle maneuvering around the crap in that closet.

Mom called my name last. The soft panels of the ball felt at home—yet awkward—in my hands.

"Coach," I called before she could dismiss us.

She looked at me and waited. I looked around the bleachers and noted all the girls honored with game balls played varsity. But what about the junior varsity? What kind of crap was it if we told them it was their job to push the varsity but then didn't pay respect when they do?

"Someone else deserves this more than me."

The team hushed in an awkward way considering we were already quiet. Mom waved her hand in a gesture that communicated I should tackle the injustices of the planet as I saw fit.

I stood, shifting the ball back and forth between my hands as I talked. "As hard as I swung and as many times as I returned the ball over the net, there was one girl there to pick it up." My teammates and coaches gawked at me. Nobody had ever given their ball away as far as I knew, but that didn't mean nobody ever could. Or *should*. "Melanie?" The sophomore's eyes widened. "This is for you." I spiked the ball at her, and she caught it with a laugh.

"Thanks," she mumbled, her cheeks reddening.

I nodded at her.

"That was generous, Julia," Mom said with a smile, "especially since that means you will join the others in taking down the net."

The prospect didn't thrill me, but Melanie deserved that ball.

"One more business item," Coach said. "Captains."

On the first day? Ally turned to me from the front row wearing her usual worried expression. As if the team needed preseason camp to choose a leader. Ally planned the music. The outfits. The socials. The fundraisers. She organized everything for the team and worked out harder than anyone. She was our captain. End of story.

"Like you, I read the sports section. People expect a lot from you all this year. Expectations can be uplifting. Or they can cripple a team. Our captain will be tasked with leading and representing this team. Select an advocate you trust and one you support." She and Coach Steve distributed ballots and pencils. "Everyone vote for two. The top candidate will be the captain, and the second highest will be assistant captain." She shooed us, and girls disbursed around the bleachers. Some thought longer than others. Longer than me. I wrote Ally's name—only hers—and dropped my folded white paper into the basket.

Once the net was tucked away, I headed for the locker room. Before I reached my locker, someone called my name. The voice and the tone were unmistakable. I poked my head into my mom's office. She sat behind the desk under the dim lighting. Behind her, newspaper articles from the ten years she'd coached decorated the wall. Including those about our mother-daughter/coach-player dynamic the first year I played varsity, a profile about me when I started standing out, and a preview of this season with a headline that read, *Great Expectations!*

They might have been printed on paper that could blow away in the wind, but they were somehow still heavy enough to bear down on my shoulders.

"Yes?"

"Sit."

I complied, slumping backward into the torn lining of the olive-green chair.

"Do you have something to say about my awards system? A system that has worked for this team for years?"

"Mom..." I tried to find the words to explain it wasn't personal, that it felt like the right thing to do at the time, but she didn't give me time to say anything.

"Julia, if you want to question me, it's best to do it off the court. You know that."

Any other girl on the team could ask her a question. Suggest an idea. But not me. Not her daughter. Playing a sport for your parent-slash-coach placed you into one of two categories: either people despised you for receiving special treatment or the parent-slash-coach worked so hard to eliminate any possible inkling of special treatment that you were mistreated.

Hello, me.

"I didn't mean to question you. I thought Melanie deserved to be rewarded for her efforts."

Mom gave an exaggerated sigh. "Maybe you're right. The tradition has always been to award the starters, but it doesn't have to stay that way."

The clock stopped ticking. The earth jerked to a stop from its usual spinning. Did my mother just embrace change?

"Don't look so surprised. I'm a reasonable person." She relaxed into her chair. "We haven't had much time to talk with you being away. How are you feeling about the captain announcement?"

I shrugged. "Fine. Ally's the clear choice."

Mom fiddled with interlocked paper clips on her desk. "So...you don't want to be captain?"

I'd never even given it any thought. The role was always so clearly Ally's. Now, with me questioning whether I even wanted to play, I'd be an imposter captaining the team. But from Mom's nonchalant question, I assumed she wanted the team to elect me.

"Mom..." I had to tell her—not that I considered quitting, but that volleyball wasn't the same. "Lately, things have felt different here."

"Sure," she said. "You're adjusting to being home after a month away. And it's your senior year."

"That's not what I meant."

Coach Steve poked his head into the side door of Mom's office, where he couldn't see into the girls' locker room. "Votes are in."

Mom nodded to him. "I don't mean to rush you, honey, but can this wait until we get home?"

"Yeah. Sure. Of course." I didn't feel rushed. More like ignored completely.

"We would have more time to really talk there, but if you want to—"

"It's fine, Mom." I stepped out of her office as if the doorway satisfied her need for some weird barrier between us. "I'll go wait with the team."

I left the office, stuffed my knee pads and deodorant into my gym bag, and closed my locker. I wanted out of the gym, but Coach Steve blocked the exit and pointed to a group of girls chatting and sharing snacks on the bleachers. Ally sat in the center of the group, discussing the season in that overwhelming way she had, and out of sheer friendly duty, I climbed the bleachers to sit next to her. A few of the other varsity girls gradually and politely diverted the conversation to something a little more interesting and slightly less stressful—boys.

"Speaking of," Ally said, "did you hear that hot Christian Santos is the student trainer for the football team this year?"

Some of the girls sighed. Others voiced disappointment.

"I know," Ally continued. "I wanted him to get assigned to us."

"Who's Christian Santos?" I asked.

"He graduated two years ago," Ally said. "He's premed now and doing a sports-medicine internship or part-time job or something. Who cares? He's here. A lot. And..." She sighed in exaggerated disappointment.

"Absolutely gorgeous," Sam said.

Ally pointed at her and nodded.

"Not that that's a concern of Miss Julia, who has her own little slice of perfection."

"Gross," Ally said.

Sam waggled her eyebrows at me. "How are things with you and Owen?"

Last night I'd found a classic Owen note, complete with torn edges, in my bag. It'd said, *Watching you jump into the water.* Like so many days at the beach, our time at the park had been...magical. A memory of him pressing me against the tree and teasing my bottom lip with his tongue and later us swimming alone with his hands exploring my bare skin had heat rushing to my cheeks.

"I knew it! Just thinking of him gets you all hot," Sam laughed and dramatically laid down on the bleacher with the back of her hand pressed to her forehead.

"Don't encourage them, please," Ally said. "They are ridiculous."

"Some would say adorable," I challenged.

"Yeah. Some probably would. But they don't live with His Mopey Highness. I mean you're my best friend, and I miss having you around too. But..." She shook her head.

"He's really mopey?" I couldn't see it. I'd never seen Owen mope. He had this quiet, pensive way about him when something was on his mind.

She raised an eyebrow as if to say *Don't get me started*.

He *missed* me. Maybe I could catch him before he lifted—if practice ever ended. Coach Steve sat at a desk on the other side of the court, counting slips of paper and ticking off names on a clipboard. He ticked and *recounted*. By then all the girls had crowded around, and my mother returned from the locker room for the news. She wouldn't count the votes. She would learn the identity of our captain with the rest of us. How else would she ensure integrity of the election, she would say. I would say if someone wanted to believe she was capable of cheating for me, then wouldn't they assume she was capable of making her assistant coach cheat for me?

Whatever.

"I counted the votes three times to be sure," Coach Steve said. "It was close, but our assistant captain for the season will be Sam Struthers." The team slapped and stomped the bleachers and shouted Sam's name. If I had cast a second vote, Sam would have taken it. Our best hitter, Sam carried herself with confidence on the court and off. Her graceful elegance attracted and impressed the younger players, and she was fun. People were in awe of her, and who could blame them? She caught my eye, and I smiled, giving her an approving nod.

"Thank you," she mouthed.

Coach Steve consulted his clipboard as if he needed a reminder of the other name. I figured he might be enjoying the suspense of it all too much. The same could not be said for my best friend. I took her hand. She wanted this. She deserved this. Coach Steve raised his clipboard, and I heard Ally suck in a quick breath.

"The captain you all elected for this season is Julia Medina."

That was not possible. Ally's hand went limp in mine. I turned to her and saw the feelings clawing around inside me etched on her face. Disbelief. Disappointment.

All sending a wave of nausea at my gut like a well-placed spike.

The girls cheered, tearing me into two very conflicted pieces. Should I show appreciation for the leadership they entrusted to me or refuse the position out of loyalty to my best friend? But even if I refused, Ally wouldn't be captain. Sam would.

Ally released my hand and mumbled congratulations. Coach Steve congratulated me, then talked about the practice, our goals for tomorrow, and other stuff that made him sound like an adult from an episode of *Charlie Brown.*

Wa. Wa. Waaa. Wom. Wa.

CHAPTER SEVEN

🏈

WHEN YOU'VE GOT SOMETHING TO PROVE, THERE'S NOTHING GREATER THAN A CHALLENGE.
—TERRY BRADSHAW

I COULDN'T BRING MYSELF TO CALL ALLY. OR OWEN.
Had Ally told him I'd stolen the role she'd coveted for the last three years? For what? Giving Melanie the game ball? Ally served the team every day. One kind gesture on my part, and it was as if all her work disintegrated. I floated through the house like gravity had nothing on the hot mess that was me. The mess's force was too strong.

Before dinner, I popped my head into Jake's room, where the trophies, news articles, and blown-up action shots of him in mid-throwing motion confirmed for anyone who might not already know this was sacred sports territory. I ran my fingertips along the books on his desk shelf. *The Everything Kids' Football Book.* A classic. I learned most of the basics from that book. The other books boasted covers with football greats like Nick Saban, Urban Meyer, Bill Cowher, Brett Favre, Peyton Manning, and of course Vince Lombardi. Tucked in the corner, a dull, brown leather binding that contrasted against the vibrant colors of the commercially published books caught my eye. My heart leapt into my throat. One of Jake's football notebooks.

At the advice of my father, all three of my brothers had preserved the moments of their football lives. Each notebook was filled with their thoughts on specific drills, challenges they faced, games they played, words that motivated them—all the way back to their Pop Warner days. No surprise, Jorge wasn't as committed to the notebooks as my other brothers, but zen master Jake was meticulous. In fact, I couldn't believe he didn't take this one to school with him.

The cover was cool and soft in my hands. I flipped it open to a quotation by Terry Bradshaw: *When you've got something to prove, there's nothing greater than a challenge.*

Jake always played like he had something to prove. As the youngest of three quarterbacks, he probably did. He wanted people to know he didn't get the position because of his last name but because of his talent.

Now I felt like I had something to prove too. I wasn't sure exactly what that was yet.

I looked around me at the quiet room and the quiet house. Nothing—no one—was around me. I tucked the notebook to my chest and realized I didn't just miss my brothers. I missed the bickering over *EA Sports* games gone bad. The teasing about who had the better stats. The debates about the best quarterbacks to ever play in the NFL. The constant need to duck as a football was thrown somewhere in the house. The spur-of-the-moment pickup games we played in the backyard. Other guys from the team showing up and jumping in. Two guys on that team. Two guys on this one. Until there were so many people in my backyard my parents had to order a stack of pizzas. My house had been Grand Central Stadium.

My brothers left, and football went with them.

I held the notebook close against my chest, grateful for the revelation sparked by the soft leather in my hands—it wasn't just my brothers I missed.

I missed football.

****

LATER THAT NIGHT, UNDER THE SPOTLIGHTS ON OUR garage, I propped up my phone on a stack of boxes and cranked up the volume. A few taps at the screen and my brothers' faces appeared. Juan from outside his apartment about an hour away. Jorge from sunny Florida, and Jake from Western Penn's gymnasium. Some friendly—or not-so-friendly—competition between my brothers provided the perfect distraction until Owen finished practice.

"Who's timing?" Jake asked.

"I got it," Jorge said and moved his face so close to the camera lens we saw his nose hair.

"Need a trim there, buddy," Juan said, the teasing of my brothers like a magic elixir capable of erasing every stress and frustration in my life.

"Shut up," Jorge said. "Everyone ready?"

I stepped up to the crack in the cement Jake chiseled for me when we were kids. "That's where girls throw from," he'd said. Bullshit. That's where girls who kicked his ass threw from.

"Go!" Jorge called, echoing through our speakers and microphones.

I shot the basketball, and it sailed through the net at the perfect angle to bounce off the garage door and come back to me. Bonus! I grabbed the rebound and took another shot. Rapid fire. That was the key to winning.

"Nobody better be cheating," Juan scolded.

"Scared to lose?" Jorge responded, but zen master Jake stayed quiet. He didn't talk smack when we all competed. Ever.

And I didn't want to, either. I wanted to win. When Jorge's alarm rang out, I'd made nine baskets. Breathing heavy with our red-cheeked faces close to the cameras, we typed our numbers into the chat box and hit Send on Juan's command.

"Seventeen, Jake?" Jorge yelled. "Liar!"

Arguments ensued, as usual. He wasn't lying. He was lying. He cheated. He didn't cheat. Juan suggested we go another round, but Jorge and Jake kept up the verbal target practice. Why would Jake go again when he already won? And why try if nobody believed him? Why would Jorge play if Jake was going to cheat to win? And so on.

Despite the arguing, we played a few more rounds before Juan and

Jorge bailed, leaving Jake and me to continue our digital connection over snacks. Jake ate in the cafeteria, and I headed to our kitchen. I told my brother about the big captain reveal at practice and how I hadn't spoken to Ally since she mumbled her congratulations.

"You think she's pissed at you?" Jake asked between bites of pizza and greetings to friends and acquaintances who passed him by.

"Probably. I mean, this was her life."

Jake nodded while I crunched tortilla chips dipped in our father's homemade salsa.

"And what does Lover Boy say?" my brother asked.

"I don't know. Haven't talked to him yet."

"If someone hurt my little sister, we'd have a problem."

"I didn't hurt her," I argued. "And she's not his little sister. She's older."

"By five minutes."

"Still. And," I smiled sweetly at him, "thank you for looking out for me."

"Any time, Little J." He exaggerated a smile. "You still thinking about quitting?"

I peeked into the living room to be sure Mom and Dad weren't around to hear Jake's question. Fortunately—and miraculously—we had some privacy.

Not only quitting. I chewed and harnessed the courage to tell my brother something I barely allowed myself to think, let alone say out loud. "I, um, well, I'm thinking of trying something new."

The little picture of me on the bottom corner of the screen bounced from the excitement. As my resident philosopher, Jake would be the ultimate gauge, which is totally why I needed to tell him first.

"Like what?" he said.

"Football."

He spit his chocolate milk at the screen, leaving droplets on the camera and him swearing in Spanish.

"Yo, Medina. You all right?" asked a beefy kid wearing a Western Penn football shirt.

"Fine," my brother answered.

Suddenly three faces peered into the camera and smiled at me.

"Your girl's cute," one of them said.

"She's my sister, man." Jake ushered the guys away, but one lingered, waving over my brother's turned back. Then, he blew me a kiss.

"I can see you on the screen," Jake said.

"Great friends you have."

"Don't change the subject."

I couldn't. I wouldn't. As fearful I was of his reaction, I needed to see it. If Jake couldn't be convinced I had a shot, then I wasn't sure anyone could.

"You're bold. You know that?" He shook his head.

"Yes. I do."

"Jules, why would you want to play football?"

A good question. One that didn't have a logical answer. Sure, my brothers played. My father coached in years past. But I was a volleyball player. A standout on the team. The captain.

A girl.

Logic dictated I'd play volleyball, score a scholarship, and be the fourth Medina in the family to play collegiate ball. I wasn't sure how I'd pay for college if I didn't play volleyball, but my heart couldn't commit to five more seasons of the sport. Like Jake had said, maybe I was burned out. Or maybe playing volleyball was too easy. Not that I executed every play perfectly, but overall, the sport came as simply to me as a free ball arced over the net right into my waiting arms.

Even with all of that, the decision wasn't intellectual. It was all heart. "It feels...*different*."

Jake actually stopped eating and gave me his full attention. "How?"

"Exciting. Unpredictable. Challenging. I mean, when we played in the backyard Saturday, I dropped back and had to assess so much in that moment. Make such quick decisions, you know? Of course, you know. It's like so much is happening in no time at all. And what I'm doing is a small part of everything happening on the field. It's exhilarating yet calming. A total contradiction."

And this would solve Owen's problem. He needed a quarterback. My heart did an end zone dance at the thought I'd be the one throwing him touchdowns this year.

Recovering from my ramble, I looked back at the screen to see

Jake grinning. "I should have seen it before," he said. "I know your last name's Medina and you know more about the game than half of the lug heads on the team, but you're still a girl, Jules."

"Last I checked," I said, annoyed but also expecting this reaction. "Spare me the whole 'girls can't play football' speech."

"I planned on it, but you know I'm in the minority." He laughed and shook his head in an *I can't believe this is happening* way. "You're really going to do this? Quarterback, obviously?"

I winked at him. "Is there any other position?"

CHAPTER EIGHT

WHEN YOU WALK UP TO OPPORTUNITY'S DOOR—DON'T
KNOCK ON IT. KICK THAT BITCH IN, SMILE, AND INTRO-
DUCE YOURSELF.
—DWAYNE JOHNSON

A RUSTIC, WOODEN PICTURE FRAME THAT RECORDED
the moment the Medina football legacy began rested on the top of
Juan's bookshelf until he moved away to college. I didn't remember
the moment in the picture. At the time it was taken, I concerned myself
more with formula, rattles, and how quickly someone could replace
the soggy diaper on my butt than what transpired around me. My
mother took the pictures of Dad and Juan in the backyard, which was
a big field at the time—long before my parents inherited the money
that turned our house into a training facility. Rays of sunlight set Juan
aglow as he stood tall next to our father's kneeling frame. Dad rested
one hand on Juan's shoulder and held a worn football in the other.

That was the first photo. The second showed Juan holding the ball
and smiling at Dad. And in the third, Juan threw the ball through the air.

My oldest brother had told me the story many times.

"Dad saw me throwing stuff around the house and figured he
better come up with a plan before I broke something Mom couldn't

replace. He took me to the backyard, knelt next to me, and with a hand on my shoulder explained the simple truth that's dominated my life. 'Being the quarterback's the best, son. There's nothing like it.'

"He said it was the best position on the field, and he had it almost right. For me, quarterback's the *only* position."

Dad and Juan threw the ball for hours that afternoon. And several afternoons for the next fifteen-plus years. Jorge joined them. Then Jake. Then me. Dad was hesitant about letting his daughter play at first, but my brothers insisted. They taught me the throwing motion, stance, footwork, routes, reads. While my friends were painting nails onto their plastic dolls, I practiced a three-step drop.

I guess I should have known it then, and maybe I always did know but was too afraid to own it. Like my brothers, for me, the quarterback was *the* position. The challenge would be making everyone else accept that. My parents. My team. Ally. Owen.

Would Owen be okay with me playing? Would he be too afraid I'd get hurt to actually focus on the game? Or would that be a cover for how he really felt—girls shouldn't play football?

No. Owen wasn't like that.

He wanted to catch touchdowns. He needed a quarterback who could read defenses, make good decisions, and execute plays with accuracy.

That could be *me*.

My phone chirped. A text from Owen: *Practice was killer. Pool and hot tub?*

I looked at the clock. Nine p.m. My parents imposed a 10:30 curfew to work myself into a school year routine. Early to bed. Early to rise. But nothing relaxes a person like a dip in the hot tub, right?

Sure. I'll be out back.

I dug through the yet-to-be-unpacked suitcases on my floor until I found the red string bikini—the one I'd worn when Owen and I snuck into the hotel pool. I jogged through the house, my pace matching the chaotic rush of emotion I felt, and found my parents, sharing a bottle of wine in the kitchen and beaming with pride at me.

"Captain Julia. I can't believe it," Dad said, shaking his head.

He seemed surprised although we had already discussed the news at dinner.

"We're so proud of you," Mom said.

"Your team voted you their leader, mija. Such a vote of confidence should be honored and respected."

"You should be proud."

I wasn't. I felt like a poser. The girls expected me to lead them to a state championship, and I had decided not to show up for the second day of practice.

"Will you join us?" Dad asked. "We can make you a mocktail."

My chest tightened. I wished I could tell him I didn't feel like celebrating.

I wished even more the words would form in my mind to explain why.

The only words that formed were, "Owen's coming for a swim."

Mom stopped her glass in midair and, with her other hand, pressed the Home button of her cell phone to check the time.

"I thought it would be fine since it's not curfew yet. Is it? Fine?"

"Of course, mija." Dad stood to kiss the top of my head. "Have you told him the good news?"

For a second, I imagined the good news as me playing football. The fact my father would refer to that revelation as "good news" made me realize how eager I was for my parents' support and approval. And how fearful I was that I wouldn't get it.

"Nope."

Not yet.

****

A FEW MINUTES LATER, OWEN'S ATHLETIC SANDALS announced his arrival before I could even see him. From the weeks at the pool and the beach in Florida, they perpetually squeaked. He reached around the gate to unlock it and stepped into the pool area wearing a white T-shirt with the Iron Valley mascot and his Hawaiian-style orange-and-red swim trunks.

"We match," I said rising from the steaming water in the hot tub to reveal the red bikini.

He watched me with an appreciative grin and then pulled his shirt over his head. No matter how many times he did that, my stomach always flipped, and my fingers itched to trace the contours of his abs. With the pool between us, we watched each other as if it were impossible to look away.

"You're killing me." He walked off the deck into the pool. After a few seconds, he came up for air and shook the water from his head.

"You aren't joining me?" I asked.

He rested his forearms on the side of the pool. "If I came in there, we wouldn't be talking, and I might be stupid here—especially with you wearing that bikini—but I really want to talk to you."

I could do talking. I took a deep breath, prepared to tell him I'd decided to quit volleyball and, instead, play football, but Owen spoke first.

"Football is such a disaster." He rambled about the quarterback position and Coach having these open tryouts and the changes in the offense and how he wouldn't get good looks from scouts as a result. The opening on the football roster was an opportunity. I just needed to recognize it. I would be the answer to Owen's stress and frustration. Being teammates would bond us like never before. *And*...he did write that note that said his favorite thing about the day was catching a touchdown pass from me. That could be a regular thing.

A breeze chilled my shoulders, so I ducked deeper into the bubbles.

"It's warm in there, huh."

"Perfect."

"I'm cold. You look amazing. I give." He climbed the pool ladder, hustled to the hot tub, and lowered himself into the water. "Ah. My muscles can use this."

"Press your back against one of the jets," I told him.

He did and groaned. "We should do this every night."

I leaned backward and looked at the stars sparkling in the cloudless sky. "Fine by me. Every night this season. We will be in this water soothing our sore muscles."

"At least one thing to look forward to." He closed his eyes and rested his head on a pillow.

I slid across the seat next to him. "Owen?"

He opened one eye. "Yes?"

"I have to tell you something."

He reached for me under the water. "I have to tell you something too." His fingertips tickled my bare stomach, then my side, and finally up my back to the nape of my neck. Owen looked toward the house. So did I. The windows were clear. No watchful parents.

"I missed you today," he whispered.

"Me too."

Owen leaned in until his lips brushed mine. But the kiss wasn't soft and sweet. Owen deepened it and scooped his hand under my butt, pulling me upward, until my legs were around him clinging tight. Our fears and frustrations and desires fueled the moment. Football. Volleyball. Being back at home and apart. Wanting to be closer to him, I ran my hand up his back and twisted my fingers into his hair. He traced the tip of his tongue over my bottom lip, and I thought I might have actually pulled a few of his curls.

"¡Dios mío!" Abuelita said, a few feet away. Owen and I jumped apart to see my grandmother, a false smile on her classically aged face.

Owen had the decency to look embarrassed. "Abuelita Medina. I didn't see you there."

"You could not see much in that position, no?"

"Ita!" Despite my attempt at scolding her, the urge to giggle nearly won. There she was in her black tankini, one hand on her hip and the other holding a plastic pitcher of frozen piña coladas. Seventy-three years old and throwing a late-night pool party with her girlfriends, and if I knew Abuelita, she probably wished she was back to her youth and in the hot tub with a "young man" like Owen.

"Five young firecrackers will walk through that gate in minutes." She pointed to Owen. "One is your grandmother, so, you know, behave as you will." With that, she left the pitcher on a table and walked back toward the pool house. "*Mi cielo*, your mother told me you were voted captain of the volleyball. Congratulations."

Owen turned to me with wide eyes. "I didn't know that."

"I thought Ally would have told you."

He shook his head.

"Sorry."

"Congratulations." He hugged me. "That's great."

"No no, handsome. In my day, the men did not touch what was

not theirs." She tsked. "What do you girls say nowadays? If you like it, then put a ring on it?"

"Ita, I'm eighteen."

"So was I," she called on her way back to the in-law suite that masqueraded as a pool house.

"Your abuelita's something," Owen said when we were alone again.

Absolutely agreed.

"So tell me about being captain," he said. "How does it feel?"

Two possibilities tugged at me. I could honor the conventions of polite conversation and say the right thing, *It was an honor to be elected.* Or I could tell the whole truth.

"It was an honor to be elected," I said, going with both options, "but..."

"But it doesn't change how you felt yesterday?"

I shook my head. "Nope."

He wrapped an arm around me and pulled me close. "I'm sorry, Jules."

"I don't want to let the girls down."

"I hear you. Completely."

I sat there, twisted up in Owen's arms, the warm, bubbling water calming me. It was one of those moments in life that tricked you into believing everything would be okay, that stressing about the small stuff was just that—small. Until it turned big.

The pool clock read 10:20. Almost curfew. "You have to go soon." Which meant I'd have to tell him soon. Like right that minute, soon. My chest fluttered.

"Wait. Real quick," he said. "So, when I said I missed you, I meant it, but that's not what I wanted to tell you."

"Okay," I said, anticipation building even more. I'd let him tell me his news, and then I'd share my own.

He took a deep breath. "This is going to be a surprise, but bear with me, okay?"

I nodded.

He shook his head and laughed a little. "Okay. My dad and I were talking again, and he convinced me."

"Convinced you of what?" I tried to smile, but my intuition

reminded me Owen had told me about his dad's grand plan at the park. Somewhere in my brain, the reality registered, but disbelief made its best effort to suppress it. Until I heard him say the words that would destroy everything.

With a full-watt, Owen Malone dimpled smile, he answered as if it were obvious. "Tomorrow, I'm trying out to be the quarterback."

CHAPTER NINE

SOME PEOPLE SAY I HAVE ATTITUDE—MAYBE I DO. BUT
I THINK YOU HAVE TO. YOU HAVE TO BELIEVE IN YOUR-
SELF WHEN NO ONE ELSE DOES. THAT MAKES YOU A
WINNER RIGHT THERE.
—VENUS WILLIAMS

OWEN MALONE—MY BOYFRIEND—WAS TRYING OUT
for quarterback. The top receiver on the Iron Valley Vikings high
school football team. Trying out for quarterback.

Against me.

Or, more accurately, since he had announced his tryout first and he
was already on the team, logic suggested I was trying out against him.

That is, if I decided to still go through with it.

At six a.m., well before my alarm was scheduled to sound, I
tapped my brothers' names into our group video chat and hit Call,
hoping they were awake. Surprisingly, Jorge answered first, fully
dressed and drinking a glass of milk.

"What up, baby sis?"

Before I could respond, Juan and Jake both logged in, looking
more disheveled than Jorge.

"Look who rolled out of bed late this morning," Jorge pressed our brothers' buttons.

"It's six a.m.," Jake disputed.

"Did you even go to bed last night, party boy?" Juan said.

"I have workouts in the morning too," Jorge answered. "You two aren't the only footballers in the family."

Jake grinned. "Make that three. Tell 'em, Little J."

"That's why I called," I said.

"Don't tell me you want to play football," Jorge said at the same time Juan threw his hands in the air and shouted, "Yes!"

Talk about dissenting opinions.

"I'd take you on my team any day," Juan said. "You're a natural, and you're wicked smart about the game. How could you not be as my protégé?"

"Whose protégé?" Jake challenged.

"Guys, focus. There's a bit of a problem with me trying out."

And, boy, could my brothers deliver when you didn't want them to.

"You're a girl," Jorge said.

"You have volleyball offers in the works," Juan said.

"Mom will kill you," Jake offered.

"Uh, thanks for those wonderfully helpful points," I said, and they nodded as if they couldn't spot sarcasm. "But there's something else."

They waited.

"Owen's trying out too."

"Lover Boy?" Jake asked.

I nodded, and Jorge whistled. Then for the first time since Chuck Noll coached the Pittsburgh Steelers, my brothers had nothing to say.

"C'mon, guys. I need your help. I can't talk to Mom about this. Or Ally. If I tried out against him, would that mean..." I couldn't bring myself to ask if Owen could take a girl—*his girlfriend*—competing against him. Or, potentially worse, winning.

"No way Owen Malone's ego could take losing to his girl-friend," Jake said.

"No way that kid could beat you for the position," Juan said.

"You sure you want to do this, Little J?" Jorge asked.

No. I wasn't sure...or maybe I was. I had first considered football because volleyball had felt too easy, like I'd grown as much as I possibly could have in that sport and wanted a different challenge. What could be more challenging than trying an entirely new sport in an environment where superficial convention said I didn't belong? I'd quit volleyball for no other reason than I loved football. Having my brothers around gave me my fill of the sport over the years, but with them gone, I'd missed it too much. Senior year would be my absolute last opportunity to play organized football. Could I abandon that opportunity to appease my parents? Or for a volleyball scholarship that wasn't even in hand?

My head and my heart battled, but the bottom line prevailed: I wanted to play football more than volleyball. More than almost anything.

After hanging up with my brothers, I found Mom sealing snacks for the team into Ziplock bags in the kitchen. I slid onto the stool to break the news. The girls brought their own lunches, but Mom still set out healthy snacks throughout the day to ensure everyone kept their energy up. It was a trick she learned from the football team, which had a snack station in the field house. Of course, the team paid for those snacks. My mom paid for these.

Her dedication to volleyball rivaled Ally's. They both knew with the utmost certainty it was our year. My chest tightened with the guilt that I was about to destroy the perfection they envisioned. "Mom?"

"Uh-huh," she said, counting granola bars and sealing them up.

"I have to tell you something."

She pushed the bags aside and leaned against the breakfast bar. Across from her, I took a deep breath. "I'm not coming to practice today."

"Are you ill?" she asked, opening the cabinet and grabbing the thermometer from the medicine box on the top shelf.

"No." Although the nausea festering in my stomach warned me I could be any second. "I don't want to play volleyball anymore."

There. Super easy. The words floated through the atmosphere of the kitchen—raw and undeniable. I should have felt a lightness in my shoulders, an overall release of tension from holding the secret inside for days.

The look on my mother's face sparked nothing close to release.

"But...it's your senior year."

"I know, Mom."

"And...you're captain."

"Sam will make a great captain."

"Janet McPherson called to interview you for the Herald."

"Someone else can do the interview, Mom."

"You're the leader of this team, Julia."

The world paused as we worked through the reality in the space between us. Abuelita bounded through the door in her satin robe and headed for the fridge.

"*¡Dios mío!* Trouble in the big house. Don't mind me. A little cream for my coffee, and..." She cut herself off to hum her way around the room.

I avoided Mom's gaze, instead watching Abuelita retrieve a spouted measuring cup and enough cream to get her through the whole day. That way, she could hide out in the pool house and avoid the discomfort of our family arguments. She blew me a kiss and left us in silence.

Dad wandered into the kitchen in his pajamas and when he saw us, glanced at his watch. "Aren't my girls going to be late for the second day of the big season?"

He pulled a coffee cup from the cupboard and rested it on the counter, a soft sound that seemed more like a crash in the awkward quiet. Coffee pot in hand, Dad studied us. "Something wrong?"

Mom didn't answer, clearly leaving the news-breaking to me.

I cleared my throat. "I decided not to play volleyball this year."

"I see." Dad poured his coffee and went for the cream. He shook the carton and frowned. "Let me guess. My mother was here?"

Mom spun toward him, and I wished I could see the look on her face. Was she angry at his nonchalant response? Tearful? Mouthing some command to him in the way parents silently communicated?

Dad sat on the stool next to me and took my hand. "What's the problem, mija?"

"I just don't want to play."

"Just like that?" my mother said, raising her voice. "You've played this sport your whole life. We've sent you to endless summer camps to perfect your skills. You planned to play in college. You loved the sport that much, but suddenly, that's all changed?"

"Yes," I admitted.

"This is ridiculous. Does this have something to do with Owen? We should never have let you go to Florida with them."

"Mom, it's not because of Owen." Although the thought of playing on the same team as Owen did influence the decision. Initially. But competing against him wouldn't earn me any hot dates in the near future.

Of course, getting my parents to support my quitting volleyball was the first hurdle to even broaching the football conversation.

Mom looked at my dad. "She's spending too much time with that boy. No more." Then to me, she said, "I'll see you at practice."

Without another word, she slung the bags of food and game plans over her shoulder and disappeared through the side door into the garage. Her car roared to life, and then the sound faded as she left.

Dad sipped his coffee and made a *yuck* face.

"Dad?"

"Julia?"

"Hit me with it."

He sighed and set his mug back down. "You're playing." Just like that. As if he'd said, *How about pancakes for breakfast?* or *Maybe omelets this morning?*

"I'm not."

He stood and crossed the kitchen toward the living room.

"Where are you going?" I asked.

"To get dressed, so I can take you to practice and get more cream for that dreadful coffee."

CHAPTER TEN

> **THERE ARE ONLY TWO OPTIONS REGARDING COMMIT-
> MENT. YOU'RE EITHER IN OR YOU'RE OUT.
> THERE IS NO SUCH THING AS LIFE IN BETWEEN.**
> **—PAT RILEY**

WAS IT ME, OR DID MY PARENTS DISREGARD MY DECI-
sion? Like, completely. Like I hadn't even told them.

Ridiculous.

Dad reappeared after a few minutes wearing shorts and a T-shirt,
his work-from-home outfit, and shuffled the car keys in his hand.

"I'm not going," I said again, at not nearly the decibel I had
in mind.

"Julia, your mother and I have given you a lot of freedom this
summer. You spent weeks with your best friend and your boyfriend
at the beach instead of working to save money for college with the
expectation that you'd practice volleyball while there, work hard this
season, and earn a scholarship."

Guilt festered in me. Plans could change, couldn't they?

"Dad, it's not how it used to be."

He crossed his arms. "Fine. Go get cleaned up. We'll go job
hunting today."

Job hunting? If I had any chance at quarterback, I'd need to work around the clock. No time for a job. Maybe even no time for friends. Or Owen. After I dealt with my parents, I had to find a way to tell my boyfriend that I might be the person throwing him touchdown passes this year—after I beat him out for the position, of course—and hope our relationship could handle any complications that might follow.

"Dad—"

"Car. Now!"

He didn't wait for an argument. I heard his car door slam in the garage and knew I wouldn't see him again until I slid into the passenger seat next to him. The situation felt impossible—like being down by two scores with no timeouts and a minute left to play. Weighing my options, I decided it was better to appease my parents, at least temporarily. I grabbed my backpack, water bottle, and shoes and obeyed my father. He drove me to the school, dropped me off, and said "Play hard" before driving away.

I looked at the large square wing of the school that housed the gym and wondered how I'd failed so completely in telling my parents. Maybe I should have faked sick after all. My phone vibrated, and the face on the screen was Jake's.

"How'd it go?" he asked when I answered the video call.

I turned the phone to show him the gym.

"That bad, huh?"

"Dad packed me up in the car and dropped me off. They barely even yelled."

"Ouch."

"Yep."

On my screen, Jake wore earbuds, the upper floors of university buildings in Pittsburgh creating a backdrop for his serious expression as he walked to practice.

"Jules?"

"I sense a lecture coming on."

He laughed. "Are you sure you want to do this?"

"I didn't even tell them about football," I said. "Only that I wanted to quit volleyball." Would Dad be more flexible if I said I wanted to play the sport he loved? Or would he be ashamed that his daughter had the audacity to think she could do something his boys had done so well? And Mom always loved that I was her little girl—the one person in the family that felt the same way she did about volleyball. It was my last year to experience the special bond-slash-torture I had playing a sport for my parent who was also my coach. Should I really give that up?

How would Mom feel if I did?

A couple of girls on the team arrived and greeted me and Jake when they walked by. We waited until they were gone to continue the conversation. Part of me wanted to know what Jake really thought, but a larger part expected him to encourage and support me no matter what.

"Tell me the truth."

"Yes."

"Do you think I can do it?" I asked, bracing myself for his answer.

He grinned. "I already answered. I knew what you were going to ask. That's what the 'yes' was for."

My heart swelled from his silliness, how well he knew me, and his confidence. "Have you heard anything about the other guys trying out?"

"Besides Lover Boy?"

I rolled my eyes.

"All right. I'm almost at the weight room. Pressed for time. There's this kid I heard a little about. Stanford, I think. He tried out for spring ball, but he was a little too raw. Attended camps all summer and supposedly improved a lot."

Ally's fear about losing out to people who were hard at work through the summer while we were lounging on the beach played in my mind. But for me, it wasn't limited to the summer. A lot of these guys played football their whole lives, quarterback or otherwise. I had some catching up to do.

"Anyone else?"

"A few misfits. They have some strengths, but nowhere near the whole package." He paused. He looked directly into the phone. "I have faith in you, baby sis, but it doesn't matter if I believe you can do it. *You* need to believe it."

I was right about that impending lecture, and true to Jake's usual style, he had my insides twisted all up in knots of anticipation and pride.

"And you have to believe it," he continued, "so you can make the guys on the team and the coaches believe it too, Jules. And the town. Well, screw the town. You don't owe them anything. The point is, I know you can play, but I also know it's not going to be easy."

As usual, Jake was right. It might not be easy, but if it were, it probably wouldn't be worth it.

****

WHEN I TUGGED OPEN THE DOOR THAT LED TO THE hallway parallel to the gym, I could hear the familiar smacking of hands and forearms against volleyballs. I stopped next to the trophy cases and listened. I *knew* the unmistakable sound of the gym. I could close my eyes and imagine it no matter where I was in the world. The girls shouted "Mine" to program themselves for game situations. New tennis shoes screeched against the waxed hardwood. Everything echoed.

What would football practice sound like? Strange? Or welcoming? In the mirrors that lined the back of the trophy cases, I caught a reflection of myself. Smiling. In the dull, neon of the hallway, my eyes sparkled. Just at the thought of what it might be like to play.

Coach Steve's whistle blew, and the sounds quieted as feet padded across the floor to him. When I opened the gym doors, I found Coach Steve, my mom, and the whole team circled up in the middle of the court. I couldn't bring myself to look at my mom's face. Or Ally's. Or anyone's, really.

"You're late, Captain," Coach Steve called. "Get your knee pads on and warm up."

He turned back to the girls as if that was the end of it, but it wasn't. *Nothing like the captain quitting the first day on the job.*

"Coach?"

He turned back around. "Captain?"

"I have something to say to the team."

My mom held on to the metal pole that supported the net. Coach Steve stepped back, and I came forward, standing at the front of a huddle that housed some of my closest friends over the last few years. Girls I respected. Girls I loved. My throat caught, but I pushed away the lump that settled there.

"You girls have been like sisters to me. We grew up together playing this sport." Around me, my teammates nodded. "That's why it's so hard for me to say this, but I can't be your captain." My heart pounded in that loud way where you can barely hear anything else, but I saw my friends' faces. A glimpse at Ally's intensified the pangs of guilt I'd been trying to ignore.

I should have told her before today. I closed my eyes. Like that could hide me from anything.

Over their questioning mumbles, I continued, "I've thought about it, and I'm not playing volleyball this year."

"You're joking," Ally said. She stepped toward me, her eyes wide with anger.

Around me, the girls' stares darkened. A few of my teammates—former teammates—laughed like this was a joke. I wanted to turn around and run away from their glares and judgy faces. Two things stopped me. First, they deserved an explanation. Second, my mom was there, and that was as good a chance as any to show her I'd made a mature decision.

"Volleyball has been my life forever. You all voting me your captain meant so much to me, but I can't lead you if my heart's not in it."

A minute that felt like an hour passed while the team watched me wide eyed. Finally, Sam pushed through the group and wrapped her arms around me. She squeezed tight. "I'll miss you, Jules. We all will."

My eyes clouded. The rest of the team followed their new captain's lead, each hugging me in turn. Maybe I read too much into it, but Ally's hug felt disingenuous. After embracing the girls, I shook Coach Steve's hand and turned to my mom. She swiped a tear from her face, but her red complexion revealed more crying was likely. I held her and kissed her cheek.

"I'm sorry, Mom."

She nodded but didn't speak.

I backpedaled from the group, taking in the sight of them. The gym. The net. The possibility. Everything I'd chosen to leave behind. "I'll root from the stands this year. You'll do amazing."

CHAPTER ELEVEN

*I'M READY TO BE UNCOMFORTABLE. I JUST WANT TO
DO MY PERSONAL BEST AND SEE HOW MY PERSONAL
BEST MEASURES UP AGAINST EVERYONE ELSE.
—ELISABETH AKINWALE*

ON MY RUN HOME FROM SHOCKING AND DISAPPOINT-
ing the girls I'd competed with since I learned to underhand serve
from the beginner's line, I considered calling Abuelita and requesting
she reiterate to my mom her philosophy on not doing something if
you couldn't do it well.

Perhaps that would offer Mom some solace. I hadn't been prepared for how deeply my decision to quit would affect her. Anger over
sacrificing my scholarship I could understand, but what she showed
in the gym wasn't anger. Not even close.

I loved my mom.

But my life was mine. I was the one who had to live it.

I'd made my decision. It was too late to turn back even if I'd
wanted to, which I didn't. I ran home with ease, as if half of my
body weight faded. I'd declared my freedom from the expectations
of volleyball, and I was lighter for it.

With Dad hidden away in the study, I retrieved a mesh bag of footballs and a stack of cones from the shed. When the field was set, I called Juan, my only brother not at practice or lifting.

"I need your help."

"Nothing impresses a coach like accuracy," he said, not missing a beat. "No matter the route, if you can hit it on the mark, you'll gain his attention."

To test accuracy, I'd need targets. I dug them out of the shed and set them up as Juan coached me.

"You already have a fluid throwing motion, so that puts you ahead of a lot of the guys who might suffer from the delusion that quarterbacking a team is nothing but touchdowns and glory."

Were my brothers too afraid to disappoint their baby sister to admit I'd committed to a bad idea? The possibility halted my entire workout. No use setting up another target or throwing another pass until I asked. "You'd tell me the truth, right, Juan?"

"I always tell you the truth, Jules."

I tossed the football from one hand to another. "You're my brother, and that carries some bias."

Juan held his camera a few inches from his face, the digital equivalent to looking me in the eye. "I work with quarterbacks all day. I know talent when I see it. Done with the questions?"

Emotions swelled from my chest, threatening to overflow down my cheeks. Not able to speak, I nodded.

"Good. Let's work on your drop backs."

I practiced a three-step. After two reps, Juan said, "Make sure you're driving back hard and getting good depth."

I alternated between practicing the skills and scribbling every golden piece of advice he offered in Jake's notebook, which I'd commandeered. Juan even revealed Coach Vincent's favorite plays so I could practice those routes. My list of skills to prep maxed out at three pages. A lot to accomplish with seven hours until tryouts.

"All right," Juan said. "Enough writing. Let me see you do it."

I propped up my phone, so Juan had a view of me on the field, gripped a ball in my hands and got into my stance. Feet shoulder width apart and staggered.

"You're leaning too far forward," Juan said, his voice loud in the silence of the space.

I adjusted by standing a little more upright. "Better?"

"Good. This isn't backyard ball, Jules. We taught you this stuff when we were kids, but you never had to follow the fundamentals in every motion for pickup games. Playing on the team will be different. You need to break any old habits you have."

"Okay."

"Don't bend your elbows."

I straightened my arms.

"But don't fully lock them either."

I nearly sighed but caught myself with the thought that he was helping me, and better to mess up in the backyard with my brother than on the field when every snap counted toward making the kind of impression that would earn me playing time.

"Good. Do it again."

I took my stance. Again. And again. Too many times to count. And then we moved on to the three-step drop. Then the five-step.

"You've got this, Jules. But remember, you're a girl."

Thanks. I'd almost forgotten that.

"I hope it won't matter later on in the season, but Day One? The fact that you're a girl will be all anyone is talking about."

"I'd rather they talk about my ability," I countered.

"You can't control what people talk about, Jules. If you want to play this position, best to accept that yesterday. Stay focused and play your best. That's all you can do."

****

WITH MY PHONE DARK AND THE SPEAKERS SILENT, eight footballs kept me company. I took as many reps as I needed until I felt comfortable with every item on pages one and two of Juan's list. Definite progress. When I first dropped back, my drive step didn't gain enough distance, so I repped it again and again. Then, to ensure my body was controlled, I ended a three-step drop by standing on one leg. The test of balance knocked me on my booty a few times. I'd need flawless balance to execute the most intensive item on my brother's list—the Slugo Seam route. Don't get me wrong. I knew routes. Gos, slants, curls, digs, seams, wheels, posts, bang posts. In my experience, if you could throw out any word in the English language, you could connect it to the name of a football route.

The Slugo Seam was one of Coach's favorites. I'd seen my brothers execute it before. Three-step drop. Pump fake the slant. Drop back two more steps. Throw a seam. *Easy.*

Or...easy to *watch*. Not to execute. I fell so many times I think the ground was offended. My brain might have been a little rattled, too, because when I heard my Dad's voice behind me, I jumped like a receiver catching an overthrown end zone pass.

"You have no control," he said.

Thanks, Dad. My bruising gluteus maximus already informed me of that sad fact. "I thought you were working."

"I thought you were at practice."

Touché.

"Technically, I *am* practicing," I said.

He crossed his arms in an all-too-obvious *I'm your dad and plan to tell you what's up* pose. "Last I checked, volleyballs were white and round."

Maybe I thought he deserved the respect of hearing the truth in a direct way. Or, more likely, I wanted to see his face when I told him, to gauge if he thought I was making a mistake or if he had any faith in me at all. I tucked the ball against my hip and squared my shoulders. "I'm going to football practice tonight to try out for quarterback."

He closed his eyes. "Sweetie, you don't have to do that. This family is done with high school football."

Didn't *have* to do that? Seriously? As if I would make a life-altering decision like this because my last name obligated me? No doubt my brothers influenced each other in major life decisions and even minor choices—such as what toothpaste to stock in the bathroom or the best movies for a Friday night. Sports-related—*Remember the Titans*, *Rudy*, *Hoosiers*—obviously. But when it came to the choices that mattered, we'd always had the ability to distinguish ourselves. That's why Juan went to a small, Christian college and Jake chose a Division I program. And why Jorge packed up and moved to Florida for school.

"Dad, this isn't some misguided attempt to extend my brothers' legacy. Jake gets it. Juan gave me the drills."

"That doesn't mean—"

"That I can pull this off?"

He backpedaled until he was sitting on a picnic bench under one of the old oak trees in our backyard. "I'd never say that."

"You're exuding confidence right now."

"Julia."

I raised my hands in surrender. "You don't need to believe in me, Dad. I do. So please let me practice."

A car door slammed in the driveway, and the dread in my father's eyes was like looking in a mirror.

I glanced at the time on my phone. Quarter to twelve. The volleyball team's lunch time.

"Does your mother know about football?"

"No," I whispered as if talking in a low voice might prevent Mom from finding us in the big, wide-open expanse of a backyard. She never left practice during our lunch break. Never.

The back door flew open.

"What are you doing out here?" She called from the porch but didn't seem keen on an actual answer. "Julia Medina, you will go back to that gym this afternoon and apologize to those girls."

With my parents standing side by side, the urge to cave overwhelmed me.

Everything would be easier. Mom's anger would dissipate. Dad could go back to pretending he had confidence I could do anything I tried. I'd play volleyball, a sport I excelled at. I wouldn't have to hear people talk about how girls can't do what boys can. Or that boys shouldn't be able to tackle a girl. I mean, how *indecent*. Or that a girl shouldn't have a shot at one of the most treasured positions boys covet. Or how audacious a girl must be to think she had a chance against a boy.

If I said *yes, Mom, you're right*, all of that fear and anxiety and potential for ill-will would disappear.

In fact, the potential for most things would disappear.

"Mom, I already apologized to them. I'm not going back."

She threw her hands in the air. "Where is this coming from? You attended camps this summer and played every day with Ally on the beach. I thought you loved it."

"I did," I said. "For a while."

"So what? You're burned out? You don't need to quit because of it, Julia. You take a break. You don't give up your team and your scholarship."

She'd always try to convince me that volleyball was the right choice for me. That I should love the sport like she had. That I was a true talent and shouldn't squander this opportunity. The pressure of her words pushed me into a corner. "Mom, I'm trying out for quarterback."

Her reaction demonstrated a series of emotions as if she were a comedienne flexing her acting muscles. Confusion. Surprise. Disbelief. Anger. Anger stuck around for a while. Then she laughed.

"I'm not joking."

"You might as well be," Mom said. "If you think I'm going to let my daughter play a sport I hated watching my boys play, you've absolutely lost it, Julia Marie. The hits. The helmet to helmet. Sacks. Face masks. And don't get me started on the crowd. If I have to hear some idiot high school football enthusiast shout 'Just throw it' one more time, I might be a danger to society."

"I want to do this," I said.

Mom closed her eyes and pressed her palm against her forehead. After three deep breaths, she spoke quietly. "Julia, I cannot imagine the things people will say about a girl quarterback. It will be so much worse than with your brothers."

"Mom, I'm not basing my life decisions on what people might or might not say. Or think. Or do."

"You could get hurt, mija," Dad said.

He was right. I could get hurt. But I could also get hurt playing volleyball or tripping up the stairs or taking a part-time job at a restaurant where the floors could be wet and I could slip and fall.

Following zen Jake's advice, I maintained my composure, made eye contact with both of my parents, and spoke as confidently as I could. "I've made a decision to do this, and I would appreciate your support. People will count me out before they even see me throw a ball, so it would be good to know that at least my parents believe in me."

After two full minutes of waiting for their blessing and neither of them speaking a word, I held my head high and returned to my drills. Their lack of support was fuel thrown on the bonfire of my disappointment, but the four pages of notes staring at me from my open notebook reminded me I didn't have time for disappointment.

I only had time to work hard.

CHAPTER TWELVE

COURAGE, SACRIFICE, DETERMINATION, COMMITMENT,
TOUGHNESS, HEART, TALENT, GUTS.THAT'S
WHAT LITTLE GIRLS ARE MADE OF; THE HECK WITH
SUGAR AND SPICE.
—BETHANY HAMILTON

AFTER LUNCH, I DUMPED THE CONTENTS OF MY DRESS-
er onto my bed and frowned. A lifetime of playing volleyball ensured
my athletic clothes screamed spandex. Spandex shorts. And tight bra
tops. *So* not going to work for football practice. Not that I was in line
for a Victoria's Secret modeling contract or anything, but I worked
out enough to rock spandex.

Confident Coach Vincent would not appreciate that and equally
confident I wanted to downplay all lady curves, I raided my brothers'
dressers until I found a pair of Iron Valley purple shorts and a football
T-shirt. Despite my relatively large stature, they made me look like
I'd been scientifically shrunk. Good news though. No curves to be
seen. In fact, I looked like a football player.

Excellent.

In truth, it wasn't about what was under the shorts but about being
part of the team. Iron Valley football players wore baggy, shapeless

shorts, so I would wear them too.

Maybe in a smaller size. I pulled on the drawstring until it was about the length of my arm and then tied it in a knot. Two knots. Mooning the team was probably not the best tryout day approach. Lucky for me, a year ago I had insisted on a pair of spikes for playing backyard ball with my brothers. I dug them out of the closet in the mudroom and tucked them into my backpack.

Finally, decked out in Iron Valley Purple, I faced the next challenge. Telling Owen.

I tapped his name on my phone. Voicemail. A slight reprieve. I'd call him again after I found a ride to practice, since I apparently couldn't depend on him taking me. My car was in the shop, deciding whether it wanted to survive or go to that scrap yard in the sky. Mom was still at volleyball. Dad didn't exactly ooze support, so asking him could have led to an outright refusal to even go. Operating under the don't-ask-permission-now-instead-ask-forgiveness-later model, I tapped a text to Jake.

Bro. I need a ride to practice. Mom and Dad are freaking.

The little bubbles signifying Jake was typing on the other end popped up. I looked at the clock. Practice started in forty minutes, and the school was about a ten-minute drive. Plenty of time to get there, but not necessarily to find a ride. As I debated borrowing Dad's keys and hoping he and Mom didn't show up at the field to yank me out of there by my horse collar, Jake responded:

Square's on his way. Was planning to go early to lift anyway.

Square Weaver. My backyard teammate from the birthday party. Thankfully, Jake had found me a ride with someone that I had at least met before! He texted me Square's number. Seconds later, a message arrived. It simply said:

Meet me at the corner.

Thank the football gods for Square. I tried Owen again while I waited. No answer. For the heck of it, I tried once more. Last thing I wanted was to surprise Owen by showing up on the field to compete against him. Ugh. I smacked my phone as if it was to blame as Square pulled up to the curb. I climbed into the front seat of his SUV.

"Thanks for the ride," I said when we were a few blocks into the trip.

He nodded and tapped the steering wheel to the beat of some old school R&B ballad. Was Square the sweet and sensitive type? He rolled down the window, hocked, and spit something green into the street.

Eh. Maybe not.

"So, uh, Square?"

"So, uh, Medina?"

Medina? The word sounded foreign, as if the surname didn't belong to me. Nobody ever called me Medina. I was Jules. Or the baby sister in that quarterback family. Or the Medina *girl*. "I was wondering what you thought about me trying out."

He looked sideways at me, his lips curling up in an oh-so-smooth way. If I remembered correctly, our middle hitter and now captain of the volleyball team Sam Strutters had had a crush on Square and that curling lip for the better part of high school.

"You don't need my approval," he said, turning his attention back to the road.

"No. I know." I'd said as much to my parents earlier in my backyard, but now that the time had come, curiosity tugged at me. "Of course, but uh...what do you think?"

"I think you gotta stop worrying about what everyone thinks."

Good advice. And like most good advice, difficult to follow.

Square parked behind the field house, and we hopped out. Shifting my backpack on my shoulder, I followed him through the gate where I used to wait outside for my brothers. Crossing the threshold excited and unnerved me, like a fish who swam along the shore her whole life and then decided one day to transition from the water to the sand.

Okay, that wouldn't be good. Hopefully *not* like a fish but some other metaphor that worked way better for this situation. We walked up a slight incline and then turned down a ramp. Square pulled the door handle, stepped inside, and pushed the door open a bit more, timing it so I could grab it and follow him. Ahead was a long hallway with traditional, institutional tile floors and depressing grey paint on the walls. Trophy cases and team photos adorned the wall on the left. He plowed ahead, not giving them a second look. I was tempted to check them out, but I needed to stick with him to avoid getting lost.

"Square?"

He turned and crossed his arms. "Look here, Medina. You wanna play, right? Have people take you seriously?"

"Of course," I said.

"Then stop with the timid, 'Uh...excuse me...' shit."

He was right, but I immediately looked to the ground, scolded.

"Don't look down. Look me in the eyes."

I obeyed, not that the advice was new to me. I knew this stuff! Make eye contact. Offer a strong handshake. Ask questions to engage others. Abuelita trained us all on manners and etiquette. And sports demanded confidence. Yet the prospect of actually stepping onto a football field to compete against a bunch of guys clouded my thoughts and actions like a morning fog settling in the stadium.

"Coach's office is in there." He pointed to the door with *Boys' Locker Room* written on it.

Excellent. Nothing like a trip into the boys' locker room on your first day. What would Abuelita's Rules of Etiquette say about that?

"Have you thought about what you're going to say?"

"Sure," I said. "I'm going to ask—"

"No. You're not going to *ask* anything. You walk in there, look *him* in the eyes, and tell him you're here to play quarterback. Not that you want to try out. Not that you need his permission. You have one shot at making a good impression."

Square's eyes were intense yet kind. I considered telling him I wouldn't let him down, but wouldn't he say not to let myself down? His philosophical mind games disguised as thoughtful advice reminded me of Jake. No wonder he and my brother were pals.

"I got this."

"Yeah, you do. The place is probably empty. Or almost empty."

I was hoping for totally empty. He slapped my shoulder, hulked down the hallway, and disappeared into the weight room.

In the quiet, I stood in front of the boys' locker room and wondered what the hell to do. Square's advice made perfect sense. Be confident. Make a good impression. But it was the *boys'* locker room.

I reached for the door.

I stopped.

I stepped way back, staring at the handle as if some telekinesis could save me from my current situation.

Jake's face flashed in my mind. *You got this, Little J,* I heard him say. Not sure he would actually say that about going into the boys' locker room.

You got this, Julia.

You got this.

Taking a deep breath, I stepped inside to hear voices echoing off the walls. Shit. Not empty. I hopped back out into the hallway and put my face in my hands. What was I thinking? I couldn't do this.

No. Square gave me good advice. I needed to follow it. I reached for the door handle again, hoping somehow it had locked itself in the last ten seconds.

No luck.

The tile walls, an aged eggshell color, resembled the girls' locker room, but boys were in there somewhere, hidden amid the rows of metal. What if Owen was one of them? What if he was undressed? What if that's how he found out I was trying out against him? I shouldn't have gotten so caught up in everything without telling Owen. He deserved to hear the news from me. And not in a locker room with all his teammates.

Maybe I should go to the weight room, find one of the coaches, and ask him to come into the locker room and bring Coach Vincent out to me.

Or maybe I should suck it up and not make a bigger mess of things by requesting special treatment.

The coach's office was in the back corner. I kept my eyes on my target, but I was only halfway there when I heard, "Hell yeah! There's a girl in here!"

Keep walking, I thought, playing Square's confident voice in my head and ignoring the urge to puke. In my peripheral vision, I saw bare skin. The glass, look at the glass!

"Hey, Jules." The slimy, provocative voice sounded like it belonged to the team kicker, Chase. Yep. He stepped in front of me, naked from the waist up. I refused to glance at the waist down.

"Hey," I responded, dodging him and hoping I sounded way less terrified than I felt.

"You can't even get a girl to talk to you in here!" one of the other guys teased, and Chase threw a towel at him.

"That's because she can see what little he has to offer."

Ugh. Boys.

They laughed and joked, making my heart race even more. I didn't give them the satisfaction of a glance. Finally, at the office, I knocked on the open door. With his back to me, Coach Vincent sipped a cup of coffee and read emails on the computer, which was nearly hidden by messy piles of football magazines, books, binders, and loose papers with x's and o's drawn on them.

"Come in," he said.

I did, standing behind him and studying the yellowing newspaper articles on the walls until he finished reading and turned. At which point, his eyes fell on my face, and he spit his sip of coffee back into the mug. "This is the boys' locker room, young lady."

"Kind of a Catch-Twenty-Two for me since girls aren't allowed, yet this is where I had to come to get my gear." I hoped he heard confidence in my voice and didn't notice me wiping sweaty palms on my shorts.

"Your gear?"

"To play football," I said.

He nodded slightly and then leaned back in his chair as if considering my request, but I remembered Square's advice not to ask for permission. If I allowed the silence, was that equivalent to asking permission? I tried to think of something to say, but he spoke first.

"You look familiar."

I'd stood outside of the stadium every game for the past ten years. I'd walked the field with all three of my brothers on their senior nights. As much as I wanted to earn this position on my own, hiding my connection to Juan, Jorge, and Jake would be about as possible as pretending I was male.

"I'm Julia Medina."

I tried to read his expression. Recognition. Brief surprise before... acceptance? My brothers led ten of his teams to the playoffs and, in some years, beyond. Last year, Jake's team won the state championship. Vincent was a good coach, but anyone who knew anything about Iron Valley Football knew he benefitted from a decade of strong leaders in the quarterback position. People might assume Coach owed a certain loyalty to someone with the last name Medina.

Not me. I figured he owed a shot to any student at the school.

"Coach, I'm here to play and want to be treated like anyone else. No special treatment for being a Medina. Or a girl. Just a chance."

He laced his fingers behind his head. "You don't need pads today. What you're wearing is fine. Head out to the practice field. Through that door." He pointed to a door right outside his office, one that would prevent me from walking through the whole locker room. Then, he picked up the sports section, signifying the end of our conversation.

"Coach?"

"Yes?" he said from behind the paper.

"We didn't talk about what position I want to play."

He lowered the paper and raised an eyebrow. "I thought that was a given."

CHAPTER THIRTEEN

IT IS NOT THE MOUNTAIN WE CONQUER BUT OURSELVES.
—SIR EDMUND HILLARY

WHEN I EXITED THE LOCKER ROOM INTO AN OPEN LOB-by, I suppressed the urge to jump up and down, squealing. Until I could get across the hall to the girls' bathroom. Then I squealed away. Football. Football! I was going to play football. The excitement and apprehension and anticipation swirled inside me, creating an explosive mixture of energy. Volleyball hadn't elicited that feeling for, well, I didn't know that it ever had. It must have. Why else would I play? Because that's what I thought girls were supposed to do? Should I have always played football?

Too late to worry about that. I was in the field house, minutes away from my tryout. I swiped the screen of my phone to call Jake, but he'd already texted me. So had Juan. Messages of encouragement. Tips to stay calm and focused. Ways to make a good impression. And from Jake, a short video clip.

"I have to get inside to lift, but I wanted to say that I know you can do this, Little J. You've got the skills. You know the game. You can beat out anyone they can find for the position. Believe that, and they will too. Love you." He blew me a kiss from the small screen, and I caught it in my grasp.

And prayed it brought me luck.

Outside the bathroom, a massive team picture of the state champi-on Iron Valley Vikings featured him prominently in the center. Guilt crept through me, devouring every cell of excitement along the way. This had been Owen's team for two years. He played quarterback with these guys in middle school. Even if I didn't want to see it be-fore, he had potential. He wanted to be quarterback, and I was there to take it away from him.

He didn't even know it.

I tapped the home screen of my phone to try calling him one last time, and a text popped up. From Owen.

About to head onto the field. Wish me luck.

Oh. No.

****

THE QUICKEST ROUTE TO THE PRACTICE FIELD WAS through the weight room. Good thing, too, since I wanted to tell Square the news anyway. I walked in expecting something similar to the closet-sized facility the volleyball team shared with the bas-ketball, wrestling, and swim teams—dark greenish carpet expelling a sweaty, mildew smell from its many years of existence. Dated weight machines that often stuck and clicked and clacked more than they actually worked.

But the football weight room smelled more of disinfectant clean-liness than the usual weight room smell of old sweat and even older cleats. I wondered how much money it cost to maintain that aroma. The floors reflected the brilliant, fully operational overhead lights and the sunlight shone through the floor-to-ceiling windows. A bold purple-and-black Viking, the school mascot, was painted on the floor at the center of the room. Several stations of free weights sat empty with pristine, silver bars and piles of barbells beside them. And no clacking machine sounds. Only the clear, concert-like voice of AC/DC's Brian Johnson belting "Thunderstruck" from a Bose surround sound system.

Square waved me over to the bench where he was lifting, sweat glistening on his face and arms. Standing under purple block letters that said, *Some wish for it. We work for it,* he toweled himself dry and introduced me to a few other linebackers, Ward Nixon and Ethan Trout, and a defensive lineman, Jimmy Medici. While I'd seen Jimmy around, I didn't know any of the three personally. Iron Valley enrolled enough kids that I didn't know everyone on the roster, especially since Jake's state championship team graduated a bunch of seniors. Square was one of the few returning starters. Probably because of that and his silent demand for respect, everyone I met in the weight room behaved as if it were completely normal for a girl to play on their team.

Jimmy even tried to make polite conversation. "You're Malone's girl, right?"

Yep. He bought me at a yard sale is what I should have said but didn't. You know, because making friends and all that.

"Wait, Creel told me Malone was trying out for quarterback," Ward said as he finished a set of squats.

Thanks for that. The rest of the guys lifting nearby went still for a second, studying me.

"Yes," I finally answered.

A few of them laughed, enjoying the richness of the drama. I needed to find Owen.

I mumbled goodbyes and then jogged the dirt path leading from the field house, around the stadium and back to the practice fields.

Juan had said, *Quarterback coaches want to see you calm and composed.*

They can teach foot work, plays, most everything else, but not leadership, Jorge had suggested.

Jake had said, *Have fun, and bond with the guys.*

Composure, leadership, bonding. No problem, especially considering the guys were already gossiping about Owen and me competing, and two sides were undoubtedly forming. Although assuming I even had a "side" of supporters was likely flawed.

Rounding the bend of the stadium, I tried to look ahead, but the field was too far to see the players clearly. I almost stepped into a massive puddle and jumped over it at the last minute. I landed in the grass to the right of the path.

"Look out!"

I turned to see a golf cart swerve away from me and crash into a trash can. The front end climbed the overturned, crushed metal. The back of the cart was piled with coolers and first aid supplies. Rolls of tape bounced out of the cart, escaping down the sidewalk.

I rushed toward the guy behind the wheel looking frazzled. "Are you okay?"

"Do you always dart in front of moving vehicles?" he responded.

"Uh…" I mentally scolded myself for the dreaded *"uh…"* Square insisted I avoid. "No. It was an accident."

He climbed out of the cart and pushed it away from the trash can with a grunt and impressive upper body strength.

"Need some help?" I asked, bending to lift the cart too.

"No, no. I'm good." The cart and trash can back in place, he stood upright and stretched. "Besides, wouldn't want you to get dirty."

I crossed my arms. "I don't mind getting dirty."

His eyebrow raised at the unintentional innuendo, and I turned away before he could catch the warmth on my cheeks. I rounded up the stray supplies and tucked them into a bag on the back of the cart.

"Thanks," he said. "You know, the coaches don't like the cheerleaders back here during practice."

I busted out laughing. Not that it was funny. More like I was nervous. Too nervous. "Not a cheerleader." I introduced myself and extended my hand. "Sorry about the cart."

He offered a strong handshake and studied my boyish athletic gear. "Medina?"

I nodded.

"Related to Jake and Jorge?"

"Little sister."

He nodded. "You're…playing…football?"

"Appears that way."

"Hmn."

Ignoring my curiosity over what that grunt of his meant, I asked, "And you are…?"

"Christian Santos."

Christian Santos. Where had I heard that name before? Aha. "Ally knows you!"

"Excuse me?" he raised an eyebrow, and, um, Ally had been right about Christian Santos. He had messy brown hair that sort of looked like it was meant to mess up in that exact way. His grin was lazy but sincere. He was almost...pretty.

"Sorry. My best friend Ally Malone. She, well, she mentioned you were the student trainer for the team."

"Yeah, I know Ally. Cool girl." He climbed back into the driver's seat. "So you need a ride, gridiron girl?"

A little voice in my head warned me against arriving on the field my first day of tryouts as if I were a princess with a chariot. "No. But thanks."

He climbed into the driver's seat. "You sure? I give the guys rides all the time." He blushed at his own innuendo. "Not like that. You know what I mean."

In the distance, my future teammates warmed up. Being late might be worse than the whole chariot thing. "Okay. If you're sure."

He patted the seat next to him, and I climbed aboard. Christian hit the gas and splattered mud on anything within a few-feet radius. We bounced along the path at a pace that boldly declared Christian didn't do slow, mud be damned. However, I felt relieved when he stopped the golf cart behind the bleachers where we were hidden from the guys on the field.

"Jump out here if you want. We can pretend this never happened."

"Thanks for the ride."

"Anytime."

He drove away, and I peeked around the steel tower of seats, where I'd watched all three of my brothers from. A handful of guys goofed around, running routes and making extravagant passes and throws. I imagined my brothers doing the same in our backyard. In fact, the image exemplified my childhood. A tickle of excitement in my stomach grew so overwhelming there was no room for fear or apprehension. The football field was where I was meant to be.

Which might take some explaining since gaping at me from the center of the field was Owen Malone.

CHAPTER FOURTEEN

*YOU HAVE TO EXPECT THINGS OF YOURSELF BEFORE
YOU CAN DO THEM.*
—MICHAEL JORDAN

"JESUS, JULIA," OWEN SAID, SPIKING THE FOOTBALL
against the grass. "I thought they were joking."

A few of the guys I'd met in the weight room laughed and waved
from the bleachers. They'd only look more at home if they held red-
and-white cartons of fresh popcorn.

"I tried to call you," I said, shameful of the feeble response.

"Tried to call me?" He put his hands on his hips, looked to the
sky, and took a deep breath. If the goal was to curb his anger, he
failed. "No, you know what? Screw that. I stood at your house
not twenty-four hours ago and told you I was going to do this,
and you said nothing."

Heat flushed over me. Couldn't everyone find something else to
stare at?

"I didn't know then," I said, lowering my voice and stepping
closer to Owen, as if that would create any kind of privacy.

"You weren't sure you wanted to try out until I said I did?"

"No. I thought I wanted to try out, but then when you said you were, I had to think." The stares from the players nearby heaped on the pressure. I hadn't even thrown a ball yet, and already, the lone girl on the team proved a worthy show.

A boy about ten years old popped up between Owen and me, throwing me off balance literally and figuratively.

"Hi," he said.

"Hi," I answered.

"I'm Luke. Coach is my dad. Who are you?"

Of course. My brothers had told me stories about Coach's passionate son. Technically a ball boy, Luke had the reputation for keeping everyone in line, motivated, and upbeat.

"Nice to meet you. I'm Julia Medina."

He shook my hand. "Medina? Like Jake and Jorge?"

"And Juan," I said.

"I didn't know Juan." His eyes widened. "You here to play football?"

"You bet."

He studied me. "You're a girl."

"Yep."

"Hmn." Luke rubbed his fingers over his chin as if considering something very important. "Cool," he said, finally. "I'm here to get the players juiced up. I do drills and stuff too. Let me know if you need anything."

I held back a smile. "Thanks. I'll do that."

With a fist bump, Luke ran off to play with a few other younger kids hanging around the field.

If only winning everyone over would be that simple.

"Okay. Bring it in," Coach Vincent called, and the group of quarterback hopefuls huddled around him and the other coaches. I stood as far from Owen as possible, avoiding eye contact.

"We have six guys..." Coach ruffled the papers on his clipboard and then tucked it behind his back before continuing, "six *players* trying out for the quarterback position. You all know the importance of this role. The quarterback must be highly skilled both physically and mentally. The quarterback must be a leader, leading with his...*their* actions and words." Coach sighed and shook his head. "Let's get started."

He referenced his clipboard again and paired us up for drills. He called four names before mine, as if building suspense. "Julia Medina and Owen Malone."

Brilliant.

Coach assigned us warm-up laps and stretches. Owen jogged next to me in silence.

"Owen, that's not what I meant."

He didn't respond.

"Say something," I said.

"Such as...?" He clipped his words with anger, but I wouldn't apologize. Taking advice from Square and my brothers, I behaved as if I belonged. Because I *did*. Apologizing for wanting the same things Owen did had no place in my life or on the field. Despite that, I should have told him. Out of respect for him and to avoid the on-field drama. That I had to own.

"I should have told you."

"That's right you should have," he said. "I poured my heart out to you about this team and what the season means to me. To my father. To my college prospects." Neither of us spoke as we ran by the coaches, but once we were out of earshot, Owen let loose. "Jesus, Julia. What the hell are you thinking?"

"I'm thinking I want to play football."

"Fine."

"Fine."

One of the other quarterback hopefuls—Dante, I think—jogged next to us. "Yo, Malone. You see Santos is back." He smirked at me. "Coach'll let anyone in this year, I guess."

Why was Dante critical of Christian? As far as I could tell, Christian Santos was a decent guy while this kid was a tool. I ignored the dig, instead resolving to kick Dante's ass up and down the field.

When Owen stayed silent through Dante's witless remarks, he got the picture and ran ahead to annoy someone else. Alone with Owen again, I wanted to say something to bring us back to the place where things were good and easy. But I wasn't sure there were words in the English language—or any language—to do that. A few feet away from each other, we ran in step, an electricity extending between us. A weak current that threatened to disappear at any moment.

When an assistant coach called "Partner stretches" after our laps, things got even worse, starting with the guys in the bleachers laughing and hooting until Coach Vincent told them to shut up. The other quarterback hopefuls and the receivers there to help with drills hit the grass, but Owen groaned. Before I could ask why, the answer became obvious.

Partner stretches were...intimate.

For instance, Dante laid on his back and put his leg straight up in the air while his partner, Alexander Stanford, leaned forward so the back of Dante's knee pressed against Stanford's shoulder. Dante's hamstring stretched when Stanford leaned forward over him, spreading Dante's legs in the process.

So, yeah. Intimate.

Owen blushed. "Do you want to go first? Or...?"

I answered by lying down, the blades of grass tickling the back of my neck. No big deal. We could do this, I coached myself while appreciating my decision not to wear spandex.

"Uh...lift your leg." He reached for my calf to pull my leg upright, but then he stopped short of touching me.

"Owen, you've touched my leg before," I said, as uncomfortable as he looked.

"That's different."

"How would you have reacted if Coach assigned me another partner, and *he* had to touch my leg?"

His gaze darkened. "Are you trying to make this better or worse?"

Someone whistled from the bleachers. Coach Vincent responded by closing practice and throwing the onlookers out to do something more productive. Once they were gone, he rubbed his temples. Jorge's voice sounded in my ear, *Coaches want to see leadership*. If Owen wouldn't defuse the situation, then I would. I took his hand and placed it on my knee. "Treat me the same as you would anyone else on the team."

He took a deep breath and then lifted my calf onto his shoulder. He pressed his knee against my butt and pushed forward until I felt a slight pull in my hamstring and a definite spark a little higher up.

So maybe that whole *treat me like one of the guys* was misguided. Owen mumbled and twitched the whole stretch, avoiding eye contact with everyone, including me. His hands against my bare leg teased my mind back to hundreds of times that same touch made me want to pull him closer and bring his lips to mine.

So. Not. Good.

To succeed on this team, I'd need to compartmentalize him. He might've been my boyfriend off the field, but on the field, he was first and foremost my competitor. Nothing sexy about that.

"Switch!"

Minutes later, Owen pressed the heels of his feet together and spread his legs. My job was to lean over his crotch and push down on his knees to extend the stretch. After about two seconds of alternating between looking at the grass far enough away that nobody could mistake me for looking at his—you know—and admiring the bright blue of the late August sky, I wondered what the hell I'd gotten myself into. Coach Vincent, fortunately, blew his whistle signaling the end of intimate partner stretches. Excellent.

Jogging toward the coaches, the possibility and potential of being a football player disintegrated the veil of drama and stress around me. There was only me and a football. We huddled up for instructions, and I wanted nothing more than to clap, bounce, or shout. I couldn't believe I was there. Under the sun. On the grass. Getting ready to play *football*. But I suppressed my urges and focused on Coach's words instead.

The drills started simple. Three-step drop. Five-step drop. Demonstrating the throwing stance. The first time I dropped back, I snuck a glance at the coaches and appreciated the raised eyebrows and surprised expressions. Over the years, my brothers' starting quarterback positions were challenged a time or two. Billy the Kid (I didn't think that was his real name) had wanted Juan's spot. Jake had faced transfer contenders every year, and in the late hours of the night, while we watched film together, my brothers bolstered their confidence due to one simple fact: their mechanics were flawless.

"People think footwork is so easy," Juan said once, shoving a handful of popcorn into his mouth.

"That's 'cause I make it look that way, brother," Jake had responded.

Lucky for me, my brothers taught me quarterback footwork when

I was five. And they laughed at me every time I did it wrong. Years of backyard ball refined the skills, and that afternoon, I'd worked out any remaining kinks. The coaches may have been surprised, but when I jogged back to the end of the line, the glares from a few of the other contenders showed me their responses were anything but pleasant. Owen didn't even look at me.

I shook it off. Owen Malone was my competitor. I didn't need his approval.

The complexity increased to bag drills. Coach tasked us with dropping back, then weaving through a series of bags along the line of scrimmage, always keeping our eyes down field. To my disappointment, Owen excelled at them. I knew from Jake's praises and my own eyes that Owen ran great routes. His natural and refined athleticism ensured his footwork around the bags was precise.

Damn.

A junior transfer everyone called Lewis embarrassed himself by continually tripping over his own feet or the bags, even planting face down in the grass at one point.

"Are you serious with this kid?" Owen muttered from behind me in line, and his critical tone made me squirm.

In the few months we'd spent together, he had teased his sister and closest friends, but his motives had never felt unkind. Was he spouting off out of anger? Or was that how he behaved on the field? Like some competitive jackass?

Worse yet, would he say stuff like that about me when I wasn't around to hear it?

Coach led us through a few more individual drills and then brought the receivers onto the field. After catching Alexander Stanford's passes, the receivers shook the sting from their hands. His sophomore status unsettled me even more. If the coaches saw a significant improvement in him from the spring, they might invest their time and energy into cultivating his talent since they'd have three full years with him at the helm. I hoped the fact that Chucky Bass would be coming back next year as a senior negated Stanford's three-year-starter potential, but you never knew with coaches. In middle school, I'd had a basketball coach who started the first five girls out of the locker room for the game. What sense did that make?

When the receivers dropped Stanford's passes, Owen bounced up and down next to me, mumbling, "You can't drop that ball," or "Are you kidding? That was right there!" His reactions brought my thoughts back to volleyball for the first time since stepping on the field. Nothing irked me more in the gym than watching another hitter tip a good set, or worse, forearm pass it, instead of timing the perfect jump and at the peak crushing the ball into the hardwood on the other side of the net. I imagined for a seasoned receiver like Owen, watching other players drop delicious passes was a little like that.

More importantly, it solidified for me that although Alexander Stanford was clearly a quarterback, Owen Malone thought like a receiver. The danger in that revelation, though, was that I thought like a volleyball player, not a football player.

That would have to change.

CHAPTER FIFTEEN

THE ROAD TO SUCCESS RUNS UPHILL.
—WILLIE DAVIS

AFTER A FEW WARM-UP REPS, COACH SPLIT US INTO two groups of three. My line consisted of Dante, Stanford, and me, which basically gave me the prime opportunity to line up across from Owen. We dropped back together, and he threw a hitch to the right while I hit the mirrored route on the left. His pass fell to the ground, and mine dropped into the receiver's arms. We jogged to the back of our respective lines and when the time came repeated the routes again. That time, we both completed our passes. Our rhythm continued that way. Hitches. Slants. Curls. I didn't connect on every attempt, but at the end of the hour, I'd done okay.

If I wanted to win the starting position, I'd have to do a lot better.

"Bring it in," Coach called.

The quarterback contenders and the receivers hustled over, wiping away sweat and sucking down as much water as possible.

"Good practice today. To be successful, we want to transition from these sessions to team practices quickly. We need a quarterback with significant skills already, but someone who is also a fast learner. That way we can get the offense together, running plays as soon as possible."

I glanced at Owen and wondered if he thought he had an advantage since he'd studied the offensive playbook all summer. Fortunately for me, I'd studied with him. But he had varsity experience that I did not.

I could spin my head silly debating the rankings. Probably best to focus on what I could control—me.

"After tomorrow," Coach continued, "the other coaches and I will narrow this group down to three contenders."

Three? That meant half of us were done in twenty-four hours? We looked sideways at each other, beginning the calculations.

That *focus on me* plan lasted long.

I could definitely rank above two-left-foot Lewis and probably the seemingly impressive six-foot, four-inch Cody, or "Codester" as Dante called him, since he squatted so low on his drop back that we were nearly the same height in our throwing motions. Yes, definitely. During side-by-side throwing drills, the receivers caught my passes before Dante even released the ball, so I ranked myself above him too. I repressed a smile, not wanting to seem overconfident, but I was. Confident, that is, that the top three would be me, Owen, and Alexander Stanford.

But then Coach dashed my hopes with a few short words.

"Maybe even two."

****

THE NEXT TWO HOURS OF RUNNING BLEACHERS, climbing the steep hill behind the school, and sprinting gassers allowed me time to get out of my head and focus on the intense challenges for my body. After hearing the stories from my brothers, I had to admit the fact I didn't puke all over the field screamed victory.

"Medina?" Square yelled when I was toweling off on the sideline.

I looked his way.

"Ride home?"

"Sure."

"Meet me out there in ten."

Gatorade bottle in hand, Owen sauntered the ten yards between us, surprising me when he said, "I'll walk you out."

His cheeks flushed from the exercise, and his shirt was wet with sweat. It clung to his shoulders and chest. I imagined the tanned skin underneath. *What am I doing?* I thought and forced myself to look away. Competitor on the field. Boyfriend off. But...we were off the field, right?

"Sure," I said. I kept a respectable distance as we walked in silence, the space between us bloated with things I expected he wanted to say and the emotions preventing him from saying them.

And probably a good bit of sexual tension and ego weaved in there too.

Finally, behind the metaphorical curtain of Square's SUV, Owen spoke. "So you quit volleyball?"

I nodded.

He stared at me for so long I thought we might need to walk back into the field house for the next day's practice. "You quit a sport you're practically guaranteed a scholarship for...why? To compete against me?"

"I didn't want to compete against you," I said.

"But you are."

Yes. "Look. I already apologized. I know I should have told you."

He shook his head. "It's more than that. I don't know how else to say it, but this is a huge mistake."

"Excuse me?"

"You know football and don't have a bad arm, but come on, Jules. Be serious. Giving up volleyball for football? You can't win this."

Hearing him say the words I'd feared in my own mind over and over tempted me to believe them. I couldn't win the starting spot. I couldn't play football. What was I thinking? What had I done? Each question devoured my energy and fed it to the darkness that threatened to control my decisions.

If I let it.

But that's something I definitely couldn't do. In fact, I played his words in my mind again. *Be serious.*

Hellfire heat smothered me.

You can't win this.

And exploded in unencumbered fury.

"Don't tell me what I can and can't do," I spat at him.

"Jules..." he said in that tone that people used when they were trying to mollify your anger although they caused it and anger was a perfectly appropriate response to their asinine behavior.

"Don't." I climbed into the passenger side of Square's SUV.

Owen leaned through the open window, his voice low. "You try out in *my* sport, against *me*, and I'm somehow the bad guy."

"*Your* sport?" I said, hopping back out of the car and into his face. "Why didn't you say so? So, what's the protocol? Does everyone on the team need a permission slip from your agency to play?"

"You're being ridiculous."

Sometimes you had to be to make a point. And when you were too angry to see anything in the world besides the ridiculous. "And how far does this extend? Do NFL players need your permission too?"

"You know, sometimes you're a real pain in the ass."

"Maybe we have that in common," I said, and our eyes locked. His cheeks were still flushed from the exercise and the argument. His hair curled at the ends from sweat.

Maybe it was the rugged attraction between us or the fact that gazing at Owen in that way for the last six months always led to me leaning into his chest and pressing my lips against his.

Always.

So there in the parking lot of the football stadium, with my future teammates all around, and despite the wild beast of an argument between us, I leaned toward him, thinking how I fit perfectly in the cradle of his arm. Before my fingertips reached his chest, he put his hands on my shoulders and said, "It's not going to be like that, Jules."

Then he turned and walked away.

CHAPTER SIXTEEN

I'M STRONGER THAN I THINK I AM. MENTALLY. PHYSICALLY.
—MISTY MAY-TREANOR

MOM FEARED THE NEWSPAPER DURING FOOTBALL
season. She did her best, but largely failed, to ignore fans coaching
from the bleachers. For the games, she packed rolls of Tums in her
coat pocket along with concession stand change she would clink
anxiously during third-down situations. Reading sports reporter Rand
Denton's writing that morning—which had, in not so many words,
announced to the whole town that a girl had the audacity to try out
for a boy's job—the thought struck me that she might have been on
to something with the antacids.

I feared that across town in his kitchen, Owen sat at his table reading Denton's article, growing even angrier that I decided to compete
against him. I pressed the Home button on my phone as if I'd missed
a message with it a foot away.

As expected, no messages.

I finished my toast and eggs, chugged the milk in my glass, and
moved to the backyard to take out my frustration on the field. When
I hustled after a stray ball, I caught a glimpse of the pool reflecting
the hot sun. And the hot tub. Owen ran his fingers along my wet

skin in that hot tub. The memory brought an instant grin to my face before disappointment settled in my gut. We'd never fought before. Not even a stupid, short-lived disagreement, but yesterday, he'd left me standing in the parking lot of the field house. Rejected. And embarrassed.

I picked up my phone from the nearby picnic table. No missed calls. No messages. I could call him, or I could keep working out. Footsteps behind me had me spinning in the hopes I'd see Owen.

"So it's true." Ally stood across the yard holding the newspaper in her hand as if it were a weapon against me.

"Al..." I wanted to tell her I was glad she'd come, that it meant so much to me, that I had so much to talk to her about. Which of course was totally stupid. She gave a plethora of nonverbal cues— the newspaper, the hands on hips, the narrowed eyes, and even the raised voice—declaring those sentiments were unequivocally unwelcome. I'd hurt her, and no matter how much I wanted to play football, that sucked.

"You quit volleyball for this? Is this some sort of dare between you and your brothers?"

"No, Al." I wouldn't take a dare that could potentially change the trajectory of my life, especially when it came to college scholarships. Even for my brothers. My best friend should know that.

"You need to come back to the team."

"I can't."

She shook her head. "Julia, this is ridiculous. You realize that."

Now, my hands were on my hips. "I don't, actually."

"I thought if I came here, I could convince you to come to practice with me. I can see that's a waste of my time."

She paused, offering me the opportunity to contradict her. I didn't.

"Nobody will take you seriously."

"You're my best friend. You should take me seriously."

"Your best friend? You want my support, yet you don't even tell me? I find out you're quitting with the rest of the team? What the hell is that?"

I sighed. It hadn't been until that moment in the gym, looking at her and the rest of the team that I'd finally realized the same thing.

I'd been wrong. It sucked, but it was true.

"Maybe I didn't do this the right way," I said. "I'm sorry. But has anyone given me any consideration for how hard it's been?"

"Of course, it's been hard, Jules! You're a girl. You know how boys are with their football. You're nothing unless you've sweated next to them and had your block knocked off with a tough hit or whatever. *And* if you're a boy."

"*I* can play," I said calmly, as if that was the sentence that could connect all the dots. As if saying it would make it real. As if that would be enough to convince my best friend for my whole life that she should support me and stop this nonsense.

She laughed a cold, humorless sound. "You're deluded."

The verbal blow struck me with the intensity of a physical assault. My arms fell to my sides, and I backpedaled to lean against the picnic table. Ally had never said anything that cruel to me. Or in that tone.

"I think you should leave."

But she didn't. "Not to mention what this is doing to my brother. What the hell are you thinking?"

"That I should have picked a different best friend." The words felt good rolling off my tongue, like she'd hurt me, and she deserved to feel that burden too. But the second the words were spoken guilt rushed over me in a powerful, immediate wave.

"I am your friend," she said, in the quiet way she did when she tried to avoid crying. "Well, at least I was. This is me delivering my last best friend speech to help you. Stop this stupidity."

Her words pushed me back to anger. "You know, a real friend would have the decency to at least ask why I want to do this."

"Maybe, given everything you're risking, the answer doesn't matter."

"You should go," I repeated, afraid one of us would escalate this and say something even worse—something we couldn't come back from.

She shook her head in disgust and threw the newspaper over her shoulder as she walked away. The argument devoured my strength to stand. Ally Malone. My best friend. Telling me something I'd committed to didn't matter.

When I rekindled the initiative to do my drills, the passes missed the target much more than they did before she arrived. And I hated myself for it. If I got playing time—*when* I got playing time—I would need to play through distractions. And endless criticism.

Still, accuracy was not exactly happening.

"This is useless," I muttered as I walked off the field, leaving a mess of footballs and targets behind.

I did what any self-respecting female high school quarterback would do. I checked my phone again for messages—there were none, rounded up healthy snacks and Jake's notebook, and went to the one place where good advice was a guarantee. The film room.

Admittedly, our film room—complete with white board, leather recliners, and a seventy-five-inch 3D, smart television—could be described as extravagant. So could the athletic complex behind our house: a lined football field, a sand volleyball court, a swimming pool with a hot tub and covered pavilion, a shed filled with more equipment than some high school athletic departments. When my parents couldn't agree how to spend money they inherited from my great grandparents, they decided to indulge in the things their kids loved—sports. Especially considering excelling at sports could earn us college scholarships to supplement the little they could stash away for that too. And that's how our modest, middle class suburban house became equal parts athletic training facility and top-tier teenage hangout.

When in need of quality advice, there was definitely a go-to guy in my life. Jake. But he was busy at the moment pursuing his own football dreams. His written words would have to do. I flipped open the notebook I'd confiscated from his room, and a well-scrolled quotation, outlined in purple and black marker read:

THE MEASURE OF WHO WE ARE IS WHAT WE DO WITH WHAT WE HAVE.
—VINCE LOMBARDI

What did *I* have? Ability, yes. A killer film room to study? Absolutely. Support? Not so much. Not from my parents, my best friend, my boyfriend. Maybe not even my coach, although something told me not to count Vincent out. My brothers were great but also busy. Remote in hand, I turned on the TV and thought of Ally. We'd always used this room as our own movie theater. Sleepovers. Double dates. You name it. We'd even watched Misty May and Kerri Walsh win gold medals in this room.

I shook my head, dismissing the thought. Ally said my dreams didn't matter. She refused to support me. My decision to play football affected her life in a big way. We'd done everything together, and that was about to change. I got that. It weighed on me, but not enough to spend my days doing something I had no passion for. I had to make the best decision for me, and that meant being the starting quarterback of the Iron Valley Vikings. No sacrifice, no challenge, no obstacle would keep me from doing that.

Period.

With Jake's notebook in my arms, I indulged, turning the worn pages, observing doodles of footballs, plays, scoreboards, and uprights.

I settled on a row of stick figures where one was significantly shorter than the others. The short one held the football. An arrow linked the drawing to two quotations:

YOU HAVE TO BE A GREAT LEADER. YOU HAVE TO BE DETERMINED. YOU HAVE TO BE CONSISTENT EVERY SINGLE DAY. THE GUYS HAVE TO LOOK UP TO YOU. THEY HAVE TO BELIEVE IN YOU WHEN YOU STEP INTO THE HUDDLE—THIS IS OUR GUY, THIS IS THE GUY THAT'S GOING TO LEAD US.

And...

PEOPLE HAVE BEEN TELLING ME MY WHOLE LIFE THAT I'M TOO SHORT, BUT IT'S NOT BEEN A FACTOR. THAT'S JUST THE WAY I LOOK AT IT.

I didn't need to read the name scrolled beneath the quotes to know who said them. Russell Wilson. The shortest quarterback to ever win the Super Bowl. People judged Wilson for his height. He was five foot eleven—an inch shorter than me. They said he couldn't play in the NFL. He si-lenced those criticisms time and again with his actions.

Why? Because he was mentally tough. Not because he was tall. Not because he could throw—of course he could do that. And not because he was a man. Mental toughness.

Hoping Jake wouldn't mind, I scribbled those two words next to Wilson's quotes.

Mental toughness

If I was going to silence the people saying I couldn't play quarterback, I'd need mental toughness too. I pulled books from the shelves, referencing earmarked pages, drafting practice plans, marking drills I wanted to try. And looking for potential moments of leadership. If I was going to win the starting quarterback position of this team, I'd have to follow Russell Wilson's lead and instill the kind of consistency and confidence required of a team leader, so when the guys stepped into the huddle—or onto the field, if we were going hurry up—they looked up to me, they believed in me, they knew I was the *girl* to lead them.

Not to deliver a cheesy pun or anything, but that was no *short* order.

CHAPTER SEVENTEEN

IT'S NOT THE WILL TO WIN THAT MATTERS—EVERYONE HAS THAT. IT'S THE WILL TO PREPARE TO WIN THAT MATTERS.
—PAUL "BEAR" BRYANT

I WENT INTO PRACTICE THAT NIGHT INTENDING TO HIT the field with the unwavering and unapologetic confidence of Russell Wilson and the immutable enthusiasm of Brett Favre. You know, totally doable. Owen and I didn't speak. We simply coexisted in the same space, going after the same thing, while failing to acknowledge the other was there.

There were moments, although I wasn't sure whether from strength or weakness, that I considered talking to him. Complimenting him on a play or asking him a question. But then an image of how he'd pushed me away and left me standing like an idiot next to Square's SUV changed my mind.

Wanting to give us a more realistic look, Coach Vincent called for shoulder pads and helmets and added linemen to the drills. The equipment weighed me down more than I'd like to admit, but I thought of the words of inspiration from Jake's notebook and wanted to exude the kind of confidence Wilson demonstrated when he took the field.

Some of the guys gawked and giggled while I warmed up, and I considered telling them a thing or two about gender stereotypes and giggling. But I thought better of it and kept my mouth shut. Besides, I had other things to worry about.

Like sticking my outstretched hands into the center's crotch.

When I stepped up to the line for the first time, the center, Ben Jones, jumped up and walked around in circles, steeling himself for the experience.

"Let's go!" Vincent shouted. "Run it!"

Jones got back into stance.

"Red thirty-four! Red thirty-four!" I pressed my thumbs together and opened my hands wide like a bird opening its beak. My right hand grazed his ass, and he jumped as if I'd stuck his backside with a needle.

"Jones!" Coach Vincent pounded his way across the turf toward us. "What's the problem?"

The center blushed and looked sideways at me.

"Answer when I speak to you, son."

"She's a girl, Coach," Jones mumbled, making the guys nearby laugh.

"Poor guy," quipped Austin Moody, a returning safety from last season. "First time a girl touches his balls—"

"You think I can't hear you, Moody!" Coach yelled without taking his eyes off Jones. His tone settled us all into silence.

Coach took a few deep breaths. "Let me make this clear." He paced the field, and I swore he wouldn't speak again until he looked into each of our eyes. "You are all teammates. *Teammates.* I don't care if you're male, female, white, Black, Hispanic, gay, straight, tall, short, fast, slow, or anywhere in between any of those dichotomies. If you're on this team, that's all that matters."

He paced some more then glared at Moody. "I will not tolerate derogatory remarks about any player on this team. By anyone. Is that clear?"

We spoke a chorus of, "Yes, Coach."

"That doesn't sound convincing."

"Yes, Coach!"

He nodded. "Good. Run the play!"

For the first time, Jones held steady when he snapped the ball. Good thing because repetitive false start calls wouldn't win either of us points with the coaching staff, and I needed to perform flawlessly today to make the impending cut. I threw crisp passes and felt good about my reps.

Until Austin Moody, who clearly didn't listen to a word Coach said, mocked my throwing motion.

"Yo, Malone," he said on the sideline between plays. Owen didn't look eager to hear what his teammate had to say. "Just think. If Medina gets the starting spot, you'll be sleeping with the quarterback."

I gripped the laces of the ball in my hand debating whether I could get away with launching it into his junk, but Square stepped in front of me.

"That's a dangerous place to be," I said.

"Looked that way, but maybe you can work it out on the field."

Square—living up to his name.

Offering me some solace, he grabbed Moody by the jersey and pushed him back into the secondary. I got under center again and decided to throw the ball to whichever receiver Moody guarded. Stupid? Maybe. It was never a good idea as a quarterback to try and force a play, but it would feel good!

I snapped the ball, read the defense, and fortunately for me, the best throw was where I wanted to go anyway. Moody tried to reach for the ball, but the receiver grabbed it out of the air before he could and ran for a touchdown. We celebrated on our way to the sideline, and Owen jogged onto the field to take his reps.

"Luck, Medina," Moody said, squirting water into his mouth. "Throw it my way again, and it's a pick six."

Square handed me a bottle.

"I don't see how," I said, swigging a squirt. "You bobbled at least six would-be interceptions last year but couldn't hold onto the ball. Has something changed?"

A few of the guys choked on their drinks, and a couple others spit theirs out entirely. Even ever-so-serious Square smiled. Moody did not. But he did leave me alone.

When almost everyone disbursed, I caught Christian watching me. We hadn't spoken since he dropped me off behind the bleachers for tryouts the day before.

"Hello..." I said, drawing out the word.

"You shouldn't let them get to you," he said, busying his hands by ripping strips of athletic tape.

"He didn't get to me."

Christian mumbled something and turned away.

Good talk. Thanks.

Moody didn't get to me. Except he kind of did. Not that I'd admit it out loud. Hopefully what I said to him would get around and everyone would know I wasn't a pushover. Maybe that would be enough.

Or I would resort to the *precision missile to the crotch* idea.

My plan to compartmentalize Owen from my efforts on the field had the same effect as the Steelers' steel curtain. I attributed my success to a blend of grit and determination, with a side of anger.

I went hard for the rest of practice, pushing myself physically and aiming for accuracy in my footwork and my throws. When the other quarterback contenders, which were down to four since two-left-foot-Lewis didn't even come back for the second day, took their reps, I stood behind them not to scope out the competition but the defense. I read the movements and debated what decisions I would have made if given the same look. I recognized tells the defense had when they were going to blitz or drop back into coverage, and as a result, I threw three more touchdowns by making good reads.

When Coach called us in, I thought I'd done enough to score a top three spot. Or at least I hoped I had.

"Quarterbacks, stay here. Everyone else, head to the weight room."

Square patted me on the back when he walked by, and I wondered if I had been a boy if he would have hit my butt instead. I didn't even want to think about how to navigate butt slapping etiquette this season.

I glanced at Owen, wondering what he thought of the practice, what he thought of my reps, but he looked away. Did he still believe I couldn't win the position? I wanted him to approve of this because it meant so much to me, and in a moment of painful clarity I feared he wanted the same from me.

It wasn't possible for us both to get what we wanted.

What if I made the cut and he didn't? Could he handle that? What if he made it and I didn't? No. That couldn't happen. Owen was a receiver, not a quarterback. Eager for glory, Owen's dad pushed him too hard to succeed and judged him too harshly when he failed. My stomach twisted into a knot that weighed more than my shoulder pads. I didn't want to be the source of Owen's failure.

But I wouldn't allow myself to be the source of my own either.

"Medina," Coach Vincent said. "Come with me."

I followed him to the bleachers.

"So, how have the last two days gone for you?"

"Great, Coach," I said automatically and then tried to ignore the insecurities flooding my mind in contradiction.

He nodded. "How do you think you've done?"

"Not as good as I can do, but probably better than you and the other coaches expected."

The amused smile I saw on his face when I first showed up in his office returned. "You might be right about that, at least the last part. What do you think you could do better?"

I took a moment to think about it and then spoke with a confidence that would make Square—and Russell Wilson, for that matter—proud. "I could be more accurate, but that will come with time. Not only from the practice but by knowing the receivers' tendencies."

He nodded. "Anything else?"

"I want to be a leader, to earn the team's confidence. I want to show the guys that I'm capable of leading them to a victory and to long-term success."

"And you think you can do that?"

I looked right into his eyes, which were squinting in the sunshine. "I know I can, Coach."

****

COACH VINCENT TALKED TO EACH OF THE QUARTER-
back contenders one by one while the rest of us stretched on the practice field. Then, as if we were on a reality television show packed with drama, he asked us to line up on the sideline. The way he said it made me anticipate a silver tray of footballs was going to appear.

I wouldn't care if it did, as long as I got one. Coach called out two names—Cody and Dante—and my heart pounded as if I were running gassers. If I had to guess, they would be the two cut, but was Coach planning to cut two or three of us? Would he say a third name? Would it be mine? I bounced on my toes, praying, praying.

After a few seconds that felt like years, Coach walked the pair of them off the field leaving Stanford, Owen, and me behind.

Stanford collapsed onto the grass. "He had me squirming!"

Owen and I sat next to him.

"Do you think this means we're staying?" Owen asked.

"We're top three in my book," Stanford said, and I appreciated the compliment for a few seconds before considering that top three wouldn't be good enough to buy me playing time. Third, or even second best, wasn't the goal.

Coach Vincent walked back onto the field, and we all stood to greet him. "You three will run the reps in camp."

My mind did the equivalent of running in place and squealing. I. Made. The. Freaking. Cut.

"I can't make any promises. We might narrow down the field to two or even one at any point. I want you to know that going in."

"Yes, sir," we said.

I couldn't even process. Football camp would bring ridiculous pain and exhaustion—but the most beautiful kind of pain and exhaustion ever. When your body had pushed itself to the absolute brink, yet you were still standing. Hell, still running and throwing too.

And the Viking Jug. An image of it adorning our dining room table as a centerpiece of pride for Juan, Jorge, and Jake struck me. Each of my brothers had been selected by their teammates as a standout leader at football camp. As a result, they'd gotten to fill the Viking-shaped jug at camp and keep it on display in our house for one week.

I shook the fantasy away. I'd be lucky to leave camp with the respect of my teammates and coaches. Leave the Viking Jug to a veteran on the team, and keep my head focused on the goal: starting quarterback.

"It's especially important," Coach continued, "because we've decided to travel for camp this year."

And the joy and excitement partying in my brain halted as if the music had suddenly silenced. Traveling?

"Coach?" Owen said.

"The boosters secured funding for us to go back to Camp Southern Trail."

Owen glanced my way, but I couldn't bring myself to make eye contact. The exhilaration of camp transformed to dread. No way would my parents let me spend a week away at an overnight camp with roughly sixty teenaged boys. Especially not after what happened there last time the team went.

Of my three brothers, Juan was the only one to travel for camp. His senior year, some freshmen snuck in a dozen or so girls to party with the team. Their gift to the seniors, apparently, which raised all sorts of issues about how teenaged boys treated teenaged girls. And what kinds of inappropriate things the team might've been responsible for. Juan told me nothing awful happened, but the possibility something could have was enough to get overnight camp shut down.

The rules had somehow changed, giving the boys—and me—another chance to go away for football camp. Of course, I could imagine the discussions among the boosters. How could they ensure nothing would happen like last time? Easy. A strict *no girls* policy. That would do. Except, of course, the team now had a girl player.

My mother was so not going to like this.

CHAPTER EIGHTEEN

ALWAYS MAKE A TOTAL EFFORT, EVEN WHEN THE
ODDS ARE AGAINST YOU.
—ARNOLD PALMER

WHEN SQUARE DROPPED ME OFF, I TIPTOED THROUGH
the back door and peeked my head into the garage. Mom's car was
gone. I stood still and listened. No television noise from the family
room. No soft music playing from my dad's office. No creaking of
his chair from his weight shifting. Both of my parents were out.

Thankfully.

Not that it would last forever, but it bought me time at least. Time
to devise a plan to somehow convince my parents to let me go to
Camp Southern Trail, or as the team referred to it, Camp Sweat and
Tears. Coach hadn't said so, but it was understood: attending was
mandatory to win the spot. That meant I would be there. No matter
what. At the end of it, I would board the bus home as the starting quarterback for the Iron Valley Vikings. Nothing less would satisfy my
appetite for the field beneath my cleats, the ball in my hands, and the
opportunity to lead the team to a big win in front of a cheering crowd.

I threw a load of my football clothes into the wash, showered, and
dressed in the spandex I'd been avoiding for the last couple of days. A

bottle of ice-cold Gatorade in hand, I dipped my feet in the pool and attempted a mental debate of my options. That debate faltered when I imagined Owen here in the pool with me. His bare chest. The way his fingertips brushed my stomach under the water when he pulled me to him. The serious look in his eyes when he listened to my problems and frustrations. The pain he tried so desperately to hide when he downplayed how much his father's expectations weighed on him.

How much had my playing football strained Owen's already tenuous relationship with his dad?

No thinking in the pool area.

I relocated to the football field, checking my phone on the way. No messages from Owen.

I collapsed on the fifty-yard line. Maybe my parents would let me drive the hour-plus back and forth to camp each day. Yet two-and-a-half hours in the car coupled with all the workouts would exhaust me more than Owen and Stanford. I'd be at a natural disadvantage. Not to mention I would miss bonding time with the guys, which would in turn mean failing to earn their trust in my leadership.

I called my brothers. Jorge, I supposed unsurprisingly, didn't answer, although it did sting for a minute that he might've been with some girl rather than taking my calls when I really needed to talk.

I broke the news to Jake and Juan.

"No way Mom and Dad will go for that," Jake said.

"Camp Sweat and Tears." Juan's smile crept into his voice. "Good times."

"Yes," I said. "Good times I need to be a part of. Any brilliant ideas?"

Silence.

"Not instilling a lot of confidence in my decision to call you guys."

"Forget about it," Juan said. "Let's play."

Competition. How Medinas dealt with the world.

Juan, Jake, and I set up large wooden targets on our respective fields. Mine was a plywood board cut in the shape of an Iron Valley receiver, painted in purple and black with a generous-sized hole where the receiver's hands should be. Juan was at the college where he coached, and Jake set up his space in the field house of

Western Penn.

"Where the hell is Jorge?" Juan said.

"Who knows?" Jake said. "He's been strange lately."

And he had been. Maybe even more so than the playboy we'd grown used to in his college years.

"You think there's something wrong?" I asked.

"He's probably busy with practice," Jake suggested.

"We're all busy with practice," Juan countered.

"Fine. A girl, then."

Juan nodded. "Could be. We all know you don't have that problem."

"You two babies mind taking this to the field?" I said. "I'd like to play sometime today."

The game was simple. Each of us had fifteen throws: five each from ten, twenty, and thirty yards. Most hits at the target won. First up at ten yards, Juan positioned his camera on his target and made five attempts at throwing the football through the hole. The first four sailed through with ease. The last one caught the edge of the board.

"Weak!" Jake shouted and took his turn.

"The targets here are narrower," Juan challenged. "Not like at those big schools where they want everyone to feel good about themselves. Do you get trophies for showing up to practice?"

Jake offered our eldest brother an unkind hand gesture and took his turn. He scored five victories and mooned us both.

"That kind of behavior could get you kicked off your fancy team," Juan said, sparking a new round of insults.

I focused my phone camera on the wooden Iron Valley receiver and lined up ten yards away. I felt the pressure of Jake's perfect five, but more than that, despite the countless times I'd competed against my brothers, this time felt different. I wasn't playing around in the backyard. I was training.

It was real.

My first pass bounced off the receiver's helmet. The second one hit his shoulder.

"Come on, sis. You got this," Juan's voice echoed, which put on even more pressure. My brothers never cheered for me during head-to-head competition.

"Are you throwing from the girls' line?"

"No, I am not," I said. "No special treatment, remember?"

The third ball hit the rim of the opening and bounced back toward me.

"Getting closer," Jake called.

Except we weren't competing to see who was *almost* accurate. Close wasn't good enough. Two more. Fearing I'd been trying too hard, I dropped back without thinking about the steps or the motion. I let the actions flow through me naturally and delivered my first ball through the opening of the target. Both of my brothers cheered. I jumped up and down, grateful they couldn't see me. With the same natural motion, I threw the last of my five shots through the opening.

"She's getting warmed up, big brother," Jake teased after they both stopped cheering. "You might be in trouble at twenty and thirty yards out."

"Let's just see," Juan said.

"Julia Marie Medina!"

Mom's outrage stretched from the porch across the backyard. If my brothers had been there, I might have hidden behind them.

"That's her low-pitched boom voice," Jake said.

"I like to call it her rumble," Juan offered as my mother pounded toward our football field. "Anyone have popcorn ready?"

"Do you think she knows about camp?" Jake asked.

Probably a wise bet. Good thing we had a few acres of land. Otherwise, the neighbors would be able to hear the ensuing battle even with their windows closed.

"Mother..."

"Don't you 'Mother' me! Care to explain why Christina Creel and a table filled with other football moms cornered me at the Station to ask what I thought of my daughter going on an overnight football camp adventure with the entire male population of her school?"

Mrs. Creel was the president of the school board. She basically believed she owned and operated Iron Valley School District and the whole town should bow to her every whim. I imagined my parents eating dinner in the semi-fancy restaurant and being bombarded by Mrs. Creel and her cronies with the news. And from parents who didn't want me to play. They couldn't have heard from someone who thought it was a great idea to have a girl on the team. Oh. No. Not possible.

Ugh. Not sure a worse scenario could exist.

"It's not the male population," I said trying to minimize the damage. "Just the football team."

She gawked at me as if there was no distinction. I supposed for her, there probably wasn't.

"I can't believe you didn't tell us." Her voice was quiet, which Jake aptly pointed out is even more dangerous than her rumble.

"Uh..." I tried to think of an intelligent response, but Jake and Juan were both gesturing to keep my mouth shut. "I planned to as soon as you got home."

"Is her nose growing, Jake?"

"I think it might be."

"What's that?" Mom asked turning the screen toward her. "Who's there?" When she recognized the small faces on the screen, her demeanor softened. "Hi, boys."

"Hi, Mom," they answered automatically.

"Thank Jesus you're here. Talk to your sister. She's losing her mind over this football stuff."

Neither of my brothers said anything.

"Juan? Jacob?"

"Mom, they support me playing."

Mom looked at me and then the screen, incredulous. "Is that true?"

They both spoke at the same time, and it sounded like Juan might have said I was good enough to play and Jake said it would make me happy. Neither response mollified our mother. In fact, both infuriated her.

"That's enough! The mothers were meeting to plan a way to stop you going."

"What?" I expected my parents to not want me to go, but could the other mothers legitimately get me banned from camp?

"You know Mrs. Creel's oldest son got caught with one of those girls who showed up at the last overnight camp," Mom continued. "He was suspended for two games his senior season."

"That was his problem, Mom. When have you ever taught me not to go after something I wanted because some guy made a mistake years ago?"

"Of course that's not what I meant," she backtracked.

"I have as much right to play as any boy in that school, and you can tell Mrs. Creel and her cronies I said so." My stomach flipped when I thought about what a comment like that could mean for Abuelita. Did she need Mrs. Creel's support to win a position on the board? If I pushed the issue and insisted on playing football, would Abuelita's campaign suffer?

Didn't matter.

Abuelita wouldn't want me to minimize my potential for politics. Especially hers.

"Oh, Jesus, help me."

When Mom invoked Jesus into our conversations, the best advice was to shut up. Of course, I didn't. "And the insinuation my very presence is going to get a boy into trouble is offensive, Mother."

"You're a wily temptress," Juan said with a straight face.

My mother, on the other hand, wore a horrified expression.

"He's joking, Mom," I said.

"You're not going," she said.

I'd anticipated she'd say that, but when the words flung from her lips, they invoked more fear in me than I could have imagined. I had to go. Not going to football camp would guarantee Owen—or more likely Stanford—would be the starting quarterback, that quitting the volleyball team was for absolutely nothing.

"Mom, be reasonable," Jake said in his calm tone that often soothed her.

But her face reddened. She opened her mouth to continue berating me, or so I anticipated, before a semi-familiar face interrupted us from across the yard.

"Excuse me. I'm Rand Denton from the Pittsburgh Herald." He shook mom's hand and then mine before glancing at the screen. "Oh, hello there. It's been a long time."

My brothers greeted the reporter as an awkward ambiance enveloped us all. How much had he heard? How could we get rid of him? If we didn't talk to him, what would he print? And what would he print if we did open up?

Denton looked around the yard, taking in the lined field with our family name, the worn target, and the footballs strewn around. "Quite the facility you have here," he said.

We all nodded and mumbled polite appreciation.

"Julia, I'd love to see you train out here. Or maybe we could talk? I'll only take a few minutes of your time."

Mom crossed her arms. "What do you want to talk about?"

"Your daughter is the first girl in the county to try out for her high school football team, and according to my research so far, potentially the first in the state to go for QB." He smiled at me. "You're a role model."

"I'm not trying out to be a role model," I said.

"So, why are you trying out, then?"

I stared at him. Rand Denton. The sports reporter from the *Pittsburgh Herald* asked *why* I wanted to play. Coach hadn't asked. Owen hadn't. Lord knew my parents hadn't. Instead of an automatic declaration of why playing football was a bad idea, he wanted to know what drove me to try out. He wanted to talk about my desire and love for the game. He had actually asked why. The swelling excitement and pride in my chest told me I desperately wanted to answer.

But I had said no special treatment. When my top goal was fitting in with the guys on the team and showing them I belonged, the last thing I wanted was an article on the front of the sports page with statistics to demonstrate how I was different. Denton's question had nearly sucked me into an interview I didn't want to give, but Mom stepped between us, and for the first time in forever I felt like we were on the same team.

"Thank you for stopping by, Mr. Denton, but I don't think we have anything to say," Mom said. "I have to ask you to leave, please."

CHAPTER NINETEEN

BELIEVE ME. THE REWARD IS NOT SO GREAT WITHOUT
THE STRUGGLE.
—WILMA RUDOLPH

THE NEXT MORNING AS THE BOOSTERS WERE MEETING
to address *the situation*, I found myself watching the screen of my
phone. Playing a game of Yahtzee. Reading sports articles. Anything
to look at the screen in case Owen's name popped up without actually
staring at the screen to wait for Owen's name to pop up.

I had some pride.

His name didn't pop up.

My parents refused to attend the meeting. No point, they insisted,
since the rulebook stipulated coaches could not discriminate. The
coach had to let me play, they insisted, whether I went to camp or
not. And they were envisioning *not*.

Square picked me up for practice as usual. On the ride, he talked
about the Steelers. I listened and threw in a few points for debate here
and there, but my heart wasn't in it. I'd sacrificed my college scholarship, my best friend, my teammates—and maybe even Owen—for
a prize that seemed to slip away a little more each hour.

That evening, the boosters hovered over the practice field until coach had to, once again, declare practices closed. I loathed the idea of making so many enemies for no other reason than being a girl who wanted to play football. But I didn't loathe it enough not to play. Jake had insisted he had a plan to win my parents' signatures on the Camp Sweat and Tears permission slip. My task was to focus enough at practice to make an impression on the coaches and some of the players, so I had a shot once the permission slip was signed.

I rolled and unrolled the paper in my hands after practice while I waited outside the field house for Square. All the guys showered, but *my* shower was under construction for another week. While I waited, a group of parents, led by Mrs. Creel, talked loudly, throwing wild gestures with their hands. Square finished much sooner than usual.

"That was fast," I said.

He pointed to the boosters. "I didn't want to leave you out there with them."

"They're harmless." I hoped it wasn't a lie.

Square started the engine and reversed from his spot. "They demanded Vincent not take you to camp, threatening him with going to the school board to have him fired."

"They can't do that!"

"Apparently since there was an...*incident* between a player and a girl last time around, they think they can."

"There won't be an *incident* this time—and not to mention one between a *player* and a *girl*. I'm a player too. And a player first and foremost."

"Don't shoot the messenger."

Square was right. This wasn't about him, and if anything, he'd been a better friend and support than just about everyone else in my life—except my brothers.

"What did Vincent say?" I asked.

Square glanced sideways at me and winked. "That maybe he should leave their kids home too. They didn't like that option."

"I bet."

I watched the houses and trees pass outside the window, allowing myself to hope. Vincent had my back. At least that was something.

****

NOT THAT I DIDN'T TRUST JAKE AND THIS GRAND PLAN,
but Mom sitting on the swing in the backyard that evening beckoned me. Time to get her to see reason.

"Hey, Mom." I handed her a bottle of water from our back porch fridge, which tended to freeze drinks it was so cold. "Can I sit with you?"

She sipped the water and nodded. We settled into a rhythm on the swing as the sun settled on the horizon.

"How's volleyball going?"

"You really want to know?"

"Of course."

"I'm working through some other outside hitters, but the timing and tone is all off." She took another drink.

"Sometimes change is good. It'll take time." I tried to sound upbeat.

"But is the change necessary?"

"Mom, please."

"I don't want to fight with you, Julia. You're my only daughter, and I love you." She sighed. "Tell me the truth. Is there any chance you'll change your mind and want to come back to the team?"

She deserved the courtesy of me at least thinking it over, but that didn't take long. "I'm sorry, but no."

She sipped the water again. "I was afraid of that."

"I *love* playing football, Mom."

She exhaled, slumping her shoulders forward. "Why?"

Fireworks as grand as a Super Bowl display exploded inside of me. "It's a challenge. It's new and different. On the field, I'm one small piece of so many moving parts. I have to do my job, but I have to anticipate so many other roles at the same time. It's like a chess match but physical and moving in quadruple motion. It's complicated and intense...and fun."

When I finished, I studied my mom's expression and found, I thought, the slightest bit of acceptance there.

"I'm sorry. I know I disappointed you."

She shook her head emphatically. "Don't ever say that. You didn't disappoint me. The situation did, yes. I would have loved to have you at my side all season." She put her arm around my shoulders. "Coaching you will forever be one of the highlights of my life. But first and foremost, I'm your mom. We'll just have to make memories some other way."

I didn't even try to suppress the tears. My mom had accepted my desire to play football. My whole body felt like it was floating. I hugged her tighter than I ever had before. "Thanks, Mom."

"I love you, Julia."

"I love you too."

We smiled at each other.

"Your abuelita needs my help with a few things around the apartment."

"Wait," I said. I needed that permission slip signed for camp. "If I'm going to do this, really do it, I have to go to camp."

"Julia..."

"Mom, please."

"I know you don't understand this, but my first job is to protect you. An overnight camp with sixty teenaged boys and one girl is not a good idea. If anything happened to you."

"It won't—"

She waved her arms to shush me. "You can't guarantee that. Nobody can."

I stood to object, but my mom mumbled an apology and walked away. After twenty-four hours and the best heart-to-heart we'd had since I left for Florida, she hadn't budged. What if I couldn't convince her? What if Jake couldn't? The reality of not going to football camp—no, I couldn't even think it. Somehow, I'd get there. I had to.

A branch cracked behind me, and I jumped.

"Hey," came Owen's soft voice.

"Hey!" Seeing him standing in front of me after so many hours staring at my phone and trying to catch his eye in practice—I forgot every awful thing we'd said and ran into his arms. He held me right back. Tight. Hard. I needed Owen. "Did you hear my mom?"

"I did. I'm sorry."

"Me too." My throat did that thing where a lump got stuck, and I couldn't move for fear it would shift and turn me into a sobbing maniac.

"You'll figure it out. Don't worry." He kissed my head. "You're a formidable opponent."

"Don't do that." I stepped backward. The night air suddenly felt as warm as if we stood under the mid-afternoon sun. "I get that I should have told you before we met on the field, and I owned that. But you didn't exactly react admirably."

"I know."

"Good. So don't act that way and then come here smelling all delicious and delivering false compliments."

The smirk on his face told me my words hadn't quite succeeded at putting him in his place.

He reached for my waist. "You think I smell delicious?"

"Owen..."

Holding his hands up in surrender, he said, "Total truth. The compliment was not false."

His encouragement wrapped me in a blanket of hope, one that I desperately needed. "Fine."

He raised an eyebrow as if to ask permission to come close again. I looped my arm around his neck and brushed a light kiss against his lips.

"That was nice," I said, busying my fingers by twisting a button on his polo. "I hate to admit it, but when you pushed me away the other day in the parking lot, that hurt."

He took a deep breath. "It's okay to admit you're hurt, you know."

"You're dodging the point."

He responded by kissing me again. Slow. Sad, even. I dipped my head forward, pressing my forehead to his. I wondered if he'd spent the last few days pressing the Home button on his phone to see if I'd called. Or messaged. How much had our pride kept us apart off the field and at odds on it?

"I'm sorry about everything," he said.

"Me too." I wasn't sorry that I wanted the same things he wanted or that I was willing to fight to earn them. However, I was sorry that one of us would fall short.

And I was sorry for how we were handling the situation.

"These last few days have been so hard for me, Jules. I mean, you're a freaking Medina. I wanted to hear you endorse me for quarterback the night I came here to swim. Part of me feared I couldn't do it, but my dad insisted, you know?"

I did.

"I thought that if you had the confidence in me, then I could do it. But then you showed up to fight me for it."

"I know," I whispered. "But you're the reason I wanted to play."

He pulled me to the bench and onto his lap. "How's that?"

"You're a great receiver, but to show that, you need someone who can throw you the ball. I thought, why not me?"

He tilted his forehead to mine, and we sat there for several minutes listening to the sounds of the insects in the night and each other's breathing.

"Thank you for wanting to help me," he said. "That means a lot."

I hoped he wouldn't ask me to help him by quitting. That I couldn't do.

"This last week has been awful for me."

"Me too," I said.

He sighed, holding something back. *Please don't ask me to quit.* That would be the end of us. I shouldn't have to choose between Owen and football.

"I love you, Jules."

My whole body stilled, his words surprising me like a deflected pass that landed right in your hands. In the end zone. In the fourth quarter of the big game.

When you were down by six.

He wasn't asking me to quit the team. He loved me. He loved me! No guy had ever said those words to me before.

That metaphorical deflected pass? I bobbled.

And dropped it.

"Did you hear me?" Owen whispered.

"Uh-huh."

Despite everything I felt for Owen, my immediate reaction was not to say it back.

CHAPTER TWENTY

WE KNOW THE PATH THAT IS AHEAD OF US. IT'S A TOUGH JOURNEY, BUT I KIND OF THINK WE ARE LOOKING FORWARD TO IT.
—BILL COWHER

"HOW ARE THINGS GOING WITH LOVER BOY?" JAKE asked the next evening at dinner. Abuelita was hosting her traditional Sunday feast early, on Friday, to accommodate Jake's Sunday night meetings, which started that week, and her Saturday night date with the other hot grandmas in town, which was always.

I slapped a spoonful of sautéed veggies onto my plate. "Complicated." My brother and I shared a lot of things, but admitting I froze when Owen told me he loved me—not going to happen.

"I always knew Malone was a—" Jake said, scooping a hefty serving from Abuelita's incomparable *arroz con pollo*.

"Stop! Ita will die if she hears whatever word was about to come out of your mouth!" And despite the questions in our relationship lately, loyalty toward Owen stirred inside of me. The crushed look on his face when I'd stuttered a measly noncommittal, *Wow. That's nice...*

Groan.

"I never liked you dating that guy."

"A fact you also never once kept to yourself."

Jake shrugged and kept scooping food. "So you guys are done, then?"

"I never said that."

"A brother can hope."

"Enough about Owen," I said. "How are you going to convince Mom and Dad to sign the permission slip?"

He looked at me as if I'd learned nothing from him. But I had. I learned our parents were more accommodating to him and my brothers than they would ever be to their fragile baby girl.

"I got this, sis." He kissed my cheek and claimed a spot at Abuelita's grand, cherrywood table. When we were all settled, I nudged Jake. He coughed and winked at Abuelita.

Then, she winked at me.

That's when I knew I hadn't learned nearly enough. It was absolute brilliance partnering with my no-nonsense Puerto Rican grandmother. She dabbed a white cotton napkin at the corners of her mouth and looked at me.

"My darling Julia, what is this I hear of you playing the football with boys?"

Mom's fork crashed against her plate.

"Mama, we don't need to discuss this now," my father said.

"Mijo, I asked Julia, not you. Yes?"

Dad opened his mouth to further exercise futility, but Abuelita lifted the polished silver fork in her left hand in a shushing gesture. "Julia?"

"I love it, Abuelita," I said. "It challenges me."

She nodded. "Very important. You must challenge yourself. That is why I run for the school board without holding political office before. We are named after powerful and influential Puerto Rican women, no?"

Checkmate. Dad put his head in his hands, and Mom slouched in her chair. Nothing could combat Abuelita's comparison to historical Puerto Rican female powerhouses.

"Like Luisa Capetillo. She wore pants in public, and my mama loved the comfort of the pants. She named me Luisa and said always to be a trendsetter. And then you, my darling granddaughter. Named after an advocate for the civil rights."

"Mama, we're not letting our daughter go away to an overnight camp with sixty high school boys because she shares the same name as a revolutionary," Dad said.

"Or because your mother liked pants," Mom muttered.

"I heard that," Abuelita said. "These are not the reasons, of course, but symbolic of the reasons. You wish to oppress your own daughter?"

Jake snorted, and Mom gasped. "Oh, dear Lord."

"No taking the Lord's name in vain in my house," Abuelita said with a stomp of her fist on the lace tablecloth. Then she picked up her silverware and continued eating. "So, you get a chaperone. She wants to play, you find a way. Play the football, mi cielo. And I will like to come watch you play."

"Mama!"

My father's final objection was silenced by Abuelita quoting a poem I'd heard her read several times before. She'd always said it would be a powerful tool for a girl in a family of boys. She moved her fork slowly through air, like a beacon of truth in her hands and recited "The Changeling" by Judith Ortiz Cofer—a Puerto Rican poet, of course.

Cofer's poem told the story of a girl who competed for her father's attention by dressing as a boy. While the ruse worked with her father for a time, the girl's mother aimed to put the daughter right back in her societally defined place.

Abuelita smiled at me. "Julia, dear. Don't be invisible. Play the football." Then as if the conversation was settled, she asked us all, "Would anyone like more arroz?"

CHAPTER TWENTY-ONE

CHAMPIONS KEEP PLAYING UNTIL THEY GET IT RIGHT.
—BILLIE JEAN KING

ABUELITA'S POEM HAD ME THINKING ABOUT OWEN.
Probably not her intention. But still. The girl in the poem changed
herself. Was it for the attention of her father? Or to become something
she desperately wished to be? My transformation from volleyball
player to quarterback hopeful wasn't for attention. Or really even
for Owen. It was for me.

After dinner, Jake and I floated in inflatable reclining chairs in
the pool. Despite the sunshine and peaceful ambiance, contentment
eluded me. Owen Malone had said he loved me, and I didn't say it
back. I thought I could compartmentalize my feelings for him. On
the field, we were teammates. Off the field, he ran his fingers over
my skin and his lips over my mouth and made my insides crumble
to mush. Trouble was that off-the-field-inside-crumbling Owen and
on-field teammate Owen were one and the same. How could I admit
such a vulnerability as loving a boy who every day competed against
me for something I so desperately wanted?

"This is the life," Jake said, his head tilted back into the water.

"Yep," I said, not sure he caught my sarcasm.

"I'm going to miss it."

I had a measly few hours with my brother, and mentally whining about Owen was getting me nowhere. So I decided to enjoy some time with Jake. If I could. "Considering the pool will be closed in a month, I'm going to miss it too."

He splashed me. "Not what I meant. Gosh, I can't even have a moment with my baby sister." We floated silently for a few minutes. "It will be weird. Not being here all the time."

"The house is quiet without you guys. Too quiet."

Jake flipped himself into the water with a loud splash and swam to the side where he'd stashed a towel and by the looks of it, a remote control. "Then let's make some noise. Here's one for you, Little J."

The opening notes to "Sweet Child O' Mine" blared through the poolside speakers, and I tapped my toes under the water. Funny how a few notes of a song could make a drastic change in your mood. My brothers worked out to Guns N' Roses music in the backyard pretty much throughout my youth, and this song was their cue to chase me around the yard and when they caught me, they would throw me in the air or swing me around. The song acted like a lightning rod for my emotions, electrifying the nostalgia and adoration I had for my brothers.

Not that I'd admit as much in actual words. Out loud.

Jake grabbed a football and tossed it underhand to me. "Hit me with it," he said and then ran to the pool. From my floating chair, I factored in his speed and threw the ball so he caught it at the peak of his jump. Through the 80's rock playlist, we took turns throwing and jumping. Then stood at opposite ends of the pool and threw back and forth, laughing, telling stories, sharing inspiration.

I was definitely going to miss this.

****

THE NEXT MORNING, AS IF SANTA CLAUS OR THE EAS-
ter bunny had paid a visit, the signed permission slip magically appeared on the pillow next to me. I ran to the breakfast table repeating, "Thank you. Thank you. Thank you."

With looks of apprehension, both my parents hugged me and

warned me to be careful. "We talked to Coach Vincent, and he has a female chaperone lined up for you—the camp cook, I think. You will be in a cabin with her, far from the boys."

"Fine," I said, glad for whatever accommodations would secure me a spot at Camp Sweat and Tears.

"I know you're a sturdy girl, Julia," Mom said, and although most girls would be offended by being called "sturdy", the adjective worked for me. "You're strong and competitive and fast, but some of those boys are going to be even stronger. You know how some defenders can be. Their whole goal is to ring the quarterback's bell. Watching your brothers go through that was...it...I can't imagine you..."

I could tell my mom was about to cry, and I hadn't seen her do that since my grandfather's funeral. "Mom, I can't promise I won't get hurt, but I can promise I want to do this. So much."

"If you get an injury, mija, we ask that you take it seriously," Dad said. "See the trainer. Get treatment. Don't play if you're hurt. Deal?"

"Deal!"

****

AFTER A LOT OF HUSTLING AND PACKING, MOM, DAD, and Abuelita dropped me at the field house with about ten minutes to spare. They hugged me, not wanting to let me go. Mrs. Creel also didn't want to let me go—at all. She glared at us and whispered with a few other parents.

"Let me handle this," Abuelita said, pushing past all of us toward Mrs. Creel, but my father stopped her. Good thing. I thought she might have had more than a lesson on Puerto Rican feminist poetry in mind, which could land her campaign in trouble.

"Julia has handled this fine, Mama," my father said. "She has the coach's permission, and that's all that matters. Right, mija?"

I nodded to satisfy my family, although what my father had said wasn't true. What mattered was the guys around me and whether they would embrace me as their quarterback. Inside, a quiet voice whispered that I was an idiot to leave my parents for this. Then the voice got louder. And louder. The moment I feared I might actually be speaking aloud, Square stepped in front of me, greeted my parents, and scooped up two of my four bags.

"I can carry my own stuff, Square."

He pretended to drop one of the bags and wiped his brow. "Can you? What did you pack in these things?"

Owen appeared, picking up the other two bags. He smiled at me in a tentative way, almost as if asking the same question I had been asking myself all day: Are we going to get through this?

"It's tradition," Owen said. "Or at least it was when the team used to go to camp regularly. The veteran players carry the newbies' bags."

"Which you should enjoy." Square shifted my bag over his shoulder. "What's in this thing?"

"Lots of Gatorade."

My parents pretended to be strong, but Abuelita was truly a force, reciting quotations and lines of poetry as we walked, arm-in-arm, to the bus. We passed girlfriends of players. They kissed their players goodbye and glared at me as if I'd somehow tricked the system for the sole purpose of spending the week with their boyfriends. I shrugged it off. Or at least tried. When Abuelita hugged me, she delivered one of her favorite quotes. "You know, mi cielo. A wise woman once said nobody can make you feel inferior without your consent."

I smiled and hugged her tighter. If only I could remember Eleanor Roosevelt's words when the inevitable doubt would set in over the next five days.

"Not Puerto Rican, but very smart anyway," Abuelita said, her unfailing nationalism making me laugh. "Have a good time. They might be boys, but you can still beat their—"

"That's enough, Mama," Dad pleaded, and Abuelita shrugged. "We'll be there for your scrimmage."

My heart sped up against the swelling happiness in my chest. "You're really coming?"

Dad frown lines appeared. "Of course, we're coming, Julia. We wouldn't miss it for anything."

Mom smiled and nodded, and I squeezed them into a wicked hug. "Thank you. Thank you," I whispered into their shoulders. We pulled away wearing tears on our cheeks.

Abuelita tapped her toes against the pavement. "What about me, mi cielo? I will be there too."

I hugged her too. My parents were coming to the scrimmage. They were coming. I repeated the statement in my head as I climbed on the bus and waved at them through an open window.

I sat across from Square on the bus, and after a few miles of fantasizing about throwing a touchdown pass in front of my parents, of playing so well they couldn't possibly deny I'd made the right choice, a certain pressure descended. What if I didn't play well? What if I didn't convince them?

No. I would. I just would.

A few of the guys talked, but mostly, the team focused on electronic devices, which Coach had said would be taken away when we arrived. I texted with Jake and watched film from the summer seven-on-seven scrimmages I'd missed. I thought about Owen. He sat a few seats in front of me. His light brown, nearly-blond-from-the-sun head bobbed with each bump, and I wondered if he was thinking of me. What if he was? And should I have been thinking of him? If I committed my-self to focusing on football during camp and impressing my parents in the upcoming scrimmage—and not focusing on Owen—then was that a passive acceptance that our relationship wasn't worth as much as my desire to play football? If I allowed myself to think of him, was I giving everything to the game?

Was it really possible to have both Owen Malone and football?

And if it wasn't, which did I want more?

CHAPTER TWENTY-TWO

IF THE SUN COMES UP, I HAVE A CHANCE.
—VENUS WILLIAMS

CAMP SWEAT AND TEARS SAT ON NEARLY FIVE THOU-
sand primarily wooded acres with cabins and sporting facilities
throughout. The sign at the entrance listed several training sites:
football, tennis, soccer, baseball, and volleyball. I wondered who
was at the volleyball site this week.

At the football site, my cabin flirted with the edge of the woods,
forcing instant recall of every horror movie I'd watched in my life.
To the rest of the team's dismay, I resided in the counselors' cabin,
which meant more space and more amenities. Namely a bathtub—in
addition to a shower—and a television. And a screened in porch.
And a fridge. And a small library—and by small, I mean a bookshelf. In other words, by Camp Sweat and Tears standards, my cabin
belonged on the Style Network while the guys' accommodations
were not so, shall we say, *fancy*.

Coach told us to spend roughly ten minutes settling in and chang-
ing into our swimsuits. I loaded the fridge with all the Gatorade I
brought, and the case of water provided by the camp, pulled on the
most modest bathing suit I owned—a black tankini with boy short

bottoms—covered up with a team shirt and shorts and jogged past all of the boys' cabins to the Main Lodge. I wasn't the last to arrive, but close. The sun dropped low in the sky, yet the heat of the day held tightly to the humid air around us. A perfect night for a swim.

"I hope you all wore your running shoes." Coach called out to a series of groans. "Let's go."

We hustled by the football fields and the swimming pool. The still water sparkled in the evening sun, and I so wanted to jump in. But Coach ran into the cover of the trees. We followed. I checked my watch periodically. One mile. Two. The dirt path seemed endless. The evergreens blurred into an unchanging yet scenic view. Occasionally guys tripped over fallen branches, miscalculating or lacking the energy to lift their legs high enough to avoid them. Some of the team started the run chatting, but by the time we hit mile two, chatter dwindled.

Everyone except D, who despite clearly struggling to breathe always had something to say. "Anyone feel like...Freddy Krueger... about to appear...out the trees?"

"Jason Voorhees," Square said, impressing me with his horror movie knowledge.

"What?" D huffed.

"Nothing, man."

Then, a few minutes later: "This is like that movie...about the Black and white kids...trying to get along," D said, sucking wind.

I'd been thinking the same thing. "*Remember the Titans*."

"Yeah. My...man...Denzel." D paused for a breath after each word.

"I hope not," Square mumbled, with surprising ease. For a big guy, he was in good shape. "They were running to Gettysburg."

"How...far's...that?"

"One hundred and fifty miles," Square said. "Give or take."

"Hell...no."

More than conjuring memories of the movie, the surprise run also reminded me of my childhood. Juan had found humor in holding our prized possessions captive to get us up early to run with him. His enthusiasm annoyed me back then, but over the years, I learned to appreciate his efforts. He was a born coach.

My watch alerted me we hit three miles as the sound of running water contrasted against the pounding of our feet on the forest floor. A creek slowly appeared through the trees to our right. Coach stopped beside it. We gathered around him, pressing our hands to the stitches in our sides, bending forward onto our knees, leaning on trees. For a lucky few, resting on fallen trunks or large rocks.

"It's been eight years since the Iron Valley Vikings prepared for their season on this ground, and I'm glad to be back. I hope you're all good from that run. It's hot tonight. It'll be hot tomorrow. Each day your body will get more and more tired. We're going to push you physically and mentally. By the end of the week, you will be stronger in more ways than one. You'll be united. You'll be a team." Coach looked out at the water, well-lit from a break in the trees. "People might say we have a lot to live up to this year, but that's one of the reasons I wanted to come here, to get away from the expectations. Last year was just that—last year. Now's your time. It's our time."

The volume of the cheers sent the birds flying from the trees above us.

Coach raised his hand to silence us. "What do you say we celebrate it with a swim?"

The guys tore off their shoes and shirts and jumped in. D managed to find a tree swing and launched himself into the center of the swimming hole. I didn't hesitate, exactly, but the thought crossed my mind that I was about to be the singular girl at a night swim with sixty guys. Tentative, I pulled my shirt over my head and found Owen standing next to me.

"Hey," he said.

"Hey." I slid down my shorts and kicked my shoes into my pile of clothes.

Owen looked out at the water. "Just like Florida, huh?"

We both laughed. Awkwardly. But still, laughter.

"The creek is a little more crowded than the Gulf if I recall."

"You might be right about that," Owen said, holding out a hand for me.

"Owen..." I searched the crowd for the coaches and was grateful to see they weren't looking.

Owen lowered his hand and stepped closer. "Is this about what I said the other day? I mean, that I..." He blushed.

"I can't talk about that now. Not here."

He pursed his lips.

"I'm crazy about you, Owen," I whispered. I refused to declare love for him for the first time amid sixty screaming hooligans splashing in a creek. "I don't want to draw attention to myself though. Especially here."

"Seems to me trying out for quarterback of a state championship football team drew a shit ton of attention to yourself."

I tried to ignore the burning festering inside me at his dig. "Can we not fight about this, please?"

He shrugged. "I didn't come here to fight. I was trying to help you down the hillside. That's all."

A thoughtful gesture amid brutal remarks. "Thanks, but I'm good."

Owen pulled his hand away.

I jumped into the water thinking Owen might follow, but I found him about twenty yards away, splashing with some of the receivers. Not that I had much time to commiserate over his absence. Someone swam underneath me, putting his hands on my back and leg, and lifted me up out of the water. Flying through the air, I looked down to find Square laughing.

"Hey!" I yelled and took in a mouthful of creek water. Ugh. Which I promptly spit at Square's face.

"You don't want to start a spitting war with me, Medina," he said. Probably right about that. He pulled me onto his square shoulders for a game of chicken, and we won. After ten minutes, we were undefeated. Teams lined up to play us, and we sent each one packing until Coach called everyone out of the water. Christian hadn't been along for the run, but he managed to drive a golf cart of towels to us.

"Hit any trash cans on your way here?" I teased.

He threw the towel at my face, but I saw him fighting a grin.

"In ancient times, the Greeks and Romans viewed baths as recreational and social experiences," Coach said, gathering us around. "A ritual bath was thought to cleanse, not only physically but mentally and spiritually as well. Tonight, you came to this place with apprehensions about camp, pressures from your parents, and maybe even some exhaustion from your run. But once you were in this water, you laughed together. Competed. Played. Enjoyed each other's company. You feel good?"

The guys around me nodded and answered in the affirmative. I felt good too. As good as could be expected when I was the only girl on a football team trying to win the prime skill position.

"Good," Coach said, still oozing positivity. "Let's get a good night's sleep and get at it in the morning."

CHAPTER TWENTY-THREE

REMEMBER, ONCE YOU SET A GOAL, IT'S ALL ABOUT
HOW HARD YOU'RE WILLING TO WORK, HOW MUCH
YOU'RE WILLING TO SACRIFICE, AND HOW BADLY YOU
TRULY WANT IT.
—JJ WATT

THAT NIGHT, IN THE SCREENED PORCH WITH THE
sounds of the insects around me and my chaperone, Miss Nancy,
snoring from her room in the cabin, I studied the team playbook and
Jake's journal. The sharp edges of anxiety cut at my insides, but thinking x's and o's calmed me like nothing else could. For nearly an hour,
I studied the pass progressions for our more frequently called plays.
To drill the information, I drew the routes myself. First, I'd look for
this receiver. And then this one. And then this one. I drew curls and
slants. Outs and posts. I quizzed myself on how my decisions might
change based on the defense.

When I felt like my mind couldn't absorb anything else, I tucked
myself in, but before I could fall asleep, a white square in the window
caught my eye. I pushed the sheet away to investigate.

"Oh. My. Gosh!" I giggled and pried the screen open until I
could slide my hand through and grab the crumpled paper with my

name on it. Despite my trying out against him and our creek-side fight earlier, Owen had maintained our tradition. I smoothed the note flat and unfolded it.

He'd written: *Being at camp with you.*

I sighed and flopped onto the cot, which I swore exploded a cloud of dust around me. Didn't matter. Owen's favorite thing about today was having me at football camp with him. Maybe he saw the potential of us playing on the same team—what it could mean for us athletically and for, well, *us.*

Despite the noise of the ice machine—yes, the counselor's cabin also boasted an ice machine—and the magnitude of the following day, I held that note to my chest, snuggled the dusty pillow on the dustier cot, and fell asleep. I slept the night through without stirring and woke the next morning at the sound the monotone *beep-beep-beep* alarm clock, exhilarated and ready for the day ahead.

It was all very romantic. Showering in the large bathroom of the cabin to the sound of birds chirping on the roof. Slipping into my football-appropriate workout clothes that smelled a little rustic from the wooden drawers. Crunching along the gravel path to the Main Lodge for breakfast as the morning sun shone on the dew-covered grass. I relished the sense of awe over it all until I greeted my teammates. My smiles evoked scowls. One after the next. So much so I thought I might be dreaming.

"How'd you sleep last night, Medina?" Chase Creel asked as I scooped scrambled eggs onto my plate.

"Great," I said, glad someone was actually talking to me, even if it was Kicker Creel whose mother despised my presence on the roster. "How about you?"

He scoffed and walked away. Okay...

I loaded my tray and found Square at a round table near the window. The stares, scowls, and whispers multiplied as I made my way to his table. I dropped my tray with a clatter, waking him from his reverie.

"Medina."

"What's with all the glares?"

"We had to run last night."

"Who?"

He helped himself to one of the milk cartons on my tray. "The whole team. Chase was being an ass. He got caught, and the coaches woke us all up to run."

"Nobody woke me up."

"Exactly," he said and chugged the milk.

So that was my great offense? I slept through a team punishment because nobody thought to punish me? Across the room, I caught Owen's eye but couldn't read his expression. Was he pleased the team had turned on me so quickly? They needed a leader in a quarterback. I needed them to accept my leadership. Not likely after this.

"What do they think happened?"

Square shrugged. "Doesn't matter. They got punished, and you didn't."

We'd see about that. The coaches ate breakfast in a private room off the main dining area. I pushed my chair over the linoleum with a squeak and stood.

"Was Coach Vincent there?"

Square shook his head, and I felt a sense of relief. Coach Vincent didn't forget about me, but somebody did.

"Who woke you?"

"Let it go, Medina," Square said, but I couldn't. And I knew he wouldn't if he were in my situation.

"Who?"

"Draveck."

Of course. The line and strength and conditioning coach with the deadly combination of a wicked temper and the seniority that gave him the authority to pull the whole team out of bed and make them run until they puked all over the sidelines. If Chase Creel was up to no good, the last person he'd want to catch him would be Coach Draveck. That's where we had common ground. The last person I'd want to challenge for not waking me was also Draveck. Oh well. A girl had to do what a girl had to do.

I knocked on the door to the private dining room as I walked through it. Empty. The coaches must have eaten and gone to the field. I returned to Square's table and forced some food down.

"Get your protein," he said. "They'll still be there in ten minutes."

And if the world around me was any indication, so would the

stares and glares.

"Are they really all this pissed, or is someone fueling the fire?" I asked.

"Kicker Creel is a snake. Everyone was pissed at him for getting them punished, and he deflected by pointing out that you must be too good to run with us. When everyone looked around and saw you were the only teammate not there, the anger sort of festered."

Festered through the punishment. And then through the night. And this morning. It couldn't go on. I downed what I could and headed for the field. Square walked with me, a buffer between me and the team. If he hadn't been looking out for me, how different would my experience have been? I didn't want to know.

D jogged to catch up to us and talked plays with me. He wanted to focus on screen passes today because he had bobbled a few in practice the week before.

"Sure," I said. "But why aren't you angry?"

"Please. I'm in high school, not preschool. Only idiots think you opted out. Coaches need to figure it out. Yeah, you're a girl, but you're on the team. They need to work with that."

"So you know they didn't wake me?"

"I don't think they did, and you said no, I don't really feel like running right now. I'm good."

Wise words spoken. Since my birthday when I threw D that touchdown pass in backyard ball, he'd had my back. We'd even had a few heart-to-heart chats. Like for instance, I knew his dad was a fan of Donnie Shell, and D's full name was actually Donnie.

"Don't ever call me that," he'd said.

So of course, it was incredibly tempting.

"Hey, Medina. You look well-rested. What do you think this is, a beauty pageant?"

The quip came from a group of about seven players—underclassmen whose names I didn't know. A few of them snickered until D was in their faces, shutting them up with a finger pointed in their direction, a string of curse words, and a general domineering air. All laughter fizzled, and they slowed their paces to create some distance between us. D rejoined Square and me, still muttering the kind of language that would make Abuelita cross herself repeatedly and scold him into shame, but I appreciated the solidarity.

"Don't let them talk to you like that," D said, and Square nodded. Good advice but arguing with underclassmen didn't strike me as the best option to gain respect. I'd need to earn that on the field.

I dropped my bag onto a bench near where Christian set up the medical equipment. "Morning, Julia," he said, but somehow my first name didn't belong on the field. There, I was Medina.

"Christian," I said.

"You feeling good?"

"Not you too. Yes. I slept the night through, but I'm paying for it today."

He nodded, eyes wide. "Um, I was asking about how you were *physically* feeling. I'm the trainer's assistant, remember."

"Oh."

"But I'm glad you got a good night's rest. Less likelihood of injuries if your body's well-rested."

Tell that to Coach Draveck who kept the entire team up late, I wanted to say, but I couldn't say much of anything. My paranoia that everyone, even Christian, judged me for last night possessed the capacity to derail my entire morning. I headed for the coaches who were studying their laminated practice scripts, drawing plays on clipboards and generally chatting.

"Morning, Coach Vincent," I said. "Can I have a minute?"

He led me a few yards away from the cluster of coaches and locked his hands behind his back. "What is it, Medina?"

I explained the situation, trying to read his expression. For a second, I thought I saw a flash of anger, but the only revelation for certain was that he didn't know Coach Draveck let me sleep through the punishment. I expected that already, but it felt good to know for sure.

"Coach Draveck!" Vincent waved him over to us and reiterated my tale, then turned back to me. "So why come to us?"

"I should have been there. Someone should have woken me up."

"Are you questioning me?" Coach Draveck said.

"No, sir," I said, although I really wanted to. Did he not wake me because, like so many others, he didn't want me on the team? Was he in Mrs. Creel's twisted anti-feminist camp? Or did he simply forget and not want a big deal made out of his mistake. "It's not my place to question you, but it is my place to be a part of this team."

Coach Vincent nodded. "An honest mistake. You got a little extra sleep. No harm done."

"I'm sorry, Coach, but I disagree. If they have to run, I should be with them."

"Medina," Draveck said, "just because you didn't run last night doesn't mean you're not a part of this team."

"The team seems to disagree, and I can't blame them. No disrespect, Coach, but the team's opinion matters most. If they don't respect me, I can't lead them."

Not that I made the comment to earn his approval, but the look on Coach Vincent's face told me that's exactly what I'd done.

"What do you propose?" Coach Draveck asked. "That we make the team run again but this time with you?"

I heard a few groans from the players nearby, who were clearly eavesdropping on us while faking their stretches.

"Not at all, Coach. They've done their running. I owe them. And *you*. I understand the punishment was two-hundred yards of bear crawls and up-downs. How many?"

"You *want* to run?" Draveck asked.

"Yes."

"On your own?"

"Yes."

He crossed his arms, the familiar look of approval I saw seconds earlier on Coach Vincent's face reflected on his as well. "If you insist. Twenty up-downs at the starting and end lines, and one every five yards."

Brutal. The food in my stomach threatened a reappearance at the thought.

I dreaded the words I was about to speak despite the fact it was the right thing to do. The only thing to do. "With your permission, Coach, on our break today, I'll run them. On my own."

CHAPTER TWENTY-FOUR

IF YOU WORK HARD AND YOU PLAY WELL, ALL THOSE
CRITICS QUIET THEMSELVES PRETTY QUICKLY.
—PEYTON MANNING

"YOU'RE AN IDIOT," SQUARE SAID LATER, WHEN WE
watched from the backfield as Owen ran the offense. "You should
have taken the gift and run. Or not run. You know what I mean."

Sure. From the first day of camp, demonstrate to the group I want
to lead that I deserve special treatment. Not a winning plan.

On the field, Owen took his reps, and not impressively. He threw a
ball too low. Then a pick on a thirty-yard post before finally connecting on a quick out, but the junior receiver, Drew Peters, got tackled
right away. The offense lined up for another play looking bored and
listless. I bounced on my toes, wanting to get in there and coach them
up, get them moving. But what if I couldn't do any better than Owen?

No. I thought of Vince Lombardi's words. "Confidence is contagious." I would be confident. I would be the contagion.

Square squirted water into his mouth. "Anyone tell you what
Kicker Creel did to deserve the punishment?"

I wasn't sure I wanted to know. Not with two-hundred yards of
bear crawls and seemingly endless up-downs still looming over me.

But the story distracted me from the anxiety that my name could be called any minute. And the contradictory desire Coach would call me onto the field that very second.

"Creel recruited two underclassmen to assist him in a classic prank. On you."

What did I ever do to these idiots? Creel liked me just fine at my birthday party when he thought I was a hot girl, which obviously didn't translate into a ticket to try out for football.

Apparently, the idiotic trio had hidden in the shadows, sneaking all the way from their cabin at the center of camp to mine armed with a bottle of baby powder. Their mission: shake it into the fan in my window—which was blowing inward.

Owen threw another pick. This time the safety Austin Moody ran it back for a touchdown. Pity for Owen tugged at me, but I suppressed my feelings and urged Square on with his story. "So, Coach Draveck caught them before they made it to my cabin?"

Square laughed. "Nope."

"I'm confused." I woke up in a baby powder–free room, so...?

"None of the guys knew that the cook was sleeping in your cabin as your chaperone."

"No!" I covered my mouth to keep from laughing at the thought of Miss Nancy covered in white powder.

Square nodded. "They saw the fan running and thought it was your room." He laughed quietly. "Best yet, the fan was one of those two-way ones. So it was blowing air in and out."

Suppressing laughter became tougher and tougher. Moral of the story: Miss Nancy, Chase, and his coconspirators had worn a baby powder mask last night.

"That's why Coach Draveck exploded," Square said. "He saw the guys running through the camp at night, after curfew, covered in white powder and feared some sort of hazing incident. The kind that draws the attention of parents, administrators, and school board directors."

"Medina!" Coach Vincent called. "Take some reps."

The sound of Coach's growly voice saying my name killed all the silliness and laughter in me. Instead, I felt a mix of dread and anticipation that'd been foreign since Mom graduated Ally and me to varsity freshmen year. Those butterflies. The feeling that my skin wasn't enough to contain the explosion of emotions inside.

I jogged onto the field. In my head, I moved in dramatic slow motion, bouncing across the grass like in a movie. Oh, magic.

Owen's path crossed mine. "Nice job out there," I said, trying to be polite and not reveal my nerves at the same time.

"Is that why you and Square were behind me laughing the whole time?" He tossed the ball hard into my gut, but it was his words that knocked the wind out of me.

"Owen, that's not—"

He kept his pace toward the sideline. I refused to watch him. Or to give him another second of my emotional energy. Whatever the hell his problem was, it would have to be dealt with later. I had a team to lead.

On the field, the linemen didn't make eye contact, and the receivers watched me as if it were Bring a Wild Animal to Practice Day. In other words, they weren't ready for me to lead them anywhere.

"All right, guys," I said in the huddle. "Let's do this!"

In response, they looked at the field. Or the sky. Or rolled their eyes at each other. Confidence is contagious, I told myself. Then mentally repeated it. Confidence is contagious. The clap when we broke the huddle was like a rumble of claps, one after the other. Not a unified intimidation.

Something else to work on.

Thankfully, D took the reps with my group. He was a small comfort in what felt like a sea of sharks. I looked to Coach Vincent for the play. A quick slant to Josh Brighton, our top receiver, at least since Owen attempted the move to quarterback. My heart thumped at the fact Coach called a pass for my first play, and one to the lanky six-foot-two receiver with great hands.

He nodded at me and clapped, "Let's go."

The call was an opportunity. My chance to show the team I could do more than throw during drills, which is what we did every day in pre-camp. Coach Vincent wanted me to do well. Like D and Square, he had my back. Maybe it was that realization or being in the moment, but the collective clap that broke the huddle obliterated my anxiety. When I stepped up to the center and yelled, "Red 34! Red 34!" in my best Jake Medina voice, I was ready to go.

Unfailingly loyal, D pep-talked me from my sidecar in the back-field. "You got this, Medina," he said again and again, and I wanted to live up to his expectations. And destroy my competition.

I called for the snap and dropped back with my eyes downfield, refusing to stare down my target. Our outside linebacker, Ward Nix-on, barreled toward me. They probably blitzed to unsettle me, but I stayed calm, knowing a blitz from the middle of the field would leave Brighton wide open on his slant. I planted my foot as he broke into his route. He extended a hand in front of him, a leading target, and I whipped the ball into his outstretched fingers at the same moment D picked up Nixon's blitz—literally—and slammed him back into the ground with a thud.

Brighton caught the ball and with the wide-open field earned us thirteen yards. I sprinted the distance and smacked him on the helmet. We celebrated together on our way back to the line. D shook my hand and tugged me into a shoulder bump.

"Like I said, Medina. I got your back," he said. I silently thanked Coach for keeping Square on the sideline during my reps. The guilt might be too much if D had dropped him like he had Nixon or if, more likely, Square had barreled through D as he tended to do to his opponents.

I modeled D's enthusiasm, pepping my line with encouragements. On the next play, I dropped a quick screen into D's waiting arms.

"Get it!" I yelled to him, and he did. A spin move bought him ten extra yards. And just like that, another fifteen yards. Jogging into the huddle for the third play, I noticed the guys watched me, not the grass or the sidelines. Coach sent in a run play. "Let's do this, guys!" They'd clapped to break the last two huddles, but something felt different that time. The sound wasn't a rumble. We were in unison. I took the snap in shotgun and handed it off to D. Three more yards.

"I got more in me," D said. "I got more."

I smiled at his obvious need to repeat things. On the next snap, he fought his way to two more yards. Although Coach scripted the plays and we weren't officially scrimmaging, I envisioned a third-and-five game-time situation. I thought back to the night before, studying the progression of my receivers. Brighton, my primary receiver, would run a curl route off the right side, but I'd take a risk with that throw. If I was right, Moody would cheat forward, as he had been all day, after the ball was snapped, giving him a lane on Brighton. In that situation, the best decision was to look to the secondary receiver coming off the left side.

If I read the defense right.

I snapped the ball, and the safeties rotated as expected, eliminating Brighton as a safe option for me, but I didn't want the defense to know I knew that. That small victory of reading their motions correctly shot energy through me. I thought about all the times I played in the backyard with my brothers and how their endless attempts at trickery prepared me for that moment. I stared down Brighton, which encouraged the safety to come harder. I could sense his anticipation, thinking I would deliver an interception right into his hands. Sorry to disappoint, Moody. Not happening. I set my feet, turned to my left, and released the ball toward my secondary receiver on a backside skinny post. Wide open.

The ball soared through his outstretched fingers. I swore in my head. D swore out loud.

"First and goal situation," one of the coaches called.

"Let that one go, guys," I said. "Huddle up."

Coach called trips right, a play that settled in my stomach in a bad way. Only one receiver, Brighton, had had any success all morning, so lining up three receivers felt risky to me. Sure enough, I rolled out to my right with no good options downfield. Refusing to force a bad throw, I tucked and ran. When my brothers ran in their high school practices, the defense stopped before contact. That's what you did to protect your quarterback, but I wasn't *the* quarterback. Yet. The play was live, and it would end with my body crashing into someone else's or me protecting myself with a slide or a step out of bounds.

I crossed the line of scrimmage. Two yards. Four. Six. Moody closed in with wide eyes under his helmet. Two steps to the sideline and I would have been safe from the tackle, but instinctively, I knew I needed this hit. The coaches let us go live for this very reason. Nobody in the place knew if I could take a hit. Including me. I'd only ever been tackled by my brothers, and any one of them would've killed the other if I'd gotten hurt.

Eight yards.

I lowered my head and shoulder, protecting the ball with both hands as Moody and I collided, the loud crunch of plastic pads connecting. I'd heard the sound so many times from the stands, but up close, it reverberated in my head louder than I'd imagined it could. I pushed for every inch with Moody's arms wrapped around me, and we fell hard. The impact sent a ringing in my head that faded as quickly as it had appeared. I opened my eyes expecting to be between Moody and the ground. But it was the other way around. I'd run him over and landed on his chest, earning the ten yards we needed for the touchdown and an awful lot of attention from the team.

The cheers dwarfed the crashing of our pads and the ringing in my head. The guys surrounded us, offering hands to pull me up. They pounded on my shoulder pads and hooted until Coach called everyone off the field.

A touchdown. I'd scored my first touchdown!

Medinas didn't celebrate touchdowns in big ways. We clapped a few hands, smacked a few helmets, and then moved on. "Get ready for the next drive," Juan would say. "Got do it again," Jorge would add. "No points for second place," Jake would say.

But the moment felt big. Too big for a few claps or smacks. So when D grabbed my shoulder pads and crashed his face mask against mine, we screamed in each other's faces in the most beautifully obnoxious way I've ever screamed. He lifted me, squeezed, and spun around.

And I laughed and let him. Medina convention be damned.

"Stanford," Coach Vincent yelled. "You're up."

Alexander Stanford took the helm while the guys who were on the field with me grabbed water.

"Nice play, Medina," D said, which met with agreement from the other guys as they chugged.

"Please," Moody said. "You got lucky. I pulled up. Can't hit a girl like that."

His comment threatened my euphoria, nearly transforming it into a bitter anger. If I let it. But the comment wasn't about me. It was about him covering his own weakness by attacking someone else, and even better, the only girl and therefore perceived inferior in the crowd.

Original.

"You won't make that mistake again then, will you?" I asked.

"You can bet on it," Moody said.

"Good. Because next time I trample you, I don't want to hear any excuses."

More hooting and laughing from the guys. And Moody telling everyone to shut up.

"Medina!" Coach called.

I jogged to him. He pulled me aside. With his hands on my shoulder pads and leaning toward me conspiratorially, he asked, "How did that feel?"

I laughed. "Incredible."

He smiled. "Good. Get some rest and get ready to do it again. Good work."

"Thanks, Coach."

"And, Medina," he said with a smile on his face. "You'll never forget this moment."

CHAPTER TWENTY-FIVE

*I DECIDED I CAN'T PAY A PERSON TO REWIND TIME, SO I
MAY AS WELL GET OVER IT.
—SERENA WILLIAMS*

I RODE THE HIGH OF THOSE FIRST REPS THROUGH THE
rest of the morning practice. Basically, until the time came to run.
Not sure if it was due to legitimate need or procrastination, I stretched
for a few minutes before diving into the punishment running. Maybe
part of me thought that if I waited long enough, all of the guys would
be far from the field doing whatever boys do on forty-five-minute
football camp breaks. Snacking. Lounging. Gaming. Nope. Lying on
the hillside, shading their eyes from the sun, watching me.

Deep. Breath.

I stood at the end line and started my twenty up-downs. Quick
feet in place for five seconds and then to the ground for a push-up.
One. Quick feet, push-up. Two. The first few felt good, misleading
me into thinking, *I can do this* and *No big deal.* By number seven,
it was a deal the size of Jake's ego. I thought of Juan, Jorge, and
Jake. They had all done this at one point or another. If my brothers
could do it, so could I.

Eleven. Ugh. I mentally cheered myself on, thinking of how nice the pool would feel after practice. Or the huge swig of Gatorade I was going to take when it was all over. Fifteen. I looked toward the hillside on my next drop down and saw some of the guys shifted from lying down to sitting, even standing. The clapping started slowly, maybe two or three guys. But by the time I finished my twenty up-downs and dropped to all fours for the bear crawls, my cheering section had grown.

When I hit the twenty-yard line, guys lined the field, yelling for me to push it. So I did. I crawled faster. On the up-downs, I popped back up with more intensity. Fifty yards. Their support numbed the burning. It fed me the energy I needed. Ahead, Square and D jumped and cheered in the end zone. I got to them as quickly as I could, and they both hugged me.

"Let's go, rookie!" Square yelled, lining up next to me. "Let's go. Let's go!"

"What. Are you. Doing?" I asked between breaths.

"Line up!" D said, and about a dozen of the guys fanned out along the end zone.

"You don't have to do this," I managed once I caught my wind.

"We know," Square said. "We're a team."

One by one, the guys—no, my teammates—started clapping until we were a raucous of thumping hands. Stanford nodded to me, ready to go. My breath caught in my throat again.

Square leaned his head back and shouted toward the sky as if he were ordering the entire solar system to get to work. "Twenty up-downs. Get it!"

In awe, I fell behind, watching my teammates take on the punishment *for a second time* to be here for me. I wouldn't let them down. I caught up, and we panted, crawled, cheered, and dug together every yard until we collapsed as a team where I'd started all alone. When I recovered, I walked through the group, shaking the hands of every player who stood beside me, recording their names and faces in my memory. These were the teammates who had my back when they didn't have to. When they could have lounged in the sun or maybe even scored a quick dip in the cool water of the swimming pool.

Refusing to be naive, I embraced the fact I had much more work to do, but it felt good knowing I'd earned some respect. I couldn't ignore a persistent disappointment at my core that of the players who dug and fought and pushed beside me in that punishment, Owen wasn't one of them.

****

AFTER DINNER, THE COACHES RETURNED OUR CELL phones for thirty minutes of screen time. I retrieved mine from the massive box to find it had three voicemails. The first was from Abuelita.

"Mija! How is the football? Are you crushing into those boys? Show them, mija. Show them there is nothing a girl cannot do."

The second was from my dad urging me to be careful and have fun. My mom was either not there or didn't say a word. I refused to let her lack of support affect me. I wanted her voice to play on the next message more than anything. I wanted to hear her say she believed in me. That she understood.

The third voice was Rand Denton's.

I hit Delete. How did he even get my number? And when would he accept I didn't want to be the star of his article about the token girl playing football? Back on the screened back porch of my cabin, I tapped Jake's name in my video chat app. When his face appeared on the screen, he dramatically studied me.

"How can this be? Famous, yet you still look like my baby sister."

"Shut up. Hardly famous."

"It's all over social media that you crushed it today."

"Seriously?"

He nodded, tossing peanuts into his mouth. "Did you really run over Austin Moody for a touchdown?"

We both laughed. "Sort of."

"Don't be modest, Jules. There's no room for humility when you're a girl trying out for the quarterback of a powerhouse football team. You know, the team *I* warmed up for you."

"Wow," I joked. "No room for humility in your life either, I see."

He shrugged in acceptance and downed another handful of nuts.

"Do you ever stop eating?"

He burped into the screen. "Stupid questions get stupid answers."

The wooden screen door at the front of the cabin clattered from someone knocking.

"No idea who that could be," I said, walking through the main living area, but when I got closer, I saw Owen.

"You're not letting him in, are you?"

"Of course not," I whispered to my overprotective brother.

"Good," Jake said. "Go out and chat with Lover Boy. I have practice anyway. Hey, wait though."

I held up a finger, signaling Owen to give me a second. "What is it?"

"Abuelita should be calling you any minute. She's finally gotten the hang of this technology stuff. Who would've thought?"

"Great," I said, my voice flat. Talking to Ita was always an experience, but my concern was to get outside and get Owen far away from my cabin before someone saw him and brought a world of trouble down on us both.

"Kill it tomorrow, sis. I know you will."

Without saying goodbye, I tossed my phone onto the table next to the door and stepped onto the front porch.

He pecked my cheek. Or maybe he tried to kiss my mouth and missed when I turned my head.

"Aren't you going to invite me inside?" he asked.

"Coach explicitly stated no boys were to visit my cabin, let alone come inside without a chaperone present."

He stepped backward and leaned on the rail of the porch.

I looked down the path toward the main area of camp, fearful I would see Coach Vincent through the trees. Or worse, Moody and Creel spying in the chance I'd screw up. "Owen, you really need to go. The whole team had to run because of Creel last night. They're not running tonight because of me."

Owen scratched the back of his head and then massaged his neck. "About that, I should have been there to run with you today."

I crossed my arms. "Is that right?"

"Of course," he said as if the question had been a silly one. As if when I needed support, he would be anywhere else other than right beside me.

As if he wasn't competing against me every second of the day.

"Where were you?"

"Commiserating." As if making a pointed attempt to change the subject, he said, "You played well today."

"Thank you." The sincerity of his comment softened my tough exterior.

This was Owen.

In the rush of the last few days, an intense fog had settled around the memories of who we were only a couple weeks earlier. He leaned against the wooden railing on the porch of my rustic cabin at the edge of the woods, the muscles of his folded arms and the waves of his hair tugging at me. I wouldn't have guessed it possible after our weeks in the Florida sun, but one day on the field tanned the softness of his cheeks and the edges of his jaw even more. I wanted to plant my lips on his and tug him through the rickety wooden screen door where I could have him to myself.

Which was precisely why he should've been anywhere but there.

"Should I go?"

Standing next to me, he tempted me like a wide-open receiver, which seemed like a good thing. Unless that receiver was on the left side of the field when I was rolling out to the right *and* had to throw across my body to hit him.

Totally a bad idea.

"I so hate to say it, but I think that would be best."

"So when are we supposed to talk, Julia? Or can't I call you that anymore, *Medina*?"

"Don't be ridiculous." I regretted my tone immediately, but before I had a chance to say so, Owen reacted.

"So I'm ridiculous? Let me tell you what's ridiculous. Coach put you out there with D, our best backfield blocker, and Brighton, our top receiver."

"Technically, you're our top receiver," I said because I couldn't help myself. I'd appreciated Coach's lineup in my first series, but I never considered it would be used against me. Yes, I had competitors around me, but I'd made plays too.

He scowled. "Coach surrounded you with the best team and put you up against the weakest defense to give you an advantage."

Could no guy on this team get knocked down a peg yet maintain some integrity?

"Would you tell *them* they're the weakest defense? Because that might not be the best approach to winning their loyalty."

"You think you're going to win their loyalty? For what? Throwing a few good balls under no pressure?"

"You should leave," I said.

Owen turned away. His shoulders rose and fell with his deep breaths. When he spoke again, his voice was soft. "I shouldn't have said that, but you have no idea how hard this is for me, Jules. I'm trying. Really, I am. I mean, you've been my confidante for months. About my father, my family, and football. But now, it's like I can't talk to you about any of that."

I imagined losing one of my confidants—my brothers. Not being able to talk to them or feel their support and love would crush me. "You can still talk to me."

"It's not the same."

On that point, at least, we agreed.

Laughter filtered down the path, and I strained on my tiptoes to see if someone might've been coming toward us, if they could see Owen at my cabin.

"Don't worry. I'm going." Owen ambled down the path, head bowed. How many times had I watched him walk on the beach or around the pool and felt adoration? Somehow in the last week, that adoration faded. Which was when I realized our relationship was on dangerous ground.

Back inside, I picked up my phone to see how much more time I had before Coach collected it. Instead of the time, I saw Abuelita's face. She must have logged into our group call before Jake hung up, which basically put her on hold until I came back.

Listening while Owen and I argued a few feet away.

"I wonder if that young man of yours is as charming as he looks, mi cielo?"

The tears pressing against my cheeks had me wondering the same thing.

CHAPTER TWENTY-SIX

*I ALWAYS BELIEVE THERE'S A REASON WHY YOU GO
THROUGH EVERYTHING.*
—JOHN ELWAY

THAT NIGHT, THE COACHES AWARDED THE TEAM FREE
time. Motivated to bond with the team, I headed for the pool. Which
was crowded like whoa. Players occupied the chairs and umbrella
tables and played music from primitive, little radios struggling to
take the place of the more advanced smart phones that had been
confiscated. As I walked around the pool to D and Square, I heard
rap, pop, and even country music.

The water was so crowded that even a few short strokes was
impossible.

And as someone who was trying to downplay her sexuality, I felt
crazy alone. Sure, there were a few linemen who couldn't exactly
boast hot bods, but the collective of roughly forty shirtless teenaged
boys had me grateful my sunglasses were the super dark kind.

Not that I ogled them...too much.

Across the pool, I saw D and Square, side by side trying to make
a little space for themselves in the crowd. D laid back into the water,
the wetness of his finger-coiled natural hair glistening in the sun. He

looked skinny next to Square, but that was perspective, of course. His chest and abdomen were muscled under his dark skin, just not as muscled as our star linebacker's. Square pushed D under the water and tried to take the space for himself, but he had too much muscle mass to float and sank pretty much immediately. I couldn't help laughing at them both.

"How's it going?" I said when I finally reached them.

"Cramped," D said. "Don't anybody have something else to do?"

"No," Square said. "That's why we're here."

Not everyone was there. Owen was missing, for instance. I squatted down next to the water and tried to ignore the vulnerability of the position. Anyone could nudge me with a toe, and I'd tumble face first into the pool. "I have an idea. If you're up for it."

"I'm down," D said, climbing the ladder. Square followed.

"Don't you want to know what it is?" I asked.

"Don't care."

They grabbed their stuff. When we walked past Moody and Creel, they scoffed.

"What will Malone think," Moody said, but the crack didn't really get to me.

Square stopped walking, an intensity in his gaze that I was glad was not directed toward me. "Watch your mouth."

"Chill, man!" Creel said, and D stepped in his face. "See. This is the shit that happens when you let a girl on the team."

"No. This is what happens when they let you on the team," I said, nervous what might happen to my two closest friends and allies on the team if they crossed the line with Creel and Moody. Coach had a strict policy against fighting. "They're not worth it. Let's go."

Square finally broke eye contact, and to my relief, we walked away to a chorus of support from the teammates we passed.

"They're looking for a fight," said the center, Ben Jones.

"Keep doing what you do." Ward Dixon fist-bumped me.

And finally, from one of the junior receivers, Drew Peters, a comment that solicited nods from the players around him. "We got your back, Medina."

"Was there drama like this on the volleyball team?" D joked.

"Nope."

"That's why you left and came to us then, huh?"

"My top reason."

"So what's this plan?" Square asked.

I led them through the lower level of the Main Lodge toward the trainer's room where we found Christian organizing supplies. D and Square nodded to Christian and fist-bumped macho greetings.

"Christian, I have a favor to ask."

****

"WE SHOULD NOT BE DOING THIS," CHRISTIAN SAID AS he cruised along the narrow streets of Camp Sweat and Tears.

"Turn left here."

He complied, taking a corner so sharp he almost hit the curb.

"You want me to drive?"

"That is not happening."

Yeah, because I'd be any more dangerous behind the wheel than you, I wanted to say. But a favor was a favor.

We passed a sign noting the volleyball facilities were ahead. It had been about two years since I attended a summer hitting camp there, but not much had changed. Unlike the football facility, there were no cabins but instead a Main Lodge with dorm-like housing, a gym with four indoor courts, and four sand courts outside. There was also a swimming pool, which sat sparkling in the sun, completely empty.

"Hell yeah!" said D.

Christian parked the golf cart, and we all ran to the pool, peeling off clothes, dropping towels, keys, and backpacks along the way. D swam laps, relishing the opportunity to stretch out. Square inflated a float he found in the storage area beside the pool and climbed aboard, his dark skin contrasting with the light yellow of the plastic. I leaned against the side, resting my head and enjoying the sound of the water slapping against the liner.

Until Christian started talking. "The volleyball facilities, huh? You been here before?"

"Camp for hitters and blockers three years running."

"Do you miss playing?"

Since I'd chosen football, I hadn't allowed myself to think about or miss volleyball. But I guessed, in a way, I did miss it. "I guess so," I said. "Sometimes."

"I hear you. I miss playing sports too, but I really want to be a doctor, so I figured why not focus on that. Get some good experience, you know?"

"Do you want to go into sports medicine?"

"Maybe. I'm also an EMT."

Wow.

"You look surprised."

"I am. I didn't realize someone so young could be an EMT."

The conversation dwindled for a few minutes as we watched D and Square enjoy the pool they had practically to themselves. Christian leaned back against the pool steps and smiled at me, squinting his eyes as the sun sparkled off them.

Ally had called him hot.

Ally had been right.

He had a Zac Efron–esque look about him. In swim trunks. Smiling at me.

I swam away from him. I'd appreciated the look of good-looking guys at the beach. Even here at camp. I was human, after all. But those moments of appreciation went something like: *Oh, he's hot. That's nice, but he's not Owen.* And then little flutters would flicker in my chest at the thought of Owen.

When I'd *appreciated* the view of Christian just then, Owen hadn't come to mind. But the flutters did find their way to my chest.

What was I doing?

"You okay?" Christian called across the pool.

"Great," I lied. "Stretching."

He swam toward me. "Are your muscles sore from the workouts?"

They were definitely tense in that moment. Fortunately—or unfortunately, depending on how you looked at it—the doors to the nearby gym burst open, and about twenty girls in spandex and volleyball T-shirts rushed outside, clapping it up and cheering, "Grove Hill, Grove Hill, Grove Hill!"

Volleyball preseason camp for Grove Hill University.

"Oh shit," I mumbled. "We should get out of here."

"Are you kidding me, Medina? Those girls are wearing spandex,"

D said, not willing to blink and miss a second of the view.

Except then they weren't wearing spandex. They were peeling away their shirts and shorts to reveal bikinis.

"Oh, my damn," Square mumbled.

"I can see where the 'favor' thing comes in," Christian said. "You do me favors like this, and I will drive you to Alaska in that golf cart."

I was proud to say the comment sparked no jealousy. None. "Ha ha. Very funny. We can't be here."

But I wasn't not sure they could hear. Their eyes were working too hard for their ears to function. The girls ran to the pool and jumped in, turning the three guys among them into bumbling, drooling idiots. Since nobody seemed to mind our presence, I toweled off and lounged in the setting sun.

"Are you with the crashers?" asked an authoritative voice that made me jump out of the chair. In a polo and shorts with the Grove Hill University logo, head coach Gina Gentile stood hands on hips. I recognized her as one of the coaches who worked the summer hitting and blocking camps. And one of the coaches who, until I'd decided to quit playing, had been recruiting me.

"Coach Gentile."

She took off her sunglasses. "Julia Medina?"

The fact that she remembered me had me impressed for a minute until I realized that meant she could tell Coach Vincent who we were and what we'd done. Perhaps there was something to be said for being forgettable. She shook my hand and invited me to sit with her at a nearby table.

"I was surprised to hear from your coach that you quit the team. To play football?"

"Yes." I gestured to the guys in the pool. "They're my teammates. Our pool was packed, and I remembered this place from the hitting camps. I'm really sorry. I wouldn't have brought them had I known you all were here."

"I'm glad you came." She pushed a bowl of granola bars in my direction.

"You are?"

She gestured for me to eat, so I did.

"Are you sure you're done with volleyball? You're a natural at it."

Maybe it was her sincerity or her generosity for allowing us to stay, but I found myself peeling away the wrappers of three granola bars and telling Gina Gentile what it had been like to play volleyball these last few weeks and how different football made me feel. Never interrupting, she nodded and mumbled understanding occasionally.

"You needed a challenge," she finally said.

"I guess I did."

"And is football challenging you?"

I laughed, and she smiled.

"Well, I'll tell you what. At the end of the football season, if you think you might be interested in trying volleyball again, call me."

"Really?"

"Really. And..." She stood. "If you like a challenge, get back in the water. Girls," she shouted toward the pool. "Get the net."

The volleyball team lined up on the side of the net opposite Square, D, Christian, and me. We dove around for well-placed spikes and blocks, swallowing a dangerous amount of chlorinated water.

I was definitely challenged, but in the best possible way.

CHAPTER TWENTY-SEVEN

TO HAVE ANY DOUBT IN YOUR BODY IS THE BIGGEST
WEAKNESS AN ATHLETE CAN HAVE.
—SHAWN JOHNSON

THE NEXT DAY, MY QUADS BURNED WHEN I TRIED TO
stand. When I squatted to sit on the toilet, my muscles gave out, and
I crashed against the seat. My muscles from my shoulders to my
calves screamed what Square had said the day before: I was an idiot.
I should have embraced my good fortune of missing the up-downs
and bear crawl punishment. Instead, I'd taken the high road, and my
body was pissed off as hell as a result.

Then again, the pain could've also been from smashing into
Moody. But I'd do ten more rounds of punishment running before
I'd admit that aloud.

Despite the soreness in my muscles, I found a rhythm on the field.
I rocked my reps, hitting receivers on almost every kind of route. I
scrambled, took a few hits, and jumped right back up for the next
play. We scored points on the field, and I scored points of respect
with the team. Stanford played well too, but Owen struggled. The
night before, he'd left another note. This one read: *When you plowed*
through Moody. #Respect. I'd wanted to thank him for it all morning,

but my traditional way of thanking him wasn't really appropriate on the practice field. And given his poor performance, it felt wrong to remind him about my great moment from the day before. The notes weren't only romantic. They encouraged me. Even if he couldn't always show it, Owen supported me. In his own way. I wanted to find a way to do the same for him. After a poor series where he made nothing but bad decisions, I joined him at the Gatorade table.

"You wanna talk about it?" I said, remembering how he'd said he missed having a confidante.

He looked around as if the question might somehow embarrass him. "Jules, I'm on the field trying to compete."

I was not expecting that reaction. "Okay...maybe after practice, then?"

He didn't answer.

"Owen?"

He pointedly looked at Christian and said, "You sure you won't be too busy?"

His words set off a guilt grenade inside me. Christian had been watching us but turned away when I looked at him. Owen downed two cups before pulling on his helmet and jogging back onto the field.

Christian caught my gaze and mouthed, "You okay?"

I shook my head, more at the situation than to answer his question and headed back to my self-assigned spot near the coaching staff. I would not think about Owen. Or Christian, for that matter. I would focus on football. I would study the defenses and the playbook. I would go after what I wanted, even if some people didn't think I should want it at all.

****

FREE TIME THAT NIGHT GOT INTERESTING. I'D FORGOT-ten to hang up my bathing suit from the day before, so I had no choice but to reach into the depths of my bag for a...bikini. Not the red bikini, but still. Lots of skin.

Lots.

I stared at myself in the mirror for about ten minutes before I decided I was done with bullshit gender issues—at least for the night—

and that since I was, in fact, a girl I should therefore act and dress, in fact, like a girl.

The stillness of my teammates as I walked through the pool area toward D and Square told me I had also reminded them that I was, in fact, a girl.

"We're cool now," D said, "so I think I can say this: damn, girl."

Square tried not to look in my direction. "What happened to that baggy suit from yesterday?"

"It's molding on my bathroom floor."

They nodded, averting their eyes.

"I can't even look at you," D continued. "You're my teammate. Teammates ain't supposed to look like that. Damn."

But after a few minutes, he got over it and debated coverages and plays with me, which was exactly what I needed to get my mind off the mess that was my relationship with Owen. Square offered the defensive point of view. The players in the pool went back to their games and laughter and music. Once they survived the initial shock of my lady curves on display, normality embraced us once again.

Until Owen arrived.

"Here comes drama," D said, heading for the pool.

Square followed, leaving me to fend for myself.

"Cowards."

"I didn't mean to chase them away." Owen sat next to me.

"You didn't," I lied. "They needed to cool off."

"Wanna take a walk with me?"

Despite the frustration and anger that had somehow become our stasis, my stomach tingled. Given all the stress surrounding our relationship lately, that gave me hope for us.

"It sounds like you're asking me on a date," I said, making an effort to flirt with him.

His grin reminded me that he was Owen, the jock who could make an impressive percentage of the Iron Valley student body swoon with just that look. "The best version of it I can manage given the situation."

"I'm in." I pulled a pair of shorts over my bathing suit and waved to the teammates worth waving to on the way out, ignoring the remarks from Kicker Creel and his crew. "They don't quit, do they?"

Owen took the path that led toward the woods. "No. They don't. But you can't let them get to you either."

I sighed, wanting to take his hand but refusing since the team was still in view. I wondered if he wanted to take mine too. "It's nice having your support."

"I feel the same way. Today on the sideline..."

I raised my hands in surrender. "You were right. It wasn't the time or the place. Your reps were..."

"Crap," Owen laughs. "You can say it."

We passed the cover of the trees then, and Owen turned to me, cupping my ass and pulling me in for a kiss. It felt too good to re-sist—his fingertips gripping my bare skin where the shorts had ridden up, his chest pressed against me, his tongue twisting with mine. But after a few seconds, I managed to regain my sense of judgment and pulled away. "Anyone can see us here," I whispered.

"I scoped out this place for two days. Trust me. Nobody can see us."

I giggled at the thought he'd planned so thoroughly. "How did you manage that?"

"I stashed my bright orange duffle here." He kissed my neck. "And checked from all angles to get a glimpse of it."

Then we were kissing too deeply for either of us to talk.

"I miss you, Jules," he said when he pulled away. "I'm worried about us."

"Me too," I admitted. On the field, I was focused, making it easy to forget how I felt when Owen and I were together like this. The truth was I didn't know how to be his girlfriend and compete against him at the same time. "We'll figure it out though."

He didn't look so sure. "You wanna walk?"

I nodded. We stepped onto the path in silence and stayed that way. So many topics felt taboo. Football, for obvious reasons. The silly things D and Square did, because it seemed Owen envied our growing friendship. Ally, because we hadn't spoken.

"How's your Abuelita's political campaign going?" he asked.

Yes! Safe subject. Thank the Lord for Abuelita. "Good, as far as I know. She's a force."

"That she is."

"But Creel's mom tried to use the school board to punish Vincent for supporting me playing. Who knows what they'll try to do to ensure Abuelita doesn't get voted in as a director who could potentially oppose them?"

"She can handle them."

"That's the thing though. I don't want her to have to handle them because of me. This campaign means so much to her. She came to America when she was my age and spent her life living for her husband, children, and now her grandchildren. Running for the school board is the first thing she's ever done for herself, and it's her chance to be...more."

For herself.

Owen backtracked the few steps toward me. In a swift motion, he wrapped an arm around me and kissed my forehead. "It'll be okay."

"Thanks."

"Of course," he said.

"Can I ask you something?"

"Yep."

"How's Ally?"

He led us down the path again. "She misses you. She doesn't say so, but I can tell. It's tough for her to play volleyball without you."

It was tough for me to play football without her to talk to.

"The team's doing well though. Some sophomore, Melanie, I think—"

"She's great!"

He glanced at me. "Yeah? Well, she's looking like your mom's choice for your old position."

The team needed six players on the court, but the thought of Melanie with the five starters who were like sisters to me made me greener than I'd ever admit. On the other hand, maybe I should swallow that jealousy and give her a call when we got back from camp. I knew firsthand how overwhelming Ally's expectations could be. For a sophomore stepping up into my position among a roster of impressive seniors, not to mention one of them being Ally the perfectionist, that was a lot to absorb.

"I'm happy for her," I said, knowing that despite my jealousy, that was true.

We reached the end of the path at one of the narrow camp roads.

"We can head back this way to the cabins," Owen said, pointing to the left. "Or we can go for a swim in the creek . . . alone."

Kissing in the woods had felt risqué enough. The woods secluded the swimming hole, but if anyone came by—like the Grove Hill volleyball team or any of the other teams training at Camp Sweat and Tears that week—catching the two of us alone together would be difficult to explain as platonic. Not that Coach Vincent instituted any rules about dating on the team. He hadn't ever had to deal with the situation before, so I didn't think he knew what to institute. I wasn't about to set a bad precedent. "It's getting late."

Owen went silent again as we walked back. I wanted to guide us back to a happy place but didn't know how. Lately, kissing was the only thing we did well.

Ahead, Christian sped toward us in the golf cart. We stepped into the grass and out of his way, but he also clung to the other side of the street to give us as much room as possible.

"Here comes the kid doctor," Owen muttered.

"He's actually pretty nice."

Owen looked sideways at me. I'd said the wrong thing again. Out of politeness—and politeness only—I waved to Christian, who waved back and promptly crashed the golf cart into a sign.

CHAPTER TWENTY-EIGHT

*ACCEPTING CRITICISM WITH THE SAME GRACE THAT
YOU DO THE APPLAUSE IS SOMETHING EVERY YOUNG
ATHLETE NEEDS TO LEARN. SOME PEOPLE CALL IT
GROWING ANOTHER LAYER OF SKIN. I JUST CALL IT
GROWING UP.*
—DAN MARINO

IN SECONDS, I WAS ACROSS THE ROAD, PULLING HIM
upright in the seat. "Are you okay?"

"He's fine." Owen's bitter voice made my sore muscles tighten.
"Isn't that right, Santos?"

"Owen, he was in an accident."

"Which wouldn't have happened if he was watching the road
instead of checking out my girlfriend."

"I wasn't—" Christian started, but I interrupted him.

"Don't be ridiculous." The accident was clearly due to Christian's
clear lack of steering ability. "You know, you might want to stop
driving these things."

He groaned-slash-laughed. "Coach Vincent's gonna kill me."

Owen watched from ten yards away with no interest in helping.

"Is it bad?" Christian asked.

"Back it up, so we can see the damage."

He reversed to reveal a barely scratched front end.

"You got lucky!"

"I'm not feeling lucky." Christian reorganized the supplies that had shifted during the impact. "I have to drop off this stuff at the baseball camp. Apparently, they're low on supplies, so they called around. You want a ride back?"

Owen laughed. "Dude, I'm not getting in that thing if you're driving."

Christian rolled his eyes and mumbled, "See you later."

He drove off, and Owen sulked. "You shouldn't encourage him. He's totally into you."

"Did it ever occur to you that a man could be around a woman without being into her?"

"No," he said deadpan.

I couldn't tell if Owen believed that or if his behavior amounted to simple jealousy. Maybe my brothers were right—he couldn't take competing with, and potentially losing to, his girlfriend. He turned his body away from mine, and I could read the tension in his face and shoulders as clearly as I read the team playbook.

"Are you looking for a fight?" I asked.

"Me?" He pointed at me accusingly. "I could ask you the same thing. How are we supposed to have a relationship like this?"

"Like what, exactly?"

"Competing against each other. Sneaking away to have any time together. All the people around us hitting on you or checking you out or talking about your ass."

"Screw them, Owen. What's the alternative? I don't play football because it's too hard for you?"

He stepped backward as if I hit him with the words. "I can't believe you said that."

I couldn't believe we were arguing in the middle of the street. About something I couldn't even put my finger on.

"Do you love me?" Owen said quietly.

Oh. There it was.

All his jealousy. His fears and anger that I might've been choosing football over him because I didn't love him.

But I did.

Or at least I thought I did—every time he made me laugh. And when his voice calmed my fears. And when seeing him made me want to melt into his embrace. Yet did I really want to say so as an answer to a question? The first time I declared those words to him should be special. Passionate. Real. Not forced as part of some stupid fight. My brain worked at supersonic speed to send a string of appropriate words to my mouth. Apparently, that wasn't fast enough.

"That's what I thought." He shook his head. "I'm done with this."

"Owen..." I reached for his hand, but he pulled it away and, to my surprise, laughed. "What's so funny?"

"That you thought this could have ended any other way."

"It could," I said, frustrated with the pleading sound of my voice. "It still can."

"No. It can't. You don't want to be seen with me."

"Being with you just reminds everyone else here I'm a girlfriend. A girl. They see me in relation to you instead of as my own person."

He nodded. "So like I said. You don't want to be seen with me."

"Owen..."

"You won't swim in the creek with me even when the guys aren't here. And maybe all of that could be overlooked, but there's one thing that can't be."

A growing block of dread in my core warned me to end the conversation. But I didn't think I could stop Owen. His emotions plowed out of him like D plowing through a defense to score.

"Every time you step onto that field," Owen went on, "it's clear what matters most to you."

His words sparked equal parts pride from the compliment and shame that he was totally right. Without meaning to, I'd chosen football over him. Time and time again.

"I shouldn't have to choose," I said quietly.

He laughed coldly. "I'd love to have the choice. A choice would be great, Julia. You know why? I'd choose you. Every time."

Owen might have thought he would have chosen me, but I didn't believe it. For one thing, his father never would have let him.

Yet he had at least *said* he would choose me. I hadn't given him the same courtesy. I hadn't even considered it.

The silence between us grew, bloated with my shame and our anger. What if I didn't have to choose? What if I could figure out how to play football and be Owen's girlfriend? If he'd been the receiver he was supposed to be when I'd decided to try out, maybe none of this would have happened. We could have played beside each other. Supported each other. Made each other better. That was what I'd wanted.

But how could I say I shouldn't have had to choose and then ask him to?

The answer came easily. I couldn't.

"Well, given your silence, I guess there's only one other thing to say."

With wetness welling in my eyes, I looked up at him and saw the pain in his too. The sad way the corners of his lips curved downward ever so slightly. I wanted to hug him and squeeze so tightly there'd be no room for hurt. For either of us. But I didn't because I anticipated the words that rolled off his kissable lips.

"We're done."

A numb stillness settled over me. Done. After six months with someone, talking to them every day. Seeing them most days. Now, playing a sport that would keep us side by side as if we were partners in a full-time job. For too long to remember differently, my phone had buzzed with Owen's texts. He'd stopped by my house anytime. His boyfriend status had afforded him that freedom. My girlfriend status had afforded me the chance to touch him. Flirt with him. Kiss him. Talk to him about anything. Everything.

What did it mean to be done?

"Owen...?" *Tell him you love him. Tell him it could work. Tell him you choose him over football. Tell him something!*

He walked to a path in the woods but stopped and turned back to me. "Do you need me to walk you back to camp, or do you know the way?"

"I know the way."

He disappeared into the green of the trees then, leaving me in the middle of the street.

Alone.

I wondered how I'd been tangled in his arms minutes earlier and now all promises between us were voided. My competing against him couldn't have been easy, but he could have embraced it with more acceptance and class.

I didn't realize it then, but I could have too.

CHAPTER TWENTY-NINE

*FALLING IN LIFE IS INEVITABLE—STAYING DOWN IS OP-
TIONAL.*
—CARRIE JOHNSON

I ROCKED BACK AND FORTH ON THE PORCH, WISHING I
had my phone so I could talk to Jake. Or my mom. Or Ally. Despite
his flaws, Owen made me laugh, and the way he looked at me told
me I was sexy, which was not something I'd always felt growing up
a sporty girl with three older brothers. At my height and build, I tow-
ered over most of the people I knew, but not Owen. I'd admired him
for his play on the field, and he'd been to enough of his sister's games
to admire my physicality too. Yes, it was physical. Super physical, but
I'd spent countless hours listening to Owen complain about his dad's
unrealistic expectations. How he missed his mom and stepbrothers.
How he didn't know whether to stay close to Ally for college or
finally separate from his twin sister.

I'd confessed my apprehensions about volleyball, how much I
wished my brothers would all be back home with me. Our dreams.
Our fears. We shared all those things.

But I didn't tell him I loved him. Maybe if I had, that would have
been enough.

Then again, maybe not.

Owen said it himself. When I stepped onto the field, my passion for the game showed. That's what I'd wanted from day one. But I didn't realize my love for football would dull my spark with Owen. I checked my window for one of Owen's notes at least seven times, but I didn't stop there. I looked on the porches, in the doors, even—in one humbling moment—under the porch. Nothing.

We really were *done*.

The searing that had plagued my chest since Owen left me standing in the street intensified. I wouldn't lose Owen and football. When word got around, the team might expect a broken, dumped girl. I'd show them a focused, skilled quarterback.

I wiped away the wetness from my cheeks and fanned out every football handout and report I had on the table. I studied the plays, the progressions, and the personnel. I needed to know where the weak links were on the defense so I could exploit them. I ranked all the defensive players and charted the best plays against the different personnel on the field. Occasionally, a tear snuck down my face and plopped onto the pages spread in front of me. I'd watch it morph the ink into an undeniable blotch. And then I'd read the words surrounding it as if it wasn't there at all.

Blotch for blotch, I plotted for success. At practice, I planned to execute.

****

THE NEXT MORNING CONSISTED OF FREQUENT thoughts of Owen followed by appropriate reprimands. For instance, *What will it be like when I see Owen?* And, *Don't think about that. Think about doing well in practice.*

Or *Has he told the team about me?* And *What does that matter? Play hard.*

And so on.

With three potential starting quarterbacks, Coach assigned no more than six reps before we switched. In other words, I didn't have much opportunity to impress. The players around me—on both defense and offense—rotated. The constant was me and my mind, if I could keep it from steering back to thoughts of Owen. Since I was a kid, I'd used it to compete with my brothers, who were always bigger, faster, and stronger than me. I'd have to harness that experience to persevere through football camp.

I didn't only set myself up for success. With strong reads and good decisions, I made the players around me look good too. They made plays. They impressed the coaches. Given my emotional hurricane every time I glanced at Owen—or thought about him—the achievement couldn't be overlooked.

"I have to say," Christian said to me on the sideline after a good series, "you're damn good."

I choked on my Gatorade.

"It's true," he said, blushing. "Maybe it takes someone not on the field with you to say it."

Since the day we met, Christian had been a good friend. A *friend*. And Owen had me questioning that kindness. Any kindness, really. I should've been able to accept a compliment without fearing the person who delivered it had some ulterior motive.

"Thanks," I said. "You feeling okay after the little fender bender?"

"I'm good."

Coach called him, ending our conversation. Across the field, Owen stayed close to Brighton and the other receivers. I got the sense he knew where I was at all times and purposely didn't look in my direction. The team noticed.

"Trouble in paradise?" Creel muttered when I walked by him.

Moody, as usual, more brutally asked me, "The hell you expect to happen when you tried to take away the quarterback spot? Flowers?"

How eloquently put. Thank you.

The day felt more like a hot mess than one in which I played "damn good". I was distracted from football, and that had to change.

By the time our electronics were released after dinner, I relished the thought of escaping the growing gossip at Camp Sweat and Tears and Owen's presence—with a classic Medina family video chat challenge. As usual, Jake and Juan accepted. The moment I saw their faces, I wanted to blurt that Owen had broken up with me and I had no freaking idea how to deal with that standing next to him and a bunch of guys every day. I needed my mom, my abuelita, my girlfriends, Ally.

But Jake never thought Owen and I fit. Last thing I wanted to do was give him the *I told you so* satisfaction. Or burn all my electronics time on a conversation that would make me feel worse.

No. There was no medicine like competition.

Last time I competed against my brothers in our classic 10/20/30, we barely finished the ten-yard round before Mom stormed out of the house and interrupted us. I set up a few tackle dummies as targets, and the fun began. Three attempts from each distance. Under the time crunch, we each hung up our phones, set them to record a video, and threw our nine balls simultaneously. Then we connected the call again and typed our tallies through text.

"Ready to send?" I asked.

"One. Two. Three," Jake said, and then I hit Send, feeling proud. I'd missed one target at thirty yards. Otherwise, my throws were flawless.

"Eight, Jules!" Juan shouted. His tally read seven. Jake's, of course, read nine.

"She beat you, big brother!" Jake teased.

"She needed the confidence boost."

"No, no, no! Don't do that," I said. "I've been listening to excuses from boys for three days when I do something better than them."

"That bad, huh?" Juan said.

"It'll take some adjustment," Jake said from his little block on the screen. "They want to win, and if you're the person who can help them do that, they'll buy in eventually."

"I don't have until 'eventually'." I needed to impress Coach Vincent soon. For the best interest of the team, Coach would need to narrow the field. When he did, I wanted to still line up behind the center.

"Are you playing your best?" Juan asked.

"Yes."

"That's all you can do," both of my brothers said in unison.

I hated when good advice pissed me off.

"How you feeling about the scrimmage?" Juan asked.

"Haven't thought about it too much," I said, which was sort of the truth. "I'm trying to practice with the game time intensity to prepare."

My brothers nodded, and my nerves fluttered against the silence.

"So...do you think you'll be able to make it?"

Their faces froze in incredulous expressions, making me wonder if the connection ended. Jake shook his head. "I can't believe you'd even have to ask, Little J."

"I'm offended," Juan said with a smirk.

"It's not like she ever came to our games. Right, bro?"

By now, I was smiling too. And feeling aptly shameful.

We said our goodbyes, and I rounded up as many of the balls from the field that I could carry. They were coming. My parents. Abuelita. Juan. Jake. They'd all be at the scrimmage to watch *me* play football. Even Moody couldn't have chased the smile away from my face.

As I jogged back to the sideline to put them away, I realized I wasn't alone. Coach Vincent held the ball bag wide open, so I could toss them inside.

"Thanks," I said, feeling slightly embarrassed about running around the field with a silly grin on my face.

"You're welcome." He tilted his head toward my phone. "That how you got so good at this? Competing against your brothers?"

I laughed, nervously, probably because Coach Vincent had referred to me as "so good". Luckily, I didn't squeal. "Since we were kids. Anytime I messed up, I heard about it."

"I wondered about that. I'll be honest. When you wanted to try out, I thought...well, I didn't believe..." He squirmed at the verbal corner he'd placed himself in.

"You can say it."

"I thought, maybe she can throw a ball, but so many aspects of the position are learned over years of practice. Footwork being one of them."

"Juan taught me footwork when I was five."

Coach laughed.

"I know the game, Coach. When I think about it, I should have played years ago."

He walked alongside me as I finished cleaning up, the one-on-one experience feeling surreal. "Then why didn't you?"

I tossed a ball into the bag. "I don't know. It was always my brothers' domain. My place was the periphery. Until they all moved out and I realized that I loved football more than just in relation to them."

"Makes sense," he said.

"I appreciate the opportunity you've given me. So much."

He knotted the drawstring on the bag. "It shows every time you step on the field. And did I hear you beat Juan tonight?"

I laughed. "He won't be happy you know that."

He smiled, the lights creating shadows on the creases of his face. For the first time, he looked his age to me. Maybe a little older. Tired, even. I wondered if the stress of all the team changes this summer was getting to him. Or the stress of figuring out how to accommodate a girl in a role traditionally reserved for machismo.

"Your brothers gave me a lot of good years."

The sentence hung in the air like he might say more, but he didn't. What would he say? *But I'm sorry that's not enough to award you the starting position*? Or *I think you can give me at least one more good year*? Or what?

"You know, that reporter Rand Denton left me a message today about interviewing you for the paper." He offered the information as a statement, yet I sensed he was also asking a question.

"He's called me a few times too." Every night I'd picked up my phone for electronics time there had been a voicemail, text, or email from Denton.

Coach nodded. "Not interested?"

"Don't feel like I've done much to warrant news."

He grinned.

"What?"

"Not sure the rest of the town feels that way."

I didn't know how to respond without sounding rude or disrespectful. Bottom line: It wasn't about the town. It was about me and this team.

"Time's about up for electronics. Better get that phone back to the Main Lodge."

"Yes, Coach." I secured the bags in the shed, and when I finished, he waited on the hillside.

"And, Medina?"

"Yes, Coach?"

"Keep working hard."

Despite the cloud of drama surrounding me, I planned on nothing less.

****

ON THE WAY BACK TO MY CABIN, I STOPPED BY Square's. He shared with seven other defensive players. Unfortunately for me, Moody answered my knock.

"Look who came down from her castle to grace us with her presence."

"Let me guess. You're still in pain from when I ran you over."

His expression declared that topic sensitive.

"Okay, okay," Square said, pushing his way past Moody and out the door. "That's enough, children."

Moody grumbled back inside.

"You here to see me or to torment Moody?"

"Seems like a package deal. Actually, I needed a girlfriend to talk to."

Square stopped walking and glared at me. "You know I'm a six-foot, two-hundred-fifteen-pound Black dude, right?"

"Why do guys always spout off their weight like it's a GPA or something?"

"You're deflecting."

He was right.

"We got a few minutes before curfew. Go for a walk?" he suggested.

"Sure," I answered. We headed along the main path toward the pool.

"You gonna talk?"

"I beat Juan," I said, although I wanted to talk about Owen, not Juan.

He raised an eyebrow.

"Never mind. It's nothing, really. But maybe it is. Juan's the quarterback who started this Medina tradition. My brothers and I compete in everything through video chat on our phones and tablets. Tonight, I beat Juan in a target contest."

Square didn't say anything.

"Like I said. Probably nothing."

"Don't do that," he said.

"What?"

"Downplay yourself. You have enough people doing that already, and they're idiots."

His words struck me as rough and tumble as if he had come through the line untouched and sacked me on the football field. I *had* been downplaying myself. My self-deprecating comments and thoughts could be just the thing holding me back. Like Jake had told me, if I didn't believe in myself playing, then who would?

"You make quick decisions that benefit the people around you. You know the defenses and read them better than Stanford would ever think to."

Each of Square's compliments was like a warm hug, especially since he wasn't the kind of guy to blow smoke.

"On paper," he continued, "you rank with any other tryout we've had in the last few years. You're of similar height, weight—"

"Watch it."

He laughed, the soft sound contrasting the noise of our shoes crunching in the gravel. "You know what I mean. You bench and squat more than some of the guys on the team."

"Including Creel and Moody." Which could explain their unpleasant nature toward me.

"And you're smart as hell. I see your reads and your strategizing. You think everything through to the smallest details and in the speed a quarterback needs to do it. I'm glad you beat Juan, but it doesn't convince me of anything I didn't already know."

"What's that?"

"Fishing, huh?"

I shrugged. "Maybe a little."

He turned to face me, and the intensity in his eyes...wow. "You're exactly what this team needs this year. I don't say that for any other reason than what you do on the field every day."

Oh, Square. I wrapped my arms around him—well, as far as I could reach—and rested my head on his shoulder. "You are the best girlfriend I could ask for."

"Glad I could help."

I sighed, letting so much stress and fear flutter in the wind with my exhale.

"You gonna let me go?"

I shot upright. "Sorry."

"It's cool. What are girlfriends for?"

"Ha ha," I said.

We walked around the swimming pool, still and bright.

"You didn't come to see me only because you beat Juan?"

"No."

"This about Owen? I heard you two broke up."

I sucked in a breath. It was out. And it was real. Had Owen boasted about dumping me, or was Square politely using other terminology?

"You want my advice?"

"That's why I knocked on your door." I attempted a light tone but didn't pull it off.

"Focus on competing. You're earning the team's respect on the field. Keep at it. Invite a couple of the receivers out before and after practice to perfect your timing."

Not what a girl would say. Definitely not what Ally would say.

We rounded the path to his cabin, and he climbed the steps to the porch. Knowing Square, he would have walked me home if it wasn't expressly forbidden.

"Maybe you and Owen breaking up is for the best," he said. "Now you don't have to split your attention between him and football."

True. I was no longer competing against my boyfriend, but something told me challenging my ex-boyfriend would only challenge me more.

CHAPTER THIRTY

I WORKED ON MY WEAKNESSES AND MADE THEM MY STRENGTHS.
—SYDNEY LEROUX

ALL NIGHT, A SPRING IN MY BED TREATED ME LIKE I was wood that needed poking in a hot fireplace. Of course, the bed couldn't be blamed for the mid-August heat. The alarm blared long before my body felt ready to rise and shine for our lifting session, especially given that my muscles still hadn't recovered from the soreness of the strenuous last few days.

Being one of the last ones to arrive, I feared my ideal partners would be taken. A worse hell befell me. Coach Vincent paired everyone.

My partner? Owen Malone. Wearing a sleeveless T-shirt with a peekaboo effect every time he leaned over to pick up a weight and that rugged scent of his that made me want to... Couldn't he at least have the decency to look or smell like shit?

If I had any luck at all, which seemed unlikely given the pairing in the first place, a weight would fall from an impressive height and put me out of my misery. Abuelita's voice in my mind scolded me and said I should wish for the weight to fall on *his* head instead.

Her bold personality was apparently loud enough to communicate in hypothetical situations telepathically from miles away. I smiled and shook my head.

"What's so funny?" Owen asked, adding weights to the squat bar.

"Nothing."

"You find the world quite entertaining." He finished the sentence as if there were more to be said, although I couldn't imagine what. He stepped under the bar and lifted it across his shoulders.

"What's that supposed to mean?" I asked as he counted his squats, ignoring my question.

He squatted eight reps, sucking in deep breaths, his face reddening with each count. He secured the bar back on the rack. "Never mind."

When we'd disagreed as a couple, which was rarely, I could reach out to him and wrap my arms around his neck. Or take his hand. But those actions that were so natural to me days ago were forbidden. The abruptness of the change unsettled me, and I didn't want to be unsettled.

"You ready for your second set?"

He tossed his towel on a nearby chair and gripped the bar again. "Do you have to order everyone around?"

"No." I stretched my shoulders. "Only people incapable of managing themselves."

He stumbled in the middle of his set and glared at me. I kept quiet until he finished, not wanting the responsibility of him injuring himself. People like Chase Creel could make trouble on the team, but the microscope pointed at me ensured I stayed perfectly in line.

"You're up, Princess," Owen said.

How did I overlook his ability to be such a colossal ass?

I slid fifteen pounds off each side of the bar, feeling Owen's eyes (and his smirk) on me. Would I have loved to squat as much or, hell, more than my ex-boyfriend-slash-competitor? Absolutely. Was I stupid enough to risk hurting myself to prove a point? Not even. So off the weights came.

Unlike most of the girls on the volleyball team, I loved squats. The effort to perfect a squat directly correlated to the ability to explode into a higher jump, which led to better blocks and spikes. Or at least, that's how it made sense to me. So when I lowered myself into the squat, keeping my weight on my heels and my back straight, I owned the execution. I paced myself, focusing on form and breathing, and when Owen helped me secure the bar, I caught more than one of my teammates staring and a softness in my boy-friend's—ex-boyfriend's—eyes.

A softness that was best to ignore.

****

AFTER OWEN CAUGHT ME NOTICING THAT LOOK IN HIS eyes, we didn't speak the rest of the lifting session other than "Ready" or "Here I go" or some other benign comment. I forced myself to focus on the workout and not wonder what *that* look was about. No. I wouldn't speculate or freak or turn into one of those girls who overanalyzed every millisecond of her ex-boyfriend's behavior. *Does he want me back? Does he not? Do I want him back?* Blah. I'd cried over Owen Malone. I wouldn't continue doing it.

Football. That was my focus. Coach dismissed us, and I hurried up the path and away from Owen. I found Brighton at the front of the pack of players and jumped in front of him.

"Can we talk a second?"

Mason, a sophomore lineman Brighton had been talking to, gave us some distance.

"Make sure you see Christian to get taped," Brighton called. "Mom will lose it if you get hurt again."

Mason rolled his eyes but nodded as he walked away.

"Little brother?"

Brighton nodded.

"I always wanted a younger sibling."

"You the baby, then?"

"Yep," I said. "But that's not what I wanted to talk to you about."

"Imagine that."

I thought he might've been teasing, but either he had a desert dry humor or a serious—and somewhat rude—demeanor. No matter. Teenage boy attitudes were a given in this world, apparently, but one must press on. "I wanted to see if you would be interested in catching some balls either before or after practice."

He stopped walking and stared at me.

"I thought it might help our timing. Give us a feel for each other."

His eyebrow twitched at my suggestion of us "feeling" each other. Nothing like an unintended sexual innuendo to fuel even more awkwardness in the conversation. I closed my eyes tight. Not what I meant. Not only was there Owen but Brighton had a girlfriend—Melanie's sister actually.

"Why?" he asked.

"I just told you why."

"No. Why me?"

The team parted as they passed and walked around us.

"You're the strongest receiver on the team. I'm the quarterback. I want us to have good chemistry."

Was that another twitch?

"On the field. Chemistry on the field, and only there. I didn't mean—"

Brighton raised a hand to stop me. "Look, Medina. As long as you're on this team, you're one of the guys to me. I'll never hit on you and assume you're never hitting on me. Deal?"

The kind of deal I'd like to sign with every other guy here. "Absolutely. And I know you're dating Elle Corwin."

A cute little grin spread across his face. "Lucky guy that I am."

"Adorable," I said. "So are you in, or what?"

Brighton appeared thoughtful, as if the offer deserved serious consideration. I didn't see how. Either he wanted to dedicate the extra time, or he didn't.

"Look, I'm here to play. I want to do well for coach, for the team, and for myself. I want to work out with you, but if you're not game, then fine. I can ask someone else."

Apparently, *hard to get* was the way to go. Later that evening after practice, Brighton hung around the field and asked what I thought we should do first.

"How about we go through the route tree, starting with the three-steps?"

Brighton jogged into position while his younger brother sat on the sideline, presumably to help fetch balls. Josh took four reps for each route, which proved a workout for me. During our regular practices,

I usually ran the offense for six reps before Owen or Stanford took my place. Two or three of the reps would be runs, so the most I threw was four passes in a series. With Brighton, I threw four passes for the first route, a hitch. It felt good.

And I connected on all of them.

We moved to the slant next. Then a curl. Then a dig. He dropped a few balls, and I threw a couple off target, but for the most part, we did well. Until we got to the five-step routes. For a while, I feared he'd never tire.

He had the kind of intimidating stamina that made me appreciate we wore the same team jersey.

Finally, Brighton cut a couple sloppier routes. Just in time—after we attempted a few post corner routes with me throwing the ball thirty or forty yards. Not my strength.

"Running so many routes after a long day of practice has to be tough," I commiserated as we loaded the equipment into the shed.

"I kind of love it actually," Brighton said, smiling.

We hustled to the cafeteria to get some dinner before Miss Nancy packed everything away. I grabbed three pint-sized cartons of milk while Brighton loaded his tray with double that amount of chocolate milk. On second thought, he put one back in the cooler and grinned at me. "Have to watch my figure."

His sudden change in demeanor confused me. "What was with the change of heart today?"

His figure was about to suffer from the mound of chicken fingers he piled on his plate. "I don't want to get into the drama," he said.

"Does this have to do with Owen?"

"Forget about him. Square's been telling everyone he's a jealous ass, and I'm starting to agree."

"Just starting to?"

A mushed-up, half-chewed chicken strip appeared in Brighton's mouth when he laughed. "You're kind of funny, Medina."

Glad someone was laughing.

CHAPTER THIRTY-ONE

*NO MATTER WHAT ACCOMPLISHMENTS YOU MAKE,
SOMEBODY HELPED YOU.*
—ALTHEA GIBSON

THE NEXT MORNING AT PRACTICE, OWEN SEEMED QUI-eter than normal. Not that he talked to me much the day before, but that morning, he didn't talk to anyone. The urge to cross the distance between us, rest my hand on his cheek, and ask him what was wrong snuck up on me.

Throughout my high knees and lunging warm-ups, I suppressed the urge. Tried to look away. But my eyes found their way back to Owen's face. Maybe he could hide it from everyone else on the team, but I knew him well enough to see the sadness there. And I...*cared*... enough about him to want to do something about it.

I resolved to talk to him after practice. Maybe it was about us. Maybe he'd changed his mind and wanted to get back together. But what would that solve? We broke up for a reason, and that reason hadn't changed—Owen and I were competing for the same position. We wanted the same thing, and it was impossible for both of us to get it.

When Coach Vincent called out the personnel for teams, clarity struck.

"Malone and Brighton, run receiver. Stanford, take some reps."

Malone...run receiver? It was like my body stopped working for a few moments to allow my senses to clarify if I'd heard what I thought I'd heard. Had Coach Vincent cut Owen from the quarterback race?

Owen jogged toward the right hash while Stanford lined up under center, and I tried to refrain from doing a happy dance. Stanford caught my eye, and his expression revealed the same surprise I'd felt.

And the excitement. We were down to two.

Owen, on the other hand, looked far from surprised. He and Coach Vincent had clearly spoken before practice, which was to be expected, I supposed. Coach wouldn't pull any of us without a private conversation first. That was the kind of coach he was. But while Owen might have expected Vincent to place him at receiver, his demeanor demonstrated irritation with the attention Coach's decision caused.

Around us, the team clustered. Whispered. Tried to catch my gaze.

Square sidled up beside me. "You see that?"

Not only did I see it but watching Owen lined up at receiver signaled the same kind of adrenaline I experienced the first time I stepped on the practice field. With all the juices flowing, I wanted to be on the field. Despite what happened between us, Owen would undoubtedly play to win. He wouldn't belittle his own skills by dropping passes from me, especially when he knew Brighton and I were perfecting our timing. He might not have been competing against me anymore, but he was still competing.

And he was good at it.

Watching the team on the field, I clapped it up from the backfield, waiting my turn about as patiently as D waited for the cookies in the cafeteria, which he ate as an appetizer. Settled and ready to go, Stanford snapped the ball for the first play, a go route. Owen ran the route flawlessly. Gracefully. Gorgeously.

From a five-step drop, Stanford launched the ball. Although not perfectly placed, the ball still fell into Owen's waiting arms after he adjusted. Then he ran for a touchdown. The team went wild, and so did Coach Vincent. That was the longest ball any of us had delivered since camp started, about fifteen yards farther downfield than I felt comfortable throwing. Outwardly I cheered with the rest of the team, but inside, my fear stole away every ounce of calm. Yes, Owen Malone would make an incredible addition to the receiver corps, but I wouldn't be the only person to benefit from that.

Getting down to two was great, but I was still competing too. Backup quarterback had never been my goal.

I had more work to do.

****

I USED TO THINK A PERFECT SPIRAL WAS IDEAL IN football. A flick of the wrist, the ball rolling off each finger one by one, pinkie first, and there you had it—a perfect spiral. Absolutely coveted in the sport. Funny thing, then, that there was nothing to covet about my downward spiral that day.

It started with a comeback route to Brighton. I released the ball thinking about the pass Stanford had made to Owen, and despite Brighton's efforts laying out for it, the ball sailed well beyond his fingertips.

He hustled back to the huddle. "Shake it off, Medina."

If by "shake it off" he meant fumble a handoff to D on the next play, then shake it off I did. In sports, people sometimes said, "Get out of your head," and that's what I needed to do. The apprehensions and insecurities I'd suppressed since first announcing I wanted to play exploded with the power reminiscent of the fountain at Point State Park. So there they were—all of my fears—skyrocketing in my mind, so loudly that the cracking of pads and the shouting of coaches around me were a distant hum.

I was totally stuck in my head.

D slapped my back. "Let's go. Let's go."

I nodded, called a quick out, and broke the huddle.

I can do this. I can do this.

I focused on Owen's outstretched hand and calculated the time it took to throw the pass and the speed of his gait and released. Owen plucked the ball from the air, tucked it against his side, and ran eight more yards. On his way back to the huddle, he smiled at me. A gesture that sent me right back into my head. *What did that smile mean? Is he happy to be back at receiver? Or was that smile about...us?*

With the muddle in my brain, no surprise that the next ball I threw was a pick six. My first interception during camp. I left the field feeling like my legs were sinking into a gooey surface.

My teammates patted my shoulders and offered words of encouragement and wisdom. "It happens to the best of us." Or "Work out the kinks now." Or "You'll get it next time." Christian handed me a Gatorade bottle and stood beside me in silence as I drank it. Coach Vincent came by and slapped my shoulders too, but despite the sports clichés flying at me from all directions, I couldn't dig myself out of the mental slump that snuck up on me that morning. Even in drills, my accuracy declined. So much so I saw Draveck pull Coach Vincent aside and whisper something in his ear that my instincts screamed had to be about me.

Why couldn't Owen have played receiver from the beginning? Instead of being a wreck on the field, I would have been prepared. Hell, I'd have been throwing with him and Brighton before and after practices. We'd have been killing it.

Maybe we'd still be together.

Over lunch, Square and D chattered about who-knows-what, and I ignored them until they wouldn't let me anymore.

"You gotta snap out of this," Square said and then downed another pint of milk.

"Yeah," D said, cookie in hand. "It's like you worked everything you had to score the starting spot, and now that you're a step closer, you're losing your focus."

"I'm focused," I lied.

If they bought it, you wouldn't have known by them rolling their eyes at me.

"Go out there this afternoon during team and crush it," Square said.

"Definitely. Definitely."

"Do you have to repeat everything?" Annoyance laced my words, but D didn't deserve my frustrations. I smiled at him to suggest I'd been teasing. He bought it.

"No." He finished the last bite of his chocolate chip treat. "Only the important stuff."

The important stuff. D and Square returned to their chatter. I tried to listen. In the last two weeks, they'd gone from virtual strangers to two of my closest friends. They supported me and defended me, but most of all, they believed in me. And to quote yet another sports cliché, I didn't want to let them down.

CHAPTER THIRTY-TWO

YOU CAN DO MORE. YOU CAN ALWAYS DO MORE.
—DAN MARINO

NOT WANTING TO LET D AND SQUARE DOWN AND AC-tually delivering on that mental promise were apparently two different things. During afternoon reps, Owen shouted repeatedly for me to get him the ball like some veteran diva. He didn't smile at me again either.

After a failed play when I threw the ball away to prevent a sack, Owen grabbed my arm and pulled me away from the huddle. "Jules, I was wide open on that last play." My first name, especially in nickname form, felt foreign on the field where everyone else called me Medina. It was like I had two different identities. Jules wasn't welcomed here. Jules was a girl who played volleyball and spent summer days lounging by the pool. Medina worked her ass off on the field alongside the guys, hoping they didn't notice or at least call her out on the fact she was a girl.

"Sorry, *Malone*. Must have missed you."

He tugged on my arm harder. "I'm trying to help you."

Didn't really feel that way to me. "Then get back in the huddle."

We jogged to the rest of the team, and I conveyed coach's play call. The progression designated Owen as the first read. *Let's hope he'll be open again,* I thought.

He wasn't. By the time I made my second read, I felt arms wrapping around me with a force that sent my body forward and flung my head backward. With the grill of my helmet pressed into the ground, I felt a shot of pain in my ankle.

"Girls don't play football, Medina," Moody growled in my ear. "Take the hint."

When he stood, his cheap shot earned him Square's face mask crashing against his own.

"That's enough!" Coach yelled, crossing the field to break up the scrum and help me stand. "Medina, you good?"

I extended and twisted my foot this way and that to assess the damage.

Draveck sidled up next to Vincent. "Looked like she rolled her ankle."

The ache that punctuated each extension confirmed Draveck's assessment.

"She should get wrapped," Draveck said to Vincent as if I wasn't standing two feet away. As if I had no say in my own medical treatment. As if I had no voice at all.

I considered fighting through the sprain and taking more reps but resting my weight on the foot in question triggered an explosion of pain, which must have been clear on my face.

"Stanford!" Coach Vincent yelled. Alexander hustled onto the field and huddled up with the offense. *My* offense. Coach made eye contact with me and tucked his hands behind his back in that nonthreatening way of his. "Medina, how do you feel about taping that ankle?"

I almost jumped with joy at the respect he showed by asking the question, although jumping was probably not the best idea at that moment. "I want to play, so if wrapping it will help me do that, then that's what I want to do."

Vincent nodded. Draveck seemed annoyed. Perhaps he expected me to cry and ask him to carry me off the field. Hate to break it to him, but that wasn't my first rolled ankle. Nor would it be the first time I played through the pain of one.

Perpetually on the sideline, our main trainer, Leo, was already occupied treating a junior for a potential concussion. So, too busy for me. One of the underclassmen drove me to the Main Lodge in the golf cart to see Christian. My driver dropped me at the lower-level door, and I walked with as minimal a limp as possible until the cart turned the corner and I could indulge in leaning on anything and everything. Considerable swearing ensued.

In the trainers' room, Christian sorted through a closet of supplies, organizing the shelves. "What happened to you?"

"Rolled my ankle. Just need it wrapped so I can get back on the field." And get ready for the scrimmage and the opportunity to convince my parents and everyone else, too, that I belonged on this team. And to show Coach I was his quarterback.

He nodded. "Give me one sec." Then back to the organizing. Nothing like being a priority. Jake wouldn't have stood for such disregard. He would have diva-ed his way to immediate treatment, probably on the sideline with Leo, concussion be damned.

Careful not to put too much weight on my right ankle, I hopped to the exam table, which was already occupied by a mannequin, the kind people used in CPR training classes. Mom had insisted my brothers and I attend CPR classes once a year, which always turned into an afternoon of goofing off, Jorge being the biggest offender. While we performed the chest compressions, Jorge danced behind us. Feeling the urge, I leaned over the mannequin, pressing the heel of my left hand over its chest and then my right hand over my left.

"You know CPR?" Christian said, moderately impressed.

I pulled my hands away from the mannequin, and Christian moved it to a nearby chair. "I'm more than a genius on the football field, you know."

He scoffed. "I guess you are, Julia."

Like it had earlier when Owen said it on the field, the sound of my first name felt foreign at football camp, but hearing Christian say it was...okay. I watched him shift things around. His arms and legs tightened with his movements, but he wasn't as muscled as Owen. Or the other players on the team who lifted constantly. Still, Christian's body was refined. He bent over to pick up a pen he dropped, offering me a prime view of the, um, refinement.

He stood and looked right at me. His gaze sort of sizzled, or maybe that was in my mind. I looked away, pretending to study some anatomy chart on the wall, all the while wondering if he'd caught me checking him out. I shook my head. What was I doing? Owen and I had *just* broken up. Then again, should I have felt badly for him? He was back on the field rocking it as receiver. Exactly where he should have been all along. Meanwhile, Owen's insecurities had painted Christian as more than what he was—a friend.

Just like Square and D and everyone else. Except...

"Why don't you call me Medina?" I asked him.

"Do you want me to call you Medina?"

Did I? No. Yes. Maybe. "Everyone else does."

"Uh-huh. And you're clearly concerned with behaving as everyone else does?"

The honesty and humor in his words made me laugh. "Touché."

"So what's with the CPR? You a lifeguard or something?" He gestured for me to hop up onto an examination table and awkwardly reached for my waist as if to help me. He stopped himself though. With red cheeks, he mumbled an apology and ruffled the hair on the back of his head, messing it up more than he probably realized.

"Christian?"

"Yeah?"

"Treat me like you would anyone on the team."

I slid onto the table and rocked from side to side to shimmy myself into the center. And waited. And waited some more. "So...I'm not an expert at this, but I think that white stuff there"—I pointed to the rolls of tape—"goes here." I gestured toward my ankle.

He grinned and shook his head. "Sorry. I've never wrapped a girl before." And his face went even redder as if the words offered some offensive innuendo. "I mean, not like, well, usually I'm assigned the guys' teams, you know, and..."

"Christian?"

He looked up at me.

"Treat me like you would anyone on the team," I repeated, and he nodded again, seemingly with more conviction this time.

"Show me how you injured it."

I complied, leaving out Moody's identity, figuring Christian would hear that on his own. He collected a few more materials out of a nearby closet and got to work spraying my foot, ankle, and calf with adhesive before applying blue pre-tape.

"Two of my brothers have heart murmurs," I said to break up the silence.

Christian stopped wrapping and looked up at me. "Huh?"

"You asked about CPR. Jake and Jorge have heart murmurs, so my mom insisted we learn CPR. I'm not sure it was really necessary, but it made her feel better."

"Sometimes that's all parents need."

Isn't that the truth?

Christian's movements were methodical as he pressed the tape down and swung the roll around my leg. Pressed and swung. Pressed and swung.

"You're good at this."

He shrugged. "It's my second year of working with the sports teams. I've wrapped a lot of inversion sprains."

"That's funny."

"What's funny?" he asked, his fingers feeling oddly intimate against my ankle to the extent that I almost forgot myself what was funny.

"It's, uh, I thought I had a rolled ankle, not a fancy...what did you call it?"

He smiled. "An inversion sprain."

Right. An inversion sprain. I didn't say anything else, afraid I might make a fool of myself if I spoke. I focused on football. That was why I was there. I needed to get taped so I could get back on the field, get out of my head, and prove myself. An image of Draveck whispering into Coach Vincent's ear irked me. Realizing Christian moved around the coaches' offices, locker room, and practice field practically invisible to everyone around him, I blurted. "What do the coaches say about me?"

His eyebrows perked up.

"Sorry. I shouldn't have asked that. I didn't mean to put you in an awkward position."

"Coach Vincent respects you." Christian massaged a strip of tape around my ankle. "Draveck's the one you need to worry about. I don't know what it is with that guy, but he's not convinced you can play."

I had suspected as much but managed a smile since Christian was convinced.

"Ultimately, it's Vincent's call anyway," he continued. "He's the head coach and the quarterbacks coach, so you're in good shape there. But you'll need to really stand out because the benefit with Stanford is that if the coaching staff invests in him this year, he can contribute to the team for two more years."

"But I'll be gone," I surmised aloud. My graduation was a factor I couldn't control, so I had convinced myself to ignore it. Maybe that logic was flawed.

"Exactly. So if Vincent names you quarterback, the team will be in the same position next year they are now."

"But Bass will be back by then."

Christian shook his head. "With Stanford or Bass, doesn't matter. If Vincent starts you this year, then he has to deal with your inexperience this year and theirs next." He finished wrapping my ankle, and the absence of his warm hands on my skin sent a surprising surge of disappointment through me.

What was that about?

Afraid he could read my mind and maybe even more afraid of what such a reading would yield, I swung my legs over the side of the exam table, turning my back to him. I expected him to walk away, to busy himself with the supplies again, but the room was quiet with our stillness.

"Julia?"

The single word held overwhelming potential. Potential for what, I didn't know. I didn't want to know. I slid off the table, catering to my injured ankle as much as possible. "I should get back out there. Thanks, Christian."

"Yeah, sure," he said. "No problem. Good luck."

Considering the pain of every tentative step, I'd need it.

CHAPTER THIRTY-THREE

*THE ONLY PERSON WHO CAN STOP YOU FROM REACH-
ING YOUR GOALS IS YOU.
—JACKIE JOYNER-KERSEE*

THE TAPE HELPED. SOMEWHAT. THE TENDERNESS IN
my ankle advocated for caution, which I wasn't sure I could deliver
since we were on our way to lift. In his speech at the creek on our first
night, Coach Vincent had promised to exhaust our bodies more and
more each day. Square and D insisted that's why my performance was
off that day, and that might even have been the cause of my injury,
but their theory didn't make me feel better. The reason the coaches
pushed us to exhaustion was to build our stamina, to ensure we could
compete every minute of every quarter of every game all season long.
If I couldn't hack it through camp, what did that mean for the season?

Not promising.

Looking around the weight room before dinner, though, I realized
misery and company really were pals. I scanned the space looking for
Owen while simultaneously coaxing myself into believing the last
thing I was doing was looking for Owen. Yeah, right. He must have
been hidden behind some machine. Not that I'd know that. Because
I totally wasn't looking for him.

Along the walls, propped on the benches, and sprawled around the open areas of the field, my teammates stretched their quads, hamstrings, and calves, in many cases massaging them while they stretched. The scent in the room was a mix of Icy Hot and smelly, bare feet, since at least half of my teammates were rubbing them. I couldn't criticize. I felt desperate for a pedicure. Ah. Soaking my toes in that warm, lavender-scented water. Having them rubbed with lotion, my ankles and calves being rubbed too. The thought had me groaning out loud.

"What's with you?" Square asked.

Oh, you know, I'm fantasizing about going to the salon. Not the kind of thing boys were likely to understand. "Nothing. Just sore."

I sensed nobody felt like lifting, but they were grateful to be inside since an afternoon rain had settled on the camp. Morale boosted when the coaches jogged into the room wearing matching shirts and old school sweatbands around their hairlines—well, for those of them who still had hairlines. Coach O'Connor, who worked with receivers and tight ends and by the looks of him had for the last sixty years, bounced back and forth from one foot to the other, jabbing the air like Rocky albeit in a much slower motion.

Coach Blackwell, the assistant line coach who, I surmised by his girth, had given up exercise at least a decade ago, held his arms high above his head, turning around in a small circle as if greeting an adoring crowd from all sides. Draveck cracked his neck, and the other coaches embraced various poses and stretches. Coach Vincent made his way to the center of the room, pulled his leg up, and pushed his arm forward mimicking the Heisman Trophy.

The mirrors on the walls trembled from the noise.

Vincent gestured for us to quiet down. "Your coaching staff and I got to talking, and we decided you all deserved a little break."

I thought the mirrors might actually burst.

"Okay. Okay." Vincent laughed. "Quiet, everyone." When we complied, he continued. "You deserve this break, not because it's late in the week, not because your bodies are tired, although I'm sure they are. You deserve this break because with every snap of the ball, with every drill, and every bear crawl, you've earned it!"

The room erupted again, genuine adoration on my teammates'

faces. Who could blame them? Vincent wasn't the kind of coach who terrified kids into respecting him. Genuinely likable, our head coach earned respect by cheering us up instead of criticizing, by challenging us but also showing care and concern. To be honest, Coach Vincent had earned my respect with every encounter since we'd met.

The team clapped, "Let's go, Coach. Let's go, Coach," while the coaches spread out over the weight room, their respective players navigating to their sides. As quarterbacks, Stanford and I stood next to Coach Vincent, our quarterback coach. I didn't dare look toward the assistant receivers' coach.

"What do you think my chances are?" Coach asked.

"Depends on the parameters of the competition," I answered, causing Coach to stop bouncing on his toes and stare at me. "Well, I've seen Coach Blackwell max on chocolate milk chugging, and he's kind of a beast. Eight pints last count. Coach O'Connor chews gum like he wants to annihilate it, and no way you're beating Coach Draveck in a hot dog eating contest. The man can eat."

Coach Vincent's grin grew as I had summarized those first two skills superior to his own, but I got sprayed when he couldn't contain his laughter at my comment about Draveck. He wiped his mouth and waved an apology. "You are your brothers' sister. That's for sure."

I could imagine any of my brothers saying something like that, so I wasn't sure which brother he meant. "Which one?"

"All of them."

That about covered it. The comparison was an honor.

Draveck called out the first challenge. Push-ups. I cheered for Coach Vincent and for the fact I wasn't the one doing the push-ups. The team counted with each rep. Blackwell dropped out after eight, which wasn't much of a surprise considering the effort it took to lift his body from any position let alone a horizontal one. O'Connor surprisingly persevered to twenty before dropping, but Coach Vincent and Draveck pressed on. Thirty. Forty. Sixty. The count slowed in the upper numbers but climbed, nonetheless.

"You got this, Coach," Stanford and I yelled, although I wasn't sure by the sweat dripping from his face to the floor that he did have it. In fact, I wondered if his and Draveck's pride would kill one of them. Finally, at seventy-eight push-ups, Draveck collapsed.

For good measure, Vincent pushed himself to eight-five, the team jumping and screaming as he finished and then hit the deck. Stanford tossed him a towel, and I held out a small paper cup of water from the nearby cooler.

Since Coach Vincent won, he dictated the next battle. "Who can nap longest," he whispered to Stanford and me before calling out for everyone else, "Grab a twenty-five-pound plate, gentlemen."

Coach Blackwell tried to cheat with a twenty-pounder, but Draveck caught him. "I have small hands," Coach Blackwell called, and everyone laughed.

"Hold the plate straight out in front of you with your arms at a ninety-degree angle from your body. If you drop below eighty-five degrees, you're done."

Coaches O'Connor and Blackwell groaned, still recovering from the push-up round. Vincent called the start. O'Connor lasted ten seconds. Blackwell lasted fifteen.

"I'm not sure if I should be angry the coaches make us work out as hard as they do when they're in such awful shape or embarrassed at how pathetic they are," Stanford said, which seemed like a valid quandary to me. As Draveck and Vincent battled for first place again, Stanford and I chirped encouragement into our coach's ear. We celebrated his victories. We teased him when he showed a vulnerability that welcomed the silliness. And when it was all over, Coach Vincent headed for the showers victorious, and Stanford extended a hand to me.

"If this were a TV movie, I'm sure I would be some evil villain terrorizing you into quitting or something," he said.

"Eh. Moody and Creel are competing for that role."

Stanford cringed. "Speaking of that cheap shot, how's your ankle?"

"A little tender. I'll be fine in no time." I had no idea if that were true, especially since all of the standing during the competition made it hurt. Bad. More than my ankle, my toes ached with the threat of cramping at any moment, and pain dulled every other sensation in my foot.

"Good. I want to be the quarterback of this team but competing against you pushes me to be better." He finished the revelation without making eye contact, as if the admission embarrassed him.

"Kind of like Draveck and Vincent?" I asked, offering some levity.

"Exactly. But I'd take our competition over theirs any day."

I nodded, thinking that the prize, or at least one of them—respect—however, was the same. I let the majority of the team filter out of the weight room toward the cafeteria for dinner before I made an attempt to leave. When Owen passed, he kept his back to me as if he was too engrossed in Brighton's story to realize I existed. I couldn't blame Owen.

I'd hurt him. I wasn't sure if I could fix that. Or even try. The reason I knew it was that he'd hurt me just as badly, and my heart told me there wasn't any fixing the damage.

Safe from prying eyes several minutes later, I sat on a bench outside the door and flexed and extended my foot, gauging the pain. How could this happen? I'd sacrificed everything to be on this team. I'd pushed myself physically and emotionally. I lost my volleyball team, my best friend, and my boyfriend. For *this*. Another extension of my foot warned me it might have been futile. No way could I drive this foot into the ground to explode into my passing motion.

Footsteps on the gravel path behind me caused me to sit still and upright.

"You have an audience," Christian whispered, his voice relaxing me until I saw Austin Moody and Kicker Creel waving from behind a tree about thirty yards away. The idiotic duo offered impolite gestures.

"Friendly," Christian said. "Can I walk you to the cafeteria?"

"I don't need an escort," I said.

"No. By the looks of it, you probably need crutches, and I'm guessing you don't want me to make that recommendation to Coach Vincent."

Scheming student trainer.

"So what will it be? Me or crutches?"

I stood, and Christian opened the door to the weight room for me. "Best if we walk through the building. The path outside is uphill, and the whole team would see you wobble by the cafeteria windows."

Good point. Hobbling through the weight room, I relieved the pressure on my foot by leaning on any machine I could. Then the wall of the hallway. When we reached the part of the building with a series of wide-open meeting rooms, my opportunity to lean was lost. Christian watched me limp along.

"Was it this bad when you came to get taped?"

"No." The injury was fresh then but not nearly as tender.

"Come by the training room after dinner, and we'll soak it."

I stumbled, and Christian grabbed my waist, his fingertips grazing my bare skin. He held me steady and gave me the first opportunity to see the depth of his eyes. A brown so dark, it was hard to tell the difference between the pupils and the irises.

"I would do this for anyone on the team," he said.

Hold them steady? Sure. Tease his hands across the smalls of their backs and stare at them with the kind of heat in his gaze that totally confirmed, once again, how right Ally had been?

I didn't think so.

Christian Santos might've been handsome, tall, smart, freaking pre-med. But he wasn't Owen Malone, who, despite trampling it, still had my heart.

"I can't do this," I said, pulling away.

Christian tilted my chin upward, so I had nowhere to look but those dark chocolate eyes. "I know."

"What the hell is this?"

Owen's voice forced me backward. I stumbled and felt shooting pain through my ankle. As I grabbed a nearby chair to right myself, Owen rushed toward Christian.

"Go ahead. Hit me," Christian said. "That won't even be the stupidest thing you've done this week."

"Owen," I said, "you know Coach's policy about fighting."

He stared at Christian as if I hadn't even spoken, as if I wasn't there. "I knew you were into her."

Relationships, breakups, all of it was too confusing. What was worse? All the confusion had impacted my game.

"Christian, can you give us a minute?"

"Fine." He glared at Owen on his way out.

Alone with Owen, my chest rose and fell sharper. My mind sprinted like D on a breakaway in the open field. Or better yet, like D spinning and rolling and bouncing off tackles along the way. Chaotic.

"Nothing happened with Christian. I stumbled. He was there."

"It doesn't matter," Owen said. "It's none of my business any-more."

"Well, regardless. It's the truth. I told him nothing could happen."

He crossed his arms. "And why's that?"

"Because of you," I blurted.

I studied the plum-colored swirly carpet, waiting for him to de-clare we could somehow fix us.

But he didn't say anything. Neither of us did. Humiliated, I at-tempted a quick getaway that likely resembled an injured quadru-ped scuffling over rough terrain. I made it three steps before Owen jumped in front of me.

"Jules, I appreciate you telling me. I do, but I don't see how things would be any different. Even with me at receiver, our problems ha-ven't gone anywhere." He sighed and closed his eyes. "I don't see how we'll get around hurting each other again."

The words had the same effect of his spikes trampling my heart.

But he had a point.

CHAPTER THIRTY-FOUR

MY BODY COULD STAND THE CRUTCHES, BUT MY MIND
COULDN'T STAND THE SIDELINE.
—MICHAEL JORDAN

SQUARE, BRIGHTON, AND D SAT AT THE TABLE WITH
the farthest walk to the food lines—because of course, why would
my luck change now—with their trays piled high. Walking from
the cafeteria door to their table without limping exhausted me and
made my ankle feel like a swollen, throbbing beast from a dramatic
kids' cartoon.

I hoped my eyes weren't equally as red and swollen. I would not
cry over Owen Malone anymore. I would not.

Who was I kidding?

"Where you been?" D asked.

A vision flashed of Owen lunging toward Christian and then me
being rejected by my ex-boyfriend who, yeah, had already dumped
me once this week.

"More importantly, where's your food?" Square asked.

"You wanna throw after dinner?" Brighton asked before stuffing
a twirled forkful of spaghetti into his mouth.

"Nothing but questions, huh?"

"You're deflecting again." Square put down his fork. "Tell me you didn't hobble your way here, which is what took so long, and you don't even have the strength to fetch chicken strips."

Part of it—the only part I was willing to admit.

D stood. "I got you." He reached into the nearby cooler and tossed me two chocolate milks and a bottle of orange Gatorade before heading for the hot food.

"So no throwing, then," Brighton surmised. "I was looking forward to it."

"Because I need the chance to redeem myself after today?" I was half joking.

Brighton's voice was serious. "No. Because you said you wanted to be the best, and so do I."

Square slapped Brighton on the back, spraying sauce from the receiver's mouth to the center of the table. Everyone pulled their trays a little closer, away from the splatter.

"You're officially inducted onto Team Medina," Square said, nodding approval.

"I didn't realize the ceremony included spraying your dinner on your friends," I teased. "Whose idea was that?"

Square raised his hand.

"Good thinking," I said.

He tapped his temple and nodded.

"Who else is in this official club?" Brighton asked, continuing to stuff his face.

Square counted on his fingers, but he lost my attention when Christian walked to the cooler behind him to grab another drink. He didn't look my way. I didn't blame him for being angry that I asked him to leave so Owen and I could talk. The season with him and Owen both on the sideline would be interesting.

"Medina, you even hearing me?" D asked, delivering my food tray.

Huh? Like one of those horrible, awkward movie scenes, they watched me as if I should have something brilliant to say. Or, at the very least, respond.

"That's a no," Square said, not looking up from his salad.

"I heard him," I disputed.

They stared me down.

"Okay. I was distracted." Although I didn't admit by what. Or whom. "What's up?"

"I'm going to borrow the golf cart to drive your injured highn-ass around," D said. "And to do some donuts on the soccer field."

That poor soccer field.

"I'm gonna ask Christian. Unless you want to?"

"Why would I want to?" I asked a little too sharply, and the guys stared with confused expressions. I suppose I should've been grateful Ally wasn't there. One outburst like that in front of her and her super-girl-power-sensors would've been all over me. She'd know. One look and she'd know.

My teammates shrugged and went back to eating.

****

"THERE IS MY SWEET IRON GRID GIRL," ABUELITA SAID, blowing me a much-needed kiss from her little square on my screen.

Jake's face appeared right around the same time Abuelita's did. In response to her comment, he laughed and shook his head. "It's *gridiron*, Abuelita."

"You men are all about the rules. Right, Julia?" She said my name as if it were spelled with an *h*, not a *j*. "My iron grid girl destroys the rules, yes, mi cielo?"

Jake lowered his head to his free hand.

"Hey!" Juan's voice boomed from the phone. "How's our littlest quarterback doing?"

"Good," I said at the same time Jake chimed in, "You can't say rookie or up-and-coming since she already beat you, big brother."

Juan disputed the statement as Abuelita declared her approval. Then she cracked us up with a story about when she stole our parents' breakfast—eggs, pancakes, bacon, and all—to share with a friend of hers from down the street. Dad stormed in demanding that enough was enough until he saw the sweet widow Mrs. Houstenstein with a forkful of his blueberry pancakes halfway to her mouth.

"They went to the Denny's, and then your father spent the afternoon cleaning Mrs. Houstenstein's gutters," Abuelita said.

When the laughter diminished, I texted Jake that I needed to talk to him alone. He took the hint, squashing the conversation in the video chat, so we were the only two left on the line.

"You look like you had a rough day," he said.

"You're awfully perceptive."

"You're my best friend. And my baby sister. There's nothing about you I can't read. What's the story?"

I feigned surprise. "You mean your superpowers are so limited that I need to tell you?"

He scowled.

"Fine. Owen's out of the running, but Stanford's killing the deep pass. I played like crap, threw my first pick six. Let's see... what else?" My ankle throbbed, reminding me of its place in the list of drama. "Austin Moody sacked me. I rolled my ankle. Yep. That should cover it."

"Was it a clean hit?"

I elevated my ankle onto a dusty couch pillow that might have been there when the Steelers won their first Super Bowl. "Square didn't think so."

Jake's face showed stoicism, but I knew he'd be boiling inside. "Moody's an ass."

"I concur."

"How bad is the ankle?"

Until I had the tape cut, I wouldn't know if it was bruised, swollen, or what. "Why don't we let the trainer determine that since I only have a couple more minutes? I need football advice."

"Only football?"

I studied his poker face. Did he know about Owen? Of course. Square. I sighed. "Owen broke up with me."

As expected, not the slightest look of surprise.

"How do you feel about that?"

"Miserable."

He nodded. "I'm sorry, Jules. But if you ask me, he did you a favor."

"Did I ask you?"

He scowled and changed the topic back to my injury. "That boy trainer isn't treating you, is he?"

My body felt super still, but hopefully, Jake didn't notice. Not like he had just said there was nothing about me he couldn't read.

"So he *is* treating you," Jake said. "Tell Vincent you want Leo to assess the injury. Seriously, Jules."

I'd had some experience with trainers, with Leo, even. I wasn't a complete moron on the subject, and Christian taped me well. He was totally professional—okay, so he almost tried to kiss me, but his lips never touched mine. Truth be told that distinction would probably be lost on my slightly older but grandiosely protective brother. He might've been surprised to have that in common with Owen.

"I thought I asked for *football* advice."

He rolled his eyes at me with purposeful drama. "Don't worry about Stanford throwing a deep ball."

"How can I not worry?"

"Jules, at the risk of sounding pompous—"

Because that would be a new phenomenon.

"I can honestly say you are better prepared mentally to start and lead the team than anyone else there. I know this because I—with some help from Juan and Jorge—have unofficially trained you for it your whole life. Give it time, and the team will realize you're the one they can depend on in the pocket."

The pain in my ankle fueled my fears that I might not have enough time.

"Besides, Square says Stanford doesn't have the mental toughness for the position. He's probably showing off to try and win the spot that way. Smart, but not enough. Not if you play your best."

"How am I going to do that on a rolled ankle?"

"Simple. You rest it until it's good enough to play your best."

My brother did not speak those words. Not possible. "*Rest* it? You're not serious."

"I am, Jules. Owen's already out of the running. Coach is down to two. No way he's going to make a decision during camp. If you rest a day or two, you might be ready to push yourself hard, and you *need* to push yourself hard to earn the starting spot."

"I need to play in the scrimmage Saturday."

"No. You don't."

My brother—the king of playing through injuries—wanted me to sit out? "What's this? Yet another double standard. Shocker!"

"Stop. Not a double standard."

"You played on rolled ankles."

"Three," he said. "Mid-season and during the playoffs. Not preseason."

"The broken finger?"

He made spirit fingers with this left hand. "Not my throwing hand."

"Pulled groin, bruised quad?"

"Midseason and playoffs."

I focused in on my memory bank, searching for some evidence I could use. Surely my brother had injured himself one of his four years during camp. Aha! "I specifically recall you cringing in the swimming pool because of bruised ribs. So, preseason." I felt victorious.

"My junior year. Nobody was hitting me during camp, which is what really hurt. Not my throwing motion."

"You wouldn't admit if I were right."

He bit into an apple with a loud crunch. "Probably not."

"This is ridiculous, Jake. I'm playing."

"You're not." He took another bite.

Infuriating! If I didn't love my brothers so much, I would want to bury them with a shovel.

A friendly knock sounded at the front of the cabin. Before I could stand to remind whoever it was about the rule prohibiting them from entering, the screen door swung open, and Square and D sauntered in.

"Look at this place!" Square spun around the center lounge area with his arms wide and peeked into the bedrooms that surrounded it.

"This like an episode of *Camp Cribs*." D pointed to the phone. "What's this? You fancy video chattin' too?"

D and Square leaned over my shoulders, calling greetings to Jake, their former teammate.

"How's that even possible?" D said. "Damn good technology to get your huge head in that little box."

Even Square lost his composure.

"Ha ha," Jake said. "You two taking care of my baby sister?"

An awkward silence lingered before both insisted they were.

"How bad was the hit?" Jake asked.

Square shook his head, and D rambled some choice words

about Moody.

"We need to turn your phone in," Square said.

"Gotta go, bro."

Jake blew me a kiss. "Love you, baby sis. Don't forget my brilliant advice."

"His head's growing too big for that little square," D said.

Jake's middle finger filled the screen. I tapped the End button, and the screen went black.

CHAPTER THIRTY-FIVE

*REMIND YOUR CRITICS WHEN THEY SAY YOU DON'T
HAVE THE EXPERTISE OR EXPERIENCE TO DO
SOMETHING THAT AN AMATEUR BUILT THE ARK AND
THE EXPERTS BUILT THE TITANIC.*
—PEYTON MANNING

HURRYING TO MAKE THE ELECTRONICS DEADLINE, WE
scrambled out the door. D and Square acted like human crutches,
not letting me put weight on my ankle for a few steps before getting
frustrated with the coordination of it all and carrying me to the golf
cart. Secured on the back seat with my leg elevated, I held tight as
D took off. First stop: dropping off our phones. Then it was off to
the trainer to assess the severity of this ankle. The thought of seeing
Christian again had me squirming in the golf cart even more than D's
erratic driving. Too much was going on. I just didn't want to deal
with any more drama.

"Come to get your tape off and soak a bit?" Christian asked when
we arrived, then added, "With an entourage?"

"I'm staying off my ankle and letting Square drive my, as D refers
to me, 'injured highness' around."

"Actually I said injured highn-ass," D clarified.

"Either way, glad to hear you decided to rest it," Christian said, fumbling through a plastic tote with rolls of tape.

I never said that.

When Christian pressed the scissors to my skin, D grabbed his hand. "Careful," he warned.

Oh, for heaven's sake.

Christian raised an eyebrow at me.

"Entourage, behave yourselves," I said, wondering if they were there at Jake's orders. They both stood behind Christian with wide stances and crossed arms, watching his every maneuver. My brother was an idiot—although in a way, I appreciated his idiocy. If I were alone with Christian, we'd have to talk about what happened with Owen.

I didn't want to talk about that embarrassment. Ever. Again.

Starting at my calf, Christian cut downward on the inside of my injured ankle. "How's it been feeling?"

"Sore. Tender."

He nodded and kept cutting. "I have the whirlpool filling for you. I can get you ice later tonight, too, though." He peeled the tape away from my skin, and the string of swear words that rolled off D's lips was as colorful as the bruise on my ankle.

"I'm gonna kill Moody," Square said. Everyone else in the room nodded agreement.

"This is bad, Julia."

No new information there. Without the tape, my ankle almost felt...floppy. Jake's urging to rest it crept into my mind. Playing on it would be a risk. I could injure it worse. Or make Stanford look so good the choice between us was obvious.

Or I could sit out and confirm what all the coaches and most of the team had been thinking for the last week—I was too fragile to play football.

I hopped off the table, careful to land on my left foot. "Where's the whirlpool?"

****

WOULD IT BE REDUNDANT TO SAY THE WHIRLPOOL

filled with ice was cold? The kind of cold you wanted to pull away from the second it touched your skin. Not dangle your foot nonchalantly in it for fifteen minutes while the chill crept up your back and your lower extremities fell asleep from the uncomfortable perch? Christian had draped a blanket over my shoulders. With the air conditioning in the building, the gesture, however kind, was nowhere near enough.

But if dipping my toes in this tundra got me back on the field faster, load up the ice. The timer buzzed, and I shivered one last time and dried my colorful ankle. Not my first sprain, but definitely the first time my skin turned that color and so quickly. Christian said Leo would check me in the morning to clear me or sit me for practice. That was if I didn't decide to sit out on my own. Any weight on my foot swelled my eyes with tears, which in turn scared and frustrated me into crying even more.

Basically, a pain in my numb ass.

Christian and my entourage had abandoned the trainer's room, so I explored, on crutches, trying to find them. Down the hall, oldies music played so quietly it took me a minute to convince myself I'd heard anything at all.

"Hello?" I called out.

The music lured me closer. Hobble, hobble. I'd get there some century. The coach's office came into view, and Coach Vincent sat behind the desk with the phone to his ear.

"You can tell Christina Creel there's no way around it. State athletic rules dictate any Iron Valley student can play, no matter the gender."

So Mrs. Creel was still pursuing my being banned from the team, and by the looks of it, her antics were stressing out Vincent.

Leaning over his desk with the phone to his ear, he pinched his eyebrows. "I get that, but—"

Who was he talking to? The athletic director? The superintendent? How far had Mrs. Creel gone to get me removed from the team?

I shouldn't have been listening, but even if I could hustle away, the conversation was about me. Didn't that give me a right to listen?

Good thing nobody was around to answer that.

"I get that too." He slammed a fist on his desk, and along with his papers and pens, I jumped. The motion must have caught his attention because he raised his hand to me in a half wave then went back to his phone call. "Listen, I can't talk about that now. Let me know when the meeting is, and I'll be there." Silence. "Fine."

He hung up the phone and waved me into his office.

"I'm sorry. I heard the music and thought Christian might be down here."

As if the apology wasn't necessary, he ignored it and pointed to the crutches. "You're on crutches now?"

"No. I mean, I am, but my foot's numb from the whirlpool. Some ice and tape, and I'll be good as new for practice tomorrow."

Coach studied my ankle. "Is the light in here that bad, or is your ankle purple? And green?"

"Bad lighting. Definitely," I said.

He grinned. "You Medinas are something, aren't you?"

"Yes, Coach."

"You determined to play on it?"

I couldn't answer him. In a way, I was, but Jake advised me to rest it. So did Christian. "I want to do what's best for the team, Coach."

He sat back in his chair, looking relaxed for the first time since I'd entered his office. "I recognize that, but you have to do what's best for you too."

Presuming I could figure out what that was.

My gaze lowered to the mobile phone on his desk. "Maybe you should consider limiting the coach's phone time too."

"Then I wouldn't have to take certain calls?" he said.

"Or any calls if you didn't want to."

He laughed. "If it were that easy."

Quiet settled on the room.

"Coach?"

"Yes?"

"I'm sorry if my playing is causing you stress."

"Are you?"

"Of course."

"But you would still play no matter what?"

"Absolutely," my mouth said before my brain could even think.

"If I let other people choose my life for me, I'd be at volleyball practice."

"Good. And don't go thinking it would be easier on me if you didn't play. Having you on that field has been the catalyst for a lot of good things. Ignore the loud mouths who think they know what's best for you, for this team. I'm the head coach." He smiled. "My loud mouth is the one that matters. You understand?"

I smiled too. "Yes, Coach."

"Rest the ankle or play on it—whatever you think is best—but know this: Your decision will not affect whether you play on this team or not. When you're healthy, you're going to play. Understood?"

"Yes, Coach."

"Good. Hobble out of my office and keep yourself out of trouble."

If he only knew how difficult those two tasks were.

CHAPTER THIRTY-SIX

*THE DIFFERENCE BETWEEN A SUCCESSFUL PERSON
AND OTHERS IS NOT A LACK OF STRENGTH, NOT A LACK
OF KNOWLEDGE BUT RATHER A LACK OF WILL.
—VINCE LOMBARDI*

THE ELUSIVE TRIO OF D, SQUARE, AND CHRISTIAN SAT
on the benches outside the weight room. Leaning against the glass, I
managed to push one of the doors open an inch before Square tugged
it for me, and I limped outside, sans crutches.

Christian scowled. "I left you crutches for a reason."

"They're right inside." The unsaid implication: I didn't want anyone outside to see me with them.

Square reached inside the door, grabbed the crutches, and handed
them off to D who was in the passenger seat of the golf cart. "We'll
bring the cart back to you in a minute, Santos."

Christian nodded at them, then walked toward me with his arm
outstretched, an invitation to lean on him.

"I'm good," I said, insisting I could get to the cart myself although, you know, probably couldn't.

I hobbled until Square extended his arm, not taking no for an
answer, led me to the cart, and boosted me into my seat. Christian

knelt in front of me as if to examine my ankle.

"How's it feeling?"

"Numb. Cold."

His smile tugged at his cheeks and brightened his eyes, like some perfect movie scene when the whole audience is meant to swoon. Not that I swooned. Just a general observation.

Possibly, I was a drama magnet.

"Almost lights out," D said, pounding the hood of the cart. "Better get this baby moving."

"I'll come by in the morning to get taped," I said louder, as if increased decibels would somehow minimize the impact of his smile.

Insisting it was his turn to drive, Square bounced the golf cart along the hilly path to my cabin. He and D climbed out to help me up the stairs and into the living room.

"Where you wanna set up?" Square asked, and I pointed to the couch.

"But you don't have to help me with that. I can manage."

They ignored me. No wonder they were friends with Jake. Peas in a pod. Square grabbed a fresh bottle of Gatorade from the fridge and put it within reach on the coffee table. D stacked pillows for me to elevate my ankle. And more pillows so I could sit upright comfortably. The setup would have my back to the front door of the cabin, which sparked my Jason Voorhees fears. But I was brave. I could deal.

"Sit," Square said.

I did, shifting my weight around until I sank into the space they created for me with the utmost comfort I could. When I did, I looked up at both of them, towering over me with mixed looks of concern and satisfaction on their faces. Also like my big brothers. "Thanks."

"Need anything else?"

"Yeah. You got some snacks or something?" D said.

Square smacked his arm. "Stop trying to steal her snacks when she can't defend them."

"I meant for her." D swatted him back.

I laughed. "Stop. I'm fine. Thank you." My playbook and Jake's journal sat on the table behind them. "Actually, if you could grab those, I could make use of my sedentary time."

They did and fist-bumped me goodbye.

I tried to study the pages, but my mind wandered back to Owen. And Christian. And how I'd managed to distract myself from my goal of playing quarterback.

A knock at the door startled me. My heart hoped it would be Owen breaking the rules because he had to see me, because we had to fix us. I craned my neck and saw Christian—probably the second biggest reason "fixing" us was staggeringly unlikely.

Not wanting to shout and wake up Miss Nancy yet unwilling to wave him on in and violate Coach Vincent's rules, I dropped my elevated foot to the floor and stood. Christian pulled open the door and rushed inside.

"No, don't get up for me. You should be elevating your ankle. That's good."

I sat back down.

"How you feeling?"

"Like Coach Vincent made the rules clear when we arrived, and you probably shouldn't be here," I said, not sure the posturing would work. Despite the "mess", a small part of me relished the company.

He pretended my words pained him. "I'm checking on my patient."

"So your boss sent you?"

He tilted his head from side to side. "Not exactly."

Good company or not, the last thing I wanted was more trouble. "You saw what happened to the team when Creel broke the rules. I'm not risking everyone being punished." Not to mention the whole Owen debacle earlier. If I knew anything for certain, it was that the team needed Owen and me to get along. That might've been a big enough task without the complication of Christian.

He picked up a bag of supplies and held it to his chest. "I'm strictly here in an official capacity." He reached into the bag. "I brought ice."

"There's an ice maker here."

"Oh." His shoulders slumped, making me feel bad.

"But if you already have it ready, probably best to use it before it melts. You can stay for as long as it takes to ice my ankle, but that's it."

"Deal." He looked toward Miss Nancy's closed door. "She

sleeping?"

"Yep. She gets up super early to start breakfast." I gestured to my bruised ankle. "Ice it up, Mr. Trainer."

"No need to rush."

"No need to stall either."

"Fair enough." He unpacked the supplies and used plastic wrap to secure a bulging bag of ice to the side of my ankle. When the cold first touched my skin, I flinched, and Christian apologized. While the ice melted and the bag shaped to the curve of my leg, Christian chatted about his experiences with the teams at the school, telling stories about the most gruesome injuries and even a few illnesses. Despite the topic, his dramatic storytelling had me laughing so hard I thought we might wake up Miss Nancy. Definitely good company.

"Julia, can I tell you something?"

The tone in the room transformed from light to tense with his words, but the hope in Christian's eyes eased my apprehensions about what he might say. A little. "Sure."

He sighed and rubbed his hands together, causing the apprehension to soar once again. "You've impressed me this week."

That I didn't mind hearing. "Thank you."

"Not just the football but how you interact with the team. In general, how you go after what you want."

Again, I thanked him. And feared where this was going.

"I know things are pretty fresh with Malone..."

"Christian, don't."

"I'm not." He shifted from sitting on the coffee table to kneeling in front of me. He braced himself with one hand on the back of the couch. "I needed to come here tonight because I know we can't keep doing *this*."

Doing what? Flirting? Being attracted to each other? Nothing had happened between us. How could it when Owen and our breakup twisted my mind into some confused, unfocused, syrupy mess?

Christian blushed and looked down at the floor. "I think you know how I feel, so I'm not going to say any more. I have no intention of pressuring you. When you're ready, though, I hope you'll consider giving me a chance."

Those dangerous flutters started flapping their wings in my gut, but I shut them down. Fast. "So, you're agreeing to give me space?"

"Yes."

"Because you coming to my cabin at night when you're techni-cally not allowed isn't actually giving me space?"

He closed his eyes and nodded. Maybe he was as confused as I was. And Owen. And every other teenager on the planet in a relation-ship/attracted to someone else at the same time. I could respect that he wanted to be clear on things. But I couldn't risk any more trouble with Owen or the team.

"Thanks for coming," I said.

Christian looked at his watch. "Yeah, definitely. All done here anyway." He cut the plastic and let the bag of watered-down ice fall to the side. He gently lifted my leg, his fingers warm against my chilled skin. I shivered.

Christian moved the blanket from the back of the couch to my shoulders.

"Thanks," I said, tucking myself in and trying to avoid eye con-tact. "I appreciate the ice..."

"You're welcome. I guess I'll head out."

Relief settled over me, but then my heart rate soared when I glanced up to say goodbye and Christian's lips pressed against mine. Tentative, he held my bottom lip between his in a slow kiss that prob-ably lasted a second but seemed like forever. Long enough for desire and guilt and fear and maybe even a little happiness to mingle and confuse me even more before I finally pushed him away.

I turned my head. "Christian..."

"Think about what I said," he whispered, his voice soft but his eyes confident.

Someone pounded on the door. The last time I'd hoped to see Owen, but now I feared it when I spun around. But the reality was so much worse.

Coach Vincent stood on the front porch, arms crossed over his chest and a furious glare, intensified from the shadows of the porch light, on his face.

CHAPTER THIRTY-SEVEN

I BELIEVE IN THE IMPOSSIBLE BECAUSE NO ONE ELSE DOES.
—FLORENCE GRIFFITH JOYNER

"OH SHIT," CHRISTIAN MUMBLED.

I tried to stand to answer the door, but Coach let himself inside. Hands on hips, he shook his head, sighed, huffed, puffed, and generally worked to contain what I assumed was the desire to rip someone's face off.

"I've fought the boosters and school board for the last week promising something like this wouldn't happen," he said after a few minutes of letting us squirm. "The rules were explicit. No boy was to enter this cabin."

"Coach, I came to check on—"

But Coach lifted a hand, silencing Christian. "You're suspended from the training staff until further notice. Go back to your cabin and stay there until you hear otherwise from me. Understand?"

Christian opened his mouth to object, and I imagined all the things he would say. He wanted to be a doctor. Working with the football team was the ultimate internship to get him into a good exercise science program at college.

"Coach," I said, but nothing else came out. What could I say to convince him when he was absolutely right?

I couldn't deny the heat of anger that spread inside me, even down to my iced ankle. I had asked Christian to leave. I had asked him for space. I didn't want this to happen. Yet I'd also let him stay. I'd enjoyed his stories and even been tempted by his kiss. As much as he was wrong, so, unfortunately, was I.

"Yes, Coach," Christian managed. "Thank you for the opportunity."

He grabbed his bag and left without another look at either of us. When the door closed behind him, Coach Vincent sat on the arm of the dated recliner and massaged the inner corners of his eyes. "You chose to play on this team, to abide by the team rules," he said quietly.

"I'm sorry I let you down, Coach. But what Christian said was true. He came here to ice my ankle."

He stared at me hard. "And what I saw when I was about to knock on the door?"

What could I say to that? Blame Christian? In that moment, he had been the instigator. But what kind of team leader laid the blame on someone else? All I could do was hold his gaze. Keep my head up.

"I've never been in this situation. I've never coached a girl before. You're a player and a damn talented one, but off the field... it's complicated."

"Am I off the team?"

Coach didn't answer right away. "I don't know."

But he was considering it. Christian could lose his internship, and I could lose everything I'd fought my friends, family, and even the town for. One stupid moment—one I wasn't even ready to have—had taken so much from both of us.

The uncertainty clawed at me.

"I'm sorry, Coach."

"As of tonight, you're suspended from the team until further notice. Miss Nancy can send someone from the kitchen with break-fast here for you. Stay in this cabin and wait to hear from me. Is that understood?"

****

IT TOOK ME ABOUT TEN MINUTES TO DECIDE I WASN'T
going home tomorrow, but I had no idea how to convince Coach
Vincent to let me stay. More importantly, I'd have to do even better
on the field. If the race between Stanford and me was close, then I
wasn't worth the stress.

I needed to be the clear, dominant choice.

In Jake's notebook, I wrote: *Potential Issues Coach Wants to
Avoid* and listed the following:

1. Romantic encounters. (Clearly.)

2. Sexual encounters. (Maybe those were the same in his book.
Oh well.)

3. Fighting with boosters.

4. Different locker room for me.

5. Fighting within the team. (i.e. Creel and Moody)

I thought that about covered it. If I could theorize ways to address
each of those issues, maybe I could stay. The thought struck me that
I shouldn't have to address them. That someone else should figure
it out, but if I were the kind of person who preferred someone else
have the ball in his hands when the game was on the line, I wouldn't
have been there in the first place.

So, what would matter most to Coach?

1. Nobody would work for him harder than I would.

2. Eventually, another girl would try out for this team, so better
to work out the kinks now.

3. He didn't want to be known as the coach who kicked a girl off
his team. (Kind of a low blow, but in a brainstorm session, everything
must be written!)

4. (Ooh, one of the Medina family favorite quotes would work
here.) I flipped through Jake's notebook to find the exact wording,
and sure enough on a page with a doodle of the moon and stars, he'd
written: *We choose to go to the moon in this decade and do the other
things, not because they are easy but because they are hard, because
that goal will serve to organize and measure the best of our energies
and skills, because that challenge is one that we are willing to accept,
one we are unwilling to postpone, and one which we intend to win.*
(Hopefully Coach liked JFK and was willing to do the hard things).

Maybe that was the key. As much as I tried to divert attention from the fact, I was a girl. With that would come some unexpected complications—like a trainer kissing me—but they were worth solving. I'd broken the rules, but so had Creel, and his punishment was team running. Why, when I broke the rules, was my punishment removal from the team? Because anything otherwise was too hard? Because fighting with the boosters was too hard?

Coach Vincent didn't cower in the face of challenges and difficulty. I'd known him a decade. He'd never cowered. I tossed and turned all night playing what I planned to say to him the next morning in my mind. I'd get it right. I'd convince him.

And I'd stay on this team.

****

THE NEXT MORNING BEFORE BREAKFAST, I HOBBLED down the path—burying my pride by using the crutches—to the coaches' office, wishing my biggest problem of the day was whether to rest my ankle, not convincing the head coach to let me stay on the team. I decided to take the shortcut to the coaches' office through the weight room, and, lucky me, saw Vincent sprinting on the treadmill through the windows. A few more hobbles bought me a closer view and the sight of Kicker Creel standing next to him.

Oh, luck, how you despise me.

Maybe by the time I maneuvered around the building to the entrance, Creel would be gone. No matter—if Coach was busy, I'd wait. I wasn't leaving the building until he listened to my reasoning. Who was I kidding? I wasn't leaving until he agreed with me. The heavy door gave me some trouble, but I eventually hopped my way through.

A thud—the kind that was loud and scary and told you something bad had happened—echoed off the walls.

Creel shouted, "Coach? Coach, are you okay? Someone help!"

I sped through the room, weaving around machines, dumbbells, and benches to find Coach Vincent lying face down on the floor, his treadmill still going full speed.

I dropped to my knees next to him. "What happened?"

"I don't know. We were talking, and he fell."

I rolled Vincent onto his back. "Shut off the treadmill." His eyes were closed, and his lips were a bluish hue. "Coach, are you okay?" I shook his shoulders.

He didn't answer. He didn't move.

"Oh my God. Oh my God," Creel kept saying from behind me.

"Listen. Go call nine-one-one, and then come back here. Okay?" Creel nodded. A group of underclassmen rushed into the weight room, swearing when they saw Coach down.

"Someone get an AED. And find Leo. Or the student trainer, Christian."

They scuttled away. I studied Coach Vincent's chest but didn't see it rising and falling. Checking his neck for a pulse, all I could hear was the sound of my own heartbeat. *Calm down. Calm down. This is Coach. He has a wife. Kids. All of us.* After a few seconds, the sound of my heartbeat faded enough for me to tell his was nonexistent. I scanned the crowd forming in the room.

"Where's Christian?"

My teammates shook their heads, looking as terrified as I felt. *He's a damn EMT, for shit's sake.* I couldn't wait. I pressed the heel of my hand against the center of Coach's chest and interlaced the fingers of my other hand on top. I started compressions. Fearing I wasn't pushing hard enough, I intensified the compressions and heard a series of cracks.

"What the hell was that?" someone asked.

Cracking cartilage. The CPR instructor my brothers and I learned from over the years had said that would happen but feeling the breaks beneath the pressure of my own hands...ugh. Instinctively, I knew the room was filled with other players and maybe even coaches, but I focused on Coach like we were the only two people there.

"I know CPR," someone said. "If you need a break."

I did. I might. Soon. My arms ached, and the compressions winded me more than up-downs and bear crawls on the field.

"Am I doing it right? Fast enough?"

"You're good. I'll count for you to keep pace."

Whoever he was, he did.

"Let me through!" The voice was Christian's, and I almost cried with relief. He knelt next to me with an AED in his hands. "Are you doing compressions only? No breaths?"

232

I gestured for the other player who knew CPR to take over, so I could answer Christian's questions. "Yes."

"How long?"

"Uh..." My head clouded as if the answers were there somewhere, but I couldn't quite see them. "I...I don't remember."

"Don't worry about it."

The player who took over compressions for me was a sophomore lineman, Michael, I realized since I could actually look at his face. Christian asked if he could continue compressions while he prepared the AED, and he said he would.

"I can help if you need me," I told him.

"I'm good. Just count."

So I did.

Christian lifted the lid to the AED as Coach Draveck pushed through the crowd. "What happened?"

"He's in cardiac arrest," Christian said, tearing Coach's shirt down the front, revealing his bare chest. "I'm a probationary EMT."

"Probationary? What does that mean?" Draveck asked.

"Someone called nine-one-one," Christian said, not really answering. "I need everyone but those performing CPR to move back, please." While Michael continued compressions, the AED instructed Christian in a robotic voice. But he performed the tasks before the instructions were even said, confirming for everyone—especially Draveck—that he knew what the hell he was doing. He attached the first pad on Coach's upper right chest and the second pad on his lower left ribcage then told the lineman to move back.

"Do not touch patient," the AED said. "Analyzing rhythm."

"Stay back, everyone," Christian reiterated.

Nobody in the room spoke or moved.

"Shock advised," came the robotic voice.

"Julia, move back. Everyone stand clear."

We all scooted farther away, and Christian pressed the flashing heart-shaped button on the AED. Coach barely flinched.

"Did it work?" someone asked. I wondered the same thing, but Christian's concern was Coach Vincent, not answering our questions. I could handle that.

"Continue CPR," the AED said, and Christian began a new series of compressions.

"I can give breaths if you want," I said, wanting to help, to feel some sense of control.

"I can do it," he said, sweat beading at his forehead. "There's a pocket mask in that bag. Follow the instructions and attach it to his face."

With fumbling fingers, I managed to secure the mask before Christian hit thirty compressions. He blew two breaths and continued compressions. The mirrors in the room reflected flashes of red and blue.

"The ambulance is here!" someone shouted.

The team cheered. Christian and I sighed with relief.

"Coming through. Make room," shouted two paramedics a few seconds later as they wheeled a gurney through the weight room. Their voices were firm. Everyone obeyed.

"We have a male, mid-forties, in full cardiac arrest," Christian reported to them in a formal tone I'd never heard him use before. "CPR was started almost immediately. I shocked him once, but there was no conversion. We continued with CPR."

"Great. Can you continue compressions while we get set up here?"

"Yes," Christian said, near breathless himself.

The female paramedic swapped the AED pads for smaller ones that wired to a monitor, while the male paramedic clipped something to his finger.

"Is he going to be okay?" I asked.

"We're going to do our best, miss."

"You've done great," the woman told Christian. "We can take it from here."

Christian and I helped each other stand, and we gave the paramedics room to work but we didn't take our eyes off Coach. I watched, waiting for him to wake up, to open his eyes and yell that we should be on the field or lifting or studying the playbook. Not watching him practically die.

"Patient's in V-fib," they said, and I wanted to tell them Coach Vincent wasn't the "patient". He was Jim Vincent, state champion head coach of the Iron Valley Vikings. A husband and father of the most adorable little boy who loved football and his dad even more.

234

An all-around good guy people adored.

The guy who'd given me a chance.

The paramedics shocked him again, but still, he didn't breathe on his own. They slid him onto a wooden board, lifted him onto the gurney, and rolled toward the ambulance, never stopping the compressions.

CHAPTER THIRTY-EIGHT

DO YOUR BEST, ONE SHOT AT A TIME, AND THEN MOVE ON.
—NANCY LOPEZ

SOMEONE HELPED ME TO THE BENCH OUTSIDE. AS THE
adrenaline wore off, the pain in my ankle increased. Christian walked
the paramedics to the ambulance, but when the back doors closed and
the flashing lights shrunk in the distance, he found me in the crowd
and hugged me tight.

"Thank you for coming," I muttered.

"You did so well, Julia. You saved his life."

I cried then, not caring if the team saw, not caring if they thought
it was because I was a girl. My coach, a man I admired and respected,
a man with a family, a man I'd stressed immeasurably twelve hours
earlier, had nearly died right in front of me. If that wasn't a reason to
cry, then I didn't know what the hell was.

"Let it out," Christian said. "The adrenaline will do that to you."

"Hey," Square called, pushing through everyone huddled around
to pull me into a bear hug. "I heard what happened. You okay?"

I rubbed my hands to mask the shaking. "I will be." I hoped.

Square looked at Christian, and they might have said something
to each other but the words didn't register with me.

The coaches ushered us into the cafeteria for breakfast, but I couldn't eat.

D, on the other hand, could. "Damn, girl," he said, offering a prime view of the pancakes turning to mush in his mouth. "Is there anything you can't do?"

"I'm pretty sure she won't be able to surpass my stellar passing records," said Jake from behind me.

My chair squealed against the floor when I pushed back from the table, barely able to breathe. Behind us, wearing Western Penn athletic clothes and a concerned expression, stood the person I wanted to see most in the world. I jumped out of my chair and fell into his arms.

"How are you here?"

"Draveck called Mom," he answered, hugging me as if his embrace had no expiration. "And since I'm twenty minutes away, she called me. They're on their way too."

"No," I said, afraid what Draveck might tell my parents about last night if they showed up here—if he even knew about Christian being in my cabin. Too big of a risk. "Please tell them I don't want to make a big deal out of it. Call them and ask them to stay home. I'll call them as soon as I can."

"You know with Abuelita in the car screaming at Dad to floor it, they're probably halfway here."

"Convince them," I urged, and my big brother being my best friend and knowing me as well as he did, accepted my telepathic message that there was more to be said—without my parents around to hear it.

He pulled his phone from his pocket.

****

IT DIDN'T TAKE LONG FOR MY BODY TO CRASH FROM the adrenaline, leaving the pain from my ankle blaring like a foghorn in my ears. Draveck announced the morning practices were canceled but the whole team should convene in the pool area.

"Bring your suits and your workout gear." As the team scattered, turning the cafeteria into a cacophony of noise, Draveck came to our table and shook Jake's hand, thanking him for coming so quickly.

"Medina," he said, talking to me then. "Go get some ice on that ankle. I have a few phone calls to make about Coach, but then I'll check in on you." He extended his hand to me and given what I knew—that he didn't support my position on the team—the gesture felt weighted. "Jim Vincent's my best friend. He's my son's godfather. What you did this morning...thank you."

I stood and shook his hand. "I'm glad I was there." Until I said the words, I didn't realize I'd felt that way. But it was true. When it came to Coach Vincent, I didn't trust anyone else to have been there in that moment.

Another revelation followed: When it came to the team, I also didn't trust anyone else to do what needed done. I *needed* to be their quarterback.

Jake helped me to the trainer's room, where Christian wrapped ice around my ankle and elevated it.

"The boy trainer's rather attentive to you," Jake said after Christian left us to retreat to his cabin, where Coach Vincent had insisted he stayed until further notice—an order he'd disobeyed to save Coach's life. Knowing my brother, the statement was more of a question. A good one.

"About that..."

Jake groaned. "And I thought Malone was bad."

"Christian and I aren't together. At all."

Jake sat next to me, lifting my feet onto his lap.

"But last night, he came to my cabin to check on me."

"And you sent him away because you knew that shit wasn't allowed."

I scrunched my face, which I knew because Jake had long ago pointed out I did that when I knew I was wrong but didn't want to admit it.

"What happened?"

I told him about the kiss and about Coach Vincent seeing us. And everything that followed.

Jake stared at me for a minute, daring me to look away, but I held his eye contact. Finally, Jake relented. "Were you going to see Coach Vincent this morning to convince him to let you stay?"

"Yep."

We sat in silence. What if I hadn't come to see Coach that morning? Would someone else have stepped in? Or would the outcome have been different? Maybe Jake was thinking the same thing, but wanting to keep our minds from going to that dark place, I asked, "Did Mom and Dad say anything to you about this earlier?"

He shook his head. "Maybe Draveck hasn't told them yet."

Yet. "What do I do?"

"Ice your ankle, but after that, you go out there like you're part of this team because until Vincent or Draveck tells you otherwise, you are."

****

I ICED AND TALKED TO MY PARENTS ON JAKE'S PHONE while he disappeared.

"Be back in two minutes," he'd said.

He was gone ten—enough time to get to Christian's cabin, give the "boy trainer" some advice about how to behave around his little sister, and get back to the Main Lodge.

"How did he take to your meddling?" I asked.

Jake played the offended big brother. "I don't know what you mean, Jules."

He drove the golf cart to the pool, my heart swelling with love and pride along the way. I seriously got the best brothers on the planet. He parked and walked around the cart to help me out. I stopped him and squeezed his hand. "Thanks for looking out for me, Jake."

"Always, baby sis," he said and then, to immediately ruin the moment, ruffled my hair.

The team crowded around us to greet Jake and congratulate me.

"You were amazing, Medina," said Drew.

"I'm not going back in the swimming pool until you're life-guarding," said Brighton.

"Yeah," Creel said, coming forward to shake my hand. "What you did this morning was for real."

Coming from Creel, that meant a lot.

"I'm glad you were there," he said.

Good thing I wasn't drinking something. I might have choked.

"I'm glad you all know how incredible my baby sister is," Jake shouted, lifting his hands high to silence the crowd. "Anyone who doesn't have her back, speak your piece so I can grab a football and light you up."

Everyone laughed.

Stanford snuck around the crowd next to me and whispered, "I didn't realize we needed campaign managers."

"Oh, Jake appoints himself manager of most things."

"You think I'm joking!" Jake kept right on taunting.

"How you doing after this morning?" Stanford asked.

I took a deep breath. "I don't know, really. Maybe after we hear some news about Coach..."

Stanford mumbled agreement.

"Who's up for some friendly competition?" Jake proposed.

Jake convinced most of the team, including Stanford and two coaches, to leave the pool for a pickup game since he didn't have to be back to Western Penn for a few hours. Creel, of all people, helped me stack towels to elevate my ankle before hustling off to play. From the sideline, I cheered when the team made a big play and when they scored—even Creel. I laughed when they laughed and yelled dissent when they fell short. Cheering from the sideline didn't make me less of a teammate. These were my brothers, my teammates. No matter what happened between Stanford and me for the starting spot, and despite what people around me believed or even hoped, I wouldn't quit football if Stanford beat me.

Whether I was on the sideline or the field, this was my team.

CHAPTER THIRTY-NINE

IF YOU HAVE EVERYTHING UNDER CONTROL, YOU'RE NOT
MOVING FAST ENOUGH.
—MARIO ANDRETTI

THE NEWS ABOUT COACH CAME SHORTLY AFTER
lunch. He was stable, and barring any complications, he should make
a full—and relatively quick—recovery. Draveck's announcement led
to the team cheering my and the lineman's names. Christian got called
into the team room for congratulations as well.

"Today's been tough and not at all what we expected," Draveck
told the team. "But Coach wants us out on that field, giving everything we have."

The team shouted agreement.

"It's our last day of practice. We're tired. We're injured. We're not
quite whole. But tomorrow, the opponent will arrive on our field not
concerned about any of those things. South Mon will come here to
win, but we won't let that happen." His face reddened as he shouted,
"Let me hear it!"

"Iron Valley!"

"I can't hear you!"

"Iron Valley!"

"Let's go!"

The team exploded to the field, pumped from Draveck's boost, and hit team practice hard. On the sidelines, players were saying, "Do it for Coach!" and the intensity from the morning fueled the afternoon in a rough and tumble way. In my seemingly usual position of elevated, iced ankle, I watched Stanford take every rep as if he was the starter and prayed that would be my last experience with the particular phenomenon. The team pushed hard. The coaches ratcheted up the intensity, but they weren't alone.

First, it was a mumble on the sidelines: South Mon had created an online profile called "No Girls Allowed," but the mumble rumbled in no time.

An underclassman heard about the page from a cousin of his who went to South Mon and texted him that morning, which he saw because we were granted electronics time to contact our parents about Coach Vincent. The cousin had asked, "Do you really have a girl quarterbacking your team?" and linked to the page.

"Did you see the site?" I asked when Square came to check on me.

"Who told you about that?"

"Not you." I gave him a pointed look.

He handed me a cup of Gatorade. "You shouldn't have to deal with that shit."

"Since my life is a world of rainbows and unicorns, I can understand how you'd feel that way."

He shook his head and tossed his cup into the trash. "Leave it, Medina."

Right. Like I've ever listened to good advice like that.

I recruited two sophomore defensive backs named Billy and Jaxon to recount the messages they'd seen on the profile.

"I don't remember," Jaxon said.

I stared him down.

"Fine. 'Guarantee she doesn't play more than one snap,' someone wrote," he said, and I waited for more. Neither of them continued.

"That's it?"

They looked at each other and shrugged. "Some idiot responded, 'When the team is already up by five touchdowns.'"

D joined us on the sidelines then. "Tell me you're not listening to this bullshit."

"Did you see it?"

"Hell yes, I saw it. I'm also going to see when you light them up tomorrow."

Fine. They didn't want me to know. I wouldn't mine them for every single post, but the taunts had hit a nerve with my team. They were angry, so I would be too.

"What was the worst post you read?"

"'What the hell is wrong with her? She must want to get hurt,'" Jaxon answered, looking down at my ankle and blushing.

"You didn't say it," I consoled. "They did. Billy?"

He squirmed a little.

"Billy!"

"'The linebackers will have fun sacking her vagina.'"

Original. And gross.

Assholes.

Guaranteed the poster was anonymous. Talk about bravery. The blood in my body moved more quickly, and my head rang with an anger I couldn't suppress. My ankle could take more weight now with only a small ache. I needed to be ready the next day. And be off suspension, not to prove myself to these idiots but to stand beside my team when we faced off. Maybe it was stupid boasting, boys being boys—whatever. All I knew is if someone opened his mouth and said something so colossally stupid, then I was going to shut it.

****

LATER THAT NIGHT, AROUND THE TEAM CAMPFIRE, I learned something remarkable about my good friend D. He told awful ghost stories. I mean, painful.

"Stop, man, please," Square pleaded after a particularly terrible tale that began with, "We was walking in the woods." It might not have been so bad if the story before hadn't been, "We was walking in the cemetery." And the one before that, "We was walking in the park."

Drew Peters could tell stories that had even the toughest lineman's arm hair perk up. While everyone shook away their shivers, I squished a marshmallow onto a stick to make a s'more.

"You should write these down, you know," I said to Drew while we roasted side by side.

"Nah," he said, modest.

"I mean it. How did you get so good at telling ghost stories?"

His marshmallow caught fire, so he blew it out quickly and smashed it between his graham crackers. I preferred the slow and steady approach and tried not to burn the slightest corner.

"I volunteer at a camp for kids every summer," Drew said. "We tell ghost stories a lot."

I examined my marshmallow, but it wasn't ready. "What kind of camp?"

Drew prepped a second s'more. "It's a grief camp for kids who've lost a loved one or suffered through some other trauma."

"Wow," I said. Not that I knew Drew all that well or anything but imagining him spending his summers volunteering to help kids in grief had me looking around at my other teammates. How did they spend their free time?

In the process, across the glow of the flames, I caught Owen's eye. He flinched and turned away. Too quickly. Did he think something was going on between Drew and me? Was he jealous? Given that he'd basically rejected me twice, what kind of sadist was I to even care?

I smashed my s'more together and dug into the deliciousness.

After too many more "We was walking in the *fill in the blank*" stories, the crowd dispersed. As we left the campfire, my ankle ached. Pain didn't shoot through with every step.

I was going to play tomorrow.

I'd ice back at the cabin, warm up with the team in the morning, and take reps against South Mon—if Coach released me from suspension. To make a case, I'd need to stay out of trouble. When I got to the golf cart that had become my ride around camp, trouble waited for me in the form of Owen Malone.

"Hey, Jules," he said in a low voice. That voice that used to make me want to curl under his arm and press a kiss against his lips.

Okay. Part of me still did.

"Hey," I said, debating if the word sounded natural. Or fake. Or suggestive. Or— Oh, forget it. "I haven't seen you much today."

"I've been...around."

More like avoiding me.

"When I heard about this morning, I wanted to come and find you."

"But you didn't."

He looked away. "I wanted to...do things that really aren't my right to do anymore."

Like what? Hold me? Kiss me? Console me? He'd relinquished those privileges by dumping me. Of course, I had helped him to that decision every time I sat with Square and D at meals instead of him. Or when I chose to focus on football and pushed our relationship aside because it was too hard for them to be in the same space.

"I'm sorry about everything," I muttered.

"Me too."

I pointed to the golf cart. "Need a ride?"

"Only if I get to drive it."

I tossed him the keys, and we rode in silence to my cabin. Learning my lesson from the night before, I didn't lead Owen up the path. Instead, we sat side by side, probably both debating how much we would say. Part of me wondered if we could have done something differently.

"Do you think things would have been different if you hadn't lost the position?" I asked.

Owen scoffed.

Anger heated my sense of peace. "I didn't realize that was funny."

"You really don't know, do you, Julia?"

"Clearly not. Enlighten me."

Owen scratched his head and sighed as if the news he was about to break would pain him like a knockout hit. "I didn't lose the quarterback position."

"You haven't taken a rep in days..." So what was I missing?

"I went to Coach and *asked* to be moved to receiver."

Bullshit. "You asked?"

"Yep."

That made no sense. "You wanted to play quarterback. Your dad pressured you. You... why?"

Owen squirmed. "I asked. Can we leave it at that?"

"Can Creel kick a fifty-yarder?"

Owen offered a soft chuckle but didn't commit to the joke.

"Owen...?"

He spoke so quietly it was as if he didn't want the universe to hear his words. "You were better than I was."

Eighty-five percent of me—probably the genetic makeup I shared with the often-pompous-but-always-lovable Jake—wanted him to repeat that. Or shout it. Or write it down, but the humbler fifteen percent of me graciously said, "Thank you."

"I told Coach I believed in you, so there was no point in me sticking around to take away your reps."

Since I'd decided to try out, all I'd wanted from Owen was that exact statement: *I believe in you.* After it was too late, he offered it, but still...he offered it. Since he'd revealed in the pool that he'd planned to try out, Owen wanted the same support from me.

My greatest mistake in our relationship was never figuring out a way to give it.

CHAPTER FORTY

I'VE WORKED TOO HARD AND TOO LONG TO LET ANYTHING STAND IN THE WAY OF MY GOALS. I WILL NOT LET MY TEAMMATES DOWN, AND I WILL NOT LET MYSELF DOWN.
—MIA HAMM

"SO, YOU'RE READY TO PLAY?" COACH DRAVECK ASKED the next morning when I bounded into the coaches' office announcing my ankle had improved.

"It's a little tender, but I'll get wrapped and be good."

He sat back in the chair and crossed his arms, looking so much like Coach Vincent I wondered if he was channeling the man. "What about the suspension?"

I scrunched my face. So he did know about that.

"Coach Vincent and I haven't been able to talk, for obvious reasons. What do you have to say for yourself about the other night?"

"The truth. Christian came to check on my ankle."

Draveck raised an eyebrow. "The truth, huh?"

Okay, so maybe it wasn't the *whole* truth. "I broke a rule. I admit that and take responsibility. But I'm not the first player on this team to break the rules. When they did it, they received a punishment on the field. I'd like that same consideration."

"Do you like running?" Draveck said with a smirk.

"Not at all."

He raised an eyebrow and studied me.

"Look, Coach. I'm here to play football. That's the truth."

He stood. "That, I believe, but I can't make any promises. Tape your ankle. Warm up with the team, and we'll see."

Too bad. I hoped for a promise. "I appreciate the opportunity, Coach."

"One more thing." Draveck tossed me a game jersey. I caught it and held it out in front of me. In the center of the purple material was a large black number twelve. My throat caught. Number twelve. It had been Juan's number. Then Jorge's and finally Jake's.

"Thanks, Coach," I managed, my voice low and unsteady.

My own number twelve jersey. As I catered to my injured ankle down the hallway to the trainer's office, I relished my swelling pride and excitement. Having the cool, soft jersey in my hands made football even more of a reality.

"Number twelve, huh? No surprise there."

Christian stood in the trainer's room when he should have been long gone from Camp Sweat and Tears. My focus so needed to be the field, not the drama occurring off it.

"Christian?"

He smiled that smile that had launched me into a world of trouble. "Hey, Julia."

Despite the wattage of his grin, my hands found my hips. "Don't 'Hey, Julia' me. Look, words are not possible for how much I appreciate you being there to help Coach Vincent, but we screwed up, Christian. Major."

"I know."

"You shouldn't have kissed me."

"I know."

First of all, I didn't expect to see Christian here. Secondly, staying angry would have come more easily if he'd stop agreeing with me.

"Look, a position opened up with the soccer team up at school. I'm gonna take it."

"Oh," I said. It sounded like a better deal for him to be close to home and school. "That's great. Congratulations."

"Thanks. One more thing."

"Yeah?"

"The day after football season ends, I'm calling you," he said. Calm. Confident. And, unfortunately for me, totally sexy. My focus was too heavily football for me to have any idea how I might feel about that call when it came, but in that moment, I felt the warmth of appreciation at the prospect.

Leo rushed into the room, holding supplies that told me he was there for something that didn't have to do with me. He looked from me to Christian, and his eyes widened.

"Just here to get taped," I said.

He gestured to the table.

"And I'm on my way out for good," Christian said, then whispered to me, "Kill them out there."

****

I'D WATCHED ENOUGH WARM-UPS FROM MY BROTH-ers' games to know they should've been boring, perfunctory, anti-climactic. The usual stretching, jogging, shuffling, backpedaling. And sure, there were always those teams that liked to talk shit any time a player neared the fifty-yard line. Jake loved throwing at those loud mouths all game long. "Shut them up on the field," he'd say. After warm-ups, we had a lot of people on the list to "shut up on the field".

"This ain't powder puff, sugar!"

"Shouldn't you be baking cookies for after the game?"

"You can't find someone with a dick to throw the ball?"

"Speaking of, sugar, why don't you suck my—" But number fifty-eight couldn't finish that sentence because his mouth was otherwise occupied with D's fist. A brawl ensued. Fists swinging. Bodies being smashed into the grass. I stood back and waited for the coaches and refs to break it up. I might've been a girl risking injury to play football, but that didn't mean I wanted to fight them. I'd never want anyone to get hurt for me but knowing my teammates wouldn't stand for other teams harassing me...emotions got in the way of words on that.

Draveck called us to the end zone and spoke in a calm but firm voice. "We will not stoop to their level. We will protect and defend every last player on this team, but we do it on the field. They think we can't throw? We'll air it out on them. They think we can't run? We're gonna shove it down their throats. You take all the rage you feel in this moment, and you channel that into the plays." Around me teammates were nodding, stone-faced. "They're taking the ball first. We shut them up with a three and out. Let me hear it!"

"Iron Valley!"

"I can't hear you!"

"Iron Valley!"

The team hustled to the sideline. The crowd, which included Juan, Jake, my parents, and Abuelita somewhere out there, chanted, "Let's go, Iron Valley. Let's go!" I'd chanted that so many times while my brothers had played, but now *I* was on the grass, fist-bumping, talking over plays, bouncing on my toes waiting for my shot on the field. *If* I got one.

"Hey, look," said Creel. "That reporter Denton's here."

Sure enough. Rand Denton roamed the sideline with a photographer at his side and a notebook in his hands.

"Focus on the game," I told Creel. He offered a sloppy salute and resumed practicing place kicks in the sideline net.

Our defense lined up for a South Mon first and ten on their own twenty-yard line.

"Medina," called Coach O'Connor from behind me. Stanford was next to him. "I'm helping with quarterbacks and offensive calls until Coach returns. We'll have four series before the JV takes the field. You will take two series each."

My stomach dropped and twisted and flipped and flopped, and holy shit, I was going to play!

"It's personal. Nobody likes what they've been saying online, so Medina, you're taking the first and last series. Start us strong and have the last word. Got it? Stanford, you're taking the heart of the reps. Keep the team motivated through the middle of the scrimmage. Got it?"

We both nodded and grinned at each other. I assumed Stanford felt as giddy as I did. Coach O'Connor walked away, and Stanford extended a hand. "I have my own challenge," he said.

"What's that?" I fist-bumped him.

"Let's score on these shitheads every series."

I laughed. "Sounds good to me." Scoring was always the goal but setting an expectation to score *every* series—especially in the first scrimmage—was no joke.

The defense deflected a pass on first down, sacked the quarterback on the second, and lined up for third down to unparalleled noise from our sideline and stands. The South Mon quarterback dropped back, looked left, pump faked, looked right, and let the ball go for a comeback route that bought them about eight yards.

Not enough for a first down.

I jogged onto the field. My teammates clapped it up from the sidelines. My school was a wave of purple behind me pushing me forward onto the field. Above all the cheers, I swore I could hear Jake's voice. "You got this, Little J!" Then Juan's. "Let's go, Julia!

I swore even Jorge's voice called to me, but that wasn't possible since he was in Florida.

D shook my hand and shoulder bumped me. "Let's go. Let's go."

Hell yeah. Let's go.

After all the advocating, the pleading, the practicing, the drama, I was about to play high school football. So it was a scrimmage, but still, a scrimmage with game-time situations.

We took the ball at the twenty. Coach O'Connor called a pass play to come out of the gate strong. In the huddle, I looked into the eyes of my line, my receivers, and especially D, Brighton, and Owen. They all had my back, and I was going to play my ass off for them too.

"West Trips Right X Slant," I called. "Break!"

At the line, their middle linebacker, good old number fifty-eight, yelled, "Watch the run."

What an ass. A guy like that with ego and stupidity? No doubt he would blitz on the first play.

"Watch fifty-eight," I called to D in the sidecar.

"Yep. Yep."

I snapped the ball, and as expected, the linebacker rushed the line. Brighton ran an arrow that pulled out another backer, which gave Owen an opening on the slant. D picked up the blitz with all the aggression Coach Draveck told him to take to the field as I delivered the ball into Owen's outstretched hand. He pulled it in and ran five yards before the safety tackled him.

Eleven yards. First down. Suck that, number fifty-eight.

Taking advantage of D's energy, O'Connor called a run for the next play, and D picked up six yards. With a quick out to Brighton, we moved the sticks for our second first down.

Number fifty-eight kept right on talking smack, but the line's intensity and dedication to keeping everyone out of the backfield coupled with my good reads had him on his ass and pissed more often than not. But when Owen came across the middle for a ball, fifty-eight put his helmet under Owen's chin and brought him down. Too hard.

The crowd offered a collective groan that turned into jeering when no yellow flags hit the field. Less concerned about the refs, I hurried to Owen, who wasn't moving. The seconds felt like minutes, but before I got to him, he rolled onto his side and pushed his way upright. Draveck called him to the sideline for evaluation.

Despite the hit, Owen had caught the ball.

"Let me run at this jackass," D said in the huddle, so I snapped the ball and handed it off to him. He broke through the line, made a jump cut, and blew past fifty-eight for a fifty-two-yard run to the end zone.

I sprinted down the field and jumped on D's back. He spun me around, all the while shouting his usual, "That's right," "Get it," and other various D-isms—in repetition, of course. We hustled off the field so Creel could come on for the extra point. Draveck congratulated me with the hugest grin I'd ever seen on his face, but D was no doubt the doll of that ball.

Creel shanked the kick...and missed. The mistake, which anyone who knew anything about football knew could be a game changer, tempered the enthusiasm from D's touchdown run, but that didn't stop him. He roamed the sidelines, pumping up the team while I went straight to Leo's table to check on Owen. Not seeing Christian there felt strange, but probably best not to mix Owen and Christian just yet.

"How you doing?" I asked.

"That guy's a prick."

"I noticed."

"Everything looks good," Leo said. "I'll let Coach know."

Owen pulled his helmet on and jumped off the table. "How's your ankle feeling?"

On the field, our defense made a good open field tackle, but South Mon earned their first first down of the day.

"Hurts a little, to be honest, but not when I'm on the field."

Owen grinned. "It's like a vortex or something. You get so focused on the game that you don't even feel what's going on. Most of the time."

I laughed. "Well, just wanted to check on you, so..." I backpedaled a few steps.

"Good drive," he said.

"Thanks. Nice catches. Way to hold on to that second one."

"Thanks."

I stood beside Coach O'Connor in case he needed to go over any offensive questions, but he mostly talked to Stanford about the next series. After a failed third-down conversion, South Mon kicked a field goal, and it was Stanford's turn to lead the team. It'd be easy to root against Stanford if he had been a jerk like Moody, but he wasn't. He was a good guy with a great arm.

Still, with him at the helm, the team didn't play with the same edge I felt with them on the field. Was it a matter of perception because I was on the sideline? Or was the difference real? I guessed that would be for the coaches to decide. Stanford and I set a goal to score on every drive, so that's what we needed to do. He threw a few good balls but then took a sack. He bounced back and hit Owen on a thirty-yard go route, putting us in the red zone. From there, though, the team couldn't convert. Even D got shut down at the line, so we settled for Creel coming in and kicking a field goal.

This time, he made it.

Two possessions. Two scores.

South Mon took the ball again on their own twenty. They compiled a decent drive earning about forty yards, but ultimately, they didn't convert on fourth and short when Square pushed through the line and tackled their running back the second he took the ball.

Square hustled off the field as the offense got into position. I smacked the side of his helmet. "Nice play!"

He slapped my helmet back and nodded. Good old Square. Get on the field. Get serious. Get down to business. He threw back a cup of Gatorade and joined me on the sideline as Stanford hit Owen on a dig.

"How you feel?"

"Good," I said, clapping. "Chewing up the field."

"And they don't like it either. I'll tell you that."

"More 'Look at that girl' comments?"

"Most of them don't care, or at least they pretend not to. I heard their coach giving them an earful about not talking shit. Seems their linebacker didn't get that message."

"It would seem."

Stanford struggled with his progression, missing a wide-open receiver, and had to throw the ball away to avoid a sack. The next play, he wasn't so lucky. He tried to force a deep ball to Brighton, and it was picked off by South Mon's cornerback, who also happened to be their punt returner. He dodged would-be tacklers through midfield. Stanford took a line straight toward him, but a South Mon defender smashed Stanford with a tough block, and the corner scored a touchdown.

Just like that, South Mon was leading ten to nine.

"Back to business," Square said, running onto the field with the rest of our defense.

Although Moody and I didn't get along off the field, I had to admit, he was like a pit bull on it. He chased people down from all over, and once he grabbed a player, he wasn't letting go until the whistle blew. He played the numbers strong, and Square dominated the middle. They weren't alone on the field, but they did impact the game significantly. Like on that drive, they forced South Mon to kick yet another field goal, which did two things. It gave them an even bigger lead and me the opportunity to lead Iron Valley to a win, but we'd need more than a field goal. We'd need a touchdown.

I snapped my helmet in place and ran onto the field.

CHAPTER FORTY-ONE

HOW MANY FOOTBALL GAMES HAD I WATCHED WITH my brothers when the game was on the line and the quarterback hustled onto the field to lead the team to victory? Quarterbacks lived for it. We wanted that opportunity to face adversity and fight side by side with people who worked as hard and wanted it as badly as we do. You were down by four in the Super Bowl. You knew you needed a touchdown. Time was limited. And as much as you wanted to soar down the field to the end zone, the defense planned to grind you into the ground every play.

It was conflict. It was passion. It was everything.

It wasn't a high school preseason scrimmage.

It was my Super Bowl.

"All right," I said to my team in the huddle. "We know what we need to do. We came here to do it. Let's get it done. West Aces H Mesh on one. Ready...break!"

We hustled to the line, across from South Mon's defense with that look in their eyes that they were coming for us. *Let 'em come,*

I thought.

From shotgun, I called for the snap and eyed the safeties and middle linebacker. They were in zone, so I knew I'd need to go through my progression. And be patient. Owen came across the middle of the field on a drive route, but the backer picked him up, which bought Brighton room on the dig. Seeing nothing but the numbers on his jersey, I fired the ball with the kind of accuracy that would crush my brothers in backyard throwing competitions. Brighton caught it with ease and turned upfield, eventually being taken down by the safety.

But not before we moved the sticks eighteen yards.

"Keep pushing. You hear me!" I demanded in the huddle. "Trips Right. T Screen Left on one. Ready...break!"

After the snap, I sat in the pocket, looking downfield—or at least that's what I wanted the defense to think. D spun off his block, and I hit him with a pass.

The play bought us another fourteen yards. Move those sticks.

The next play, D earned four yards with a run up the middle. Coach O'Connor called his number again, and he pounded the ball three more yards, which put us in a third-and-three situation.

My first third down of the day. In the huddle, my team looked at me with confidence and intensity. No apprehension. No fear. First down or third down, it didn't matter. We were there to do what needed done.

"East Trips Right Twenty-Five Fake Sprint Right Pass on one. Ready...break!"

I faked the handoff to D and then sprinted out from the pocket to the right sideline looking for my receivers, but the linebacker picked Brighton up in the flat and the corner covered Owen downfield. We needed that first down. Refusing to force the pass, I tucked the ball and ran to my right. The safety came at me quick, but I needed three yards. I crossed the line of scrimmage.

One. Number fifty-eight charged.

Two. The safety barreled closer.

No way I was letting them hit me. Not with a healing sprain. Not with half the field left to take before we scored the winning touchdown. Football was a rough-and-tumble game, but no need to tumble when you didn't have to. I stepped out of bounds at the first-down marker, so close to the defenders they crashed into their teammates on the sidelines to avoid being penalized for a late hit.

First. Down.

"Let's do this," D shouted, smacking asses—not mine. "Let's do this!"

It felt good to see the sticks move, but the first down didn't guarantee the end zone. "We have more work to do. Let's go!"

On first and ten, I dropped back and ran my progression, but the defense played man coverage, crippling the receivers. The pocket collapsed around me, so I hustled away from the traffic and, following Coach Vincent's instructions from earlier in the week, threw it away well above Owen's head to prevent the sack, but also any chance of an interception.

"Shake it off," Owen said on the way to the huddle. "Find me. I got you."

He meant it too. He and Brighton ran precise routes, pulling defenders to open up other targets on the field. Two more passes into Owen's waiting hands, and we ate away another ten yards. South Mon's defensive line growled and bickered. The secondary fidgeted before I snapped the ball. They wanted to stop us, but not everyone got what they wanted.

I kept calm. My team was pumped. One more run from D and we were in the red zone. Number fifty-eight screamed at the defense, and something he said gave me a sense of déjà vu, sending me back to those beach volleyball tournaments with Ally. How weighed down I felt playing in them. How perfunctory it all was, but in that moment on the football field, nothing was certain. I didn't know if we'd score on that drive. I didn't know if I'd earn the starting position. I didn't know if I could cut it with the tough teams on our schedule.

But I knew the appreciation I felt to be on that field. The hours I'd lost track of competing against my brothers, throwing passes with Brighton before or after practice. The way my heart rate quickened with the grass beneath me. The fact that next to my brothers, I preferred D's and Square's company over anyone's. I was certain about the things that mattered. That was enough to persevere through the unexpected.

With D beside me, my line ready to block the threats against me, and Brighton and Owen out on the numbers eager to catch the ball, I pressed on, calling for the snap and handing off to D. Two more yards. The next play was West Aces H Mesh again, the dig we earned eighteen yards with on the first play of the drive. But this time, Brighton dropped the pass.

Third and long.

"We can do this. West Aces Smash Switch on one. Ready...break!"

The play had us taking a shot. A long shot. On a pass that wasn't my strength. Owen nodded to me, and I had to trust that if I put the ball up in the end zone, he would come down with it. I snapped the ball and dropped back. Owen sprinted into his route upfield, but before he could break out to the corner, I was hit from behind—a force like solid steel between my shoulder blades. I saw sky as my head snapped backward. Then the grass. *Hold on to the ball, hold on to the ball!* Tucking it against my side, I protected it more than myself as the defender took me to the ground. Hard.

It didn't hurt. Not like I expected, or—hell, who was I kidding—not like I'd feared. The sack was nothing until the defender pushed against me to stand up, and rage soared through my sprained ankle.

Damn.

The left tackle, Bryce Pennybaker, picked me up.

"Thanks."

"Sorry about that, Medina."

"Sorry?" Owen got in the Bryce's face. "You let him in untouched."

"I'm fine," I insisted, more frustrated about the lost yards than the sack itself. I could get through one more play. Maybe two. Finish this drive, and my ankle could have as much ice as it wanted. Hell, I'd even sit in that ice bucket again.

Coach Draveck called a time-out, but instead of us going to the sideline to him, he came to us. "Pennybaker! What was that?!"

Wisely, the tackle didn't respond.

"He was rushing upfield, and you reached for him. Get a bigger kick slide on your first step, and don't let it happen again. You understand me?"

Bryce nodded.

"Do you understand me?"

"Yes, Coach!"

Draveck sighed and shook his head before turning to me. "You good?"

"Yes, Coach."

He nodded in a way that told me he might not have entirely bought it, but he wasn't going to push me on the subject either. "Malone was open on that last play, so we're going to switch it up a bit and bring him into the slot. East Aces Z Corner. Medina, be patient back here"—he looked at the line—"and you all better give her that opportunity."

"Yes, Coach."

"Malone?"

"Coach?"

"Catch the damn ball."

He would, if I could get it there. With the loss of yards from the sack, I was looking at a thirty-yard pass. Not my strongest skill, even on a good ankle. Pumped from the sack, the defense lined up across from us with renewed intensity in their eyes and confidence that outweighed my own.

If I let it.

"Red 34! Red 34! Set...hut!"

The line held the defense while Owen took off. I scanned the field, refusing to take another hit. If I couldn't hit Owen on the corner, then I'd have to earn a first down some other way. Owen took a few steps toward the post, forcing the safety to turn his hips. The shift bought Owen enough time to explode toward the open corner of the end zone. I hitched forward and planted my right foot. Ignoring the shock of pain, I launched the ball.

The safety was beat. Everything in the place stilled except Owen and the ball. Would it hit its target? Would he catch it? The ball spun a perfect spiral, hit its apex, and descended. Owen reached for it. One step. Another, and there it was. On his fingertips. In his arms.

Touchdown.

In sports movies, cameras capture every reaction to these moments. The family cheering with pride in the stands. The coaches grateful for a win despite the adversity. The defense crumbling to the ground, sweaty and on the verge of tears. But I didn't see any of those things. All I saw was Owen Malone. In the end zone. Holding the football above his head in victory. I sprinted toward him and jumped. He caught me, and we hooted and hollered together. With D. Brighton. Hell, even Pennybaker ambled down the field for the celebration, which never seemed to end.

CHAPTER FORTY-TWO

A TROPHY CARRIES DUST. MEMORIES LAST FOREVER.
—MARY LOU RETTON

AFTER LISTENING TO AN EMOTIONAL SPEECH FROM
Coach Draveck and showering, we were dismissed to join our families and the Mon Valley contingent for a potluck picnic. Standing between me and the fans, though, was Rand Denton.

"Incredible job today, Julia," he said, shaking my hand.

"Thank you."

"I enjoyed covering your brothers' teams. You play so much like them."

"Not like a girl, you mean?"

Denton's smile faltered. "Look, Julia, I want to write a story about you because you're competing for the starting quarterback position of a state championship team. More interestingly, three of your brothers played this position before, which would be worth a story if you weren't state champs last year. And, yes, more interestingly, this is the first time a girl has ever played for this team. You might not want to be an icon or a symbol, but there's no way to get around that."

"What about Stanford?" I asked.

Denton's eyes widened. "You want me to write about your

competitor?"

"Did you plan to?"

"Not for this story," he admitted.

Embracing my identity as a girl around the team and being bold enough to wear a bikini to the pool were small steps—with teammates I respected. Submitting myself to the scrutiny of a reporter for a very public display in the regional newspaper—I hated to say it—intimidated me.

"I want to write about you and why you want to play. I want to talk about your successes today and interview the coaches about your skills. I'll even talk to some of your teammates. It's a feature story."

"Can I read it before it prints?"

Denton cringed. "We usually don't do that sort of thing."

"Why not?"

"Lots of reasons, really. Tell you what, you can see the photos, and I'll confirm accuracy of every one of your quotes before it prints."

The guy was going out of his way to accommodate my insecurities. In my head, I was starting to sound like a diva. Not a good sign. "That's not necessary," I said. "You wrote great stories about my brothers. They're plastered all over the walls in my house. I trust you."

He smiled. "I'll call you Monday."

****

WHEN I LOCATED MY FAMILY IN THE CROWD, IT WAS largely due to Jake sprinting toward me. He wrapped his arms around me and jolted me into a violent brotherly squeeze. "Little J! That was incredible!"

Juan ruffled the hair that had found its way clear from my ponytail. "Impressive, sis."

My parents and Abuelita greeted me similarly.

"Mi cielo, watching you play the football..." Abuelita fanned herself then leaned close. "Did it hurt when that boy pounced on you?"

"Sacked, Abuelita," Jake corrected.

"She knows the terminology," Juan said. "How could she not at this point?"

Abuelita winked at me.

"I have to agree with the brothers on this one."

I spun to find a tall, tan, and handsome Jorge behind me. "Jorge!"

"Best quarterbacking I've seen at Iron Valley since I played," Jorge said, hugging me. Of course, Jake objected.

"What are you doing here? You should be in Florida."

Jorge looked at our parents and sighed. "I quit."

"College?"

He laughed. "No. Football."

My brother quit football? *My brother?* A Medina quit football.

"Don't look so shocked."

"We were all shocked, dude," Jake said.

"Hey, if Julia can convince you to let her play football because that makes her happy, then I should be able to quit football if that's what makes me happy. Right, Little J?"

I shrugged. "Sure." Although I'd never known my brother not to play football or not be happy doing it.

The crowd gravitated from the field toward the cafeteria where the potluck picnic food was being combined with our normal cafeteria fare. But it didn't make sense. If Jorge hadn't been at football all those times, why didn't he answer our calls? I looped my arm in his and told him so.

"I found an internship, and the hours are long."

"An internship? Like you do...professional stuff?"

He hip-checked me. "I went to college for more than football, you know?"

"No. I didn't know that." I jabbed his ribs. "Actually, I'm glad to hear it. I thought you might be dissing me for some girl."

Jorge smirked. "There's always a girl, but I'd never ditch you for her, sis."

Another hip-check. This time, my sidestep reminded me of the soreness in my ankle. I grimaced, and Jorge immediately apologized.

"What were you thinking?" Jake scolded him. "She's injured, man."

Jake and Juan pushed their way past Jorge and lifted me onto their shoulders like a queen. Jorge walked behind us, spotting me. Mom jogged ahead to take pictures on her phone. Outside the cafeteria, they set me down on my good foot.

"I want a nice picture!" Mom said, and my brothers groaned. "No.

Don't even. All my babies together? That never happens."

She positioned us so that the background was the football field. My brothers huddled around *me*. No more days of me standing on the end—the youngest, the only girl. I was in the center. And I was wearing my purple Iron Valley Vikings shirt with the huge number 12 on it.

Juan's number. Jorge's number. Jake's number.

And now, my number.

Three quarterbacks for role models. No wonder I chose the gridiron. Knowing they'd *all* sat in the stands, watching and cheering for me my first time on the field—that was poetic. While my mom pleaded for us to smile, they pushed and tugged at each other behind our backs, where our parents couldn't see, but that didn't bother me. For the first time in my whole life, I lined up for a photo, not as the kid sister to the Medina quarterbacks but as a quarterback myself. I had nothing to do but smile.

****

SQUARE GRABBED ME AFTER MY FAMILY AND I FIN-ished eating. "I want you to meet someone." He gestured to a woman bounding toward me with the kind of gait that develops after years of chasing down three sons, and the pear-shaped body from cooking and baking for them day after day.

"Finally, I get to meet the girl my boy's been talking so much about."

"Mom!" Square objected, sounding more distressed than I'd ever heard him before.

"Oh, stop," she said and swatted at his hand. "You didn't tell me how pretty she was." She grinned conspiratorially. "Although I guessed that part for myself."

He closed his eyes and shook his head.

"Really?" I joined the teasing. "He's so serious around here."

"That way at home too, honey!" She swatted him with a rolled-up program. "It wouldn't hurt you to smile once in a while." She turned back to me, all smiles and energy. "But he played well today, didn't he?"

"He always does."

Mrs. Weaver nodded. We said our goodbyes, and a few seconds later, I felt another tap on the shoulder. Ally Malone stood behind me with a tentative smile. Without a thought about what had transpired between us, I wrapped her into a bear hug.

"You were amazing, Jules," she whispered.

Over her shoulder I caught Owen's eye and the sad smile that crossed his lips.

"I missed you," I said. "Do you have any idea what it's like to be with nobody but boys for an entire week?"

"I wish! I saw the swimming pool. Were they shirtless, like, all the time?"

"Not all the time," I said.

"I'd drool. I'd absolutely drool."

Then, as if realizing she'd said something she shouldn't have, she apologized. "Owen told me you broke up. I didn't mean to be insensitive about the other guys."

"Don't worry about it."

"You think there's a chance you could work it out?"

I'd asked myself the same question. Breaking up hadn't switched off my feelings for Owen, but how could I explain to Ally that my laser focus to compete pushed Owen to the side and suppressing that focus for him would make everything I'd done in the last two weeks seem futile. And then there was that promise of Christian calling me after the season ends. Did I want him to? I shook my head to clear the mess of thoughts inside of it, but that would take more time than a few minutes with my best friend.

"I don't know," I said. "I'm trying to focus on football and go from there."

"It shows. When will Coach name a starter?"

"I don't even know when he'll be back."

As much as I wanted the coveted title, my best chances were to compete against myself. If I could improve every day, then when Coach made the call, I'd know I did everything I could. That's what it was all about.

"How's volleyball?"

Ally smiled, but I knew from many years of friendship, it was the polite smile she used to cover up a feeling she'd rather not show. "Different."

I regretted mentioning the sport that had once tied us so close together yet also in a way tore us apart. Wanting to get back to how things used to be, I asked, "Would you want to come swim tomorrow or something?"

"Can't," she said. I thought I heard some disappointment in her voice. Or maybe that was me hoping. "I'm going to my mom's with a few of the girls to bake treats for camp this week."

Right. Something I'd helped with the last two years. I refused to imagine the kitchen surfaces covered with chocolate, sugar, flour, butter, and M&Ms—Ally always insisted on her favorite M&M cookies for camp—or the way Ally's mom would fawn over the girls, encouraging and admiring us.

Er, *them*.

And I definitely would not under any circumstances think about Owen sneaking into the kitchen to steal a cookie from the cooling rack or how the girls might react at the fact he was newly single. And on the high school market again.

"What about Monday evening," Ally asked. "You free then?"

Her question brought me back to the moment and to the joy I should've been feeling over our win. "We're conditioning in the evening when it's supposed to be cooler."

She nodded, the distance between us growing in the silence.

"We'll figure something out," she suggested, hugging me goodbye, but I couldn't be sure either of us believed it.

I really wanted to.

Being the politician she was, Abuelita worked the crowd, both advocating for my support as quarterback and for votes in the upcoming election. My parents chatted with friends, and my brothers drew plays on programs, napkins, anything they could find.

I found Brighton, D, and Square on the pool deck. To help us bond, the coaches had invited South Mon's team to join us. They agreed, but they mostly ate outside while our team congregated in the cafeteria. With the guys shirtless, telling our team apart from theirs was a little more difficult. One face in particular, though, was familiar.

"Number fifty-eight," I said as he dried off and walked toward me.

My team clustered around me, forcing him to raise his hands in surrender.

"I come in peace." He offered a handshake, but I wouldn't take it, not when he didn't deserve it.

"You purposely tried to hurt one of our receivers, and you played like a dick pretty much the whole game. And that doesn't even touch on the things you said."

He scoffed. "You got spunk. I'll give you that."

I crossed my arms.

"I came to concede. You're not bad, Medina."

"You mean, for a girl?"

He extended his hand again. "No. I mean you're not bad."

"Not bad" was synonymous with "good", but I supposed the compliment stretched his comfort zone enough. For now. I shook his hand and pushed his ass into the pool. At which point, Square scooped me up, D peeled my shoes off, and then we splashed into the refreshing water together. I felt like anything was possible on such a hot day with good food, good people, and laughter.

And, of course, football.

CHAPTER FORTY-THREE

THE POTENTIAL FOR GREATNESS LIVES WITHIN EACH OF US.
—WILMA RUDOLPH

I PACKED THE LAST OF MY PURPLE IRON VALLEY ATH-
letic clothes and rolled my towels and linens into a ball as per our
cabin cleanup instructions. Two small actions that transformed my
home at Camp Sweat and Tears back into an empty bedroom as if
I'd never been there at all.

But I had been. I'd collapsed onto that awful, two-inch thick cot
after long days. I'd studied the playbook until I passed out with it
on my chest. I'd read Jake's journal and added my own flavor to the
pages. And speaking of flavor, I'd probably be leaving lots of crumbs
behind from protein bars and crackers.

"Beep! Beep!" someone yelled from outside. I favored my ankle as
I backpedaled through the cabin, committing every detail to memory.

Outside, Square threw my suitcase into the back of the golf cart.
"A lot lighter this time around."

"I drank the Gatorade."

"Not all of it, I hope," D said from behind the wheel. "I might get
thirsty on the bus. What then?"

I climbed into the seat next to him. "Then you drink your own

Gatorade."

"I thought we was cool," he mumbled and slammed his foot down on the golf cart in that way of his. We tore through the camp fast, even by D's standards.

"Let's not end up dead," Square said, and D might have slowed down a little.

Maybe not.

As we passed the guys' cabins, a few teammates begged for a ride. D flew by, leaving them in a cloud of swirling dirt.

"Cold," Square said, but we all had smiles on our faces.

Holding on with two hands, I prepared for D's abrupt stop next to the busses. My suitcase, however, flew into Square's leg. He swore. D laughed. Good times.

Once we were all settled on the bus, the coaches released the electronics. The earbuds went in, and it was like the world had reclaimed us from the bubble Coach Vincent and the staff had attempted to create. But not for long. The bus driver steered us deeper into the property—not toward the exit. Slowly, the team noticed, and the questions started.

"Where are we going?"

"You know the exit's the other way, right?"

"You don't think they're making us run again, do you?"

My ankle and I hoped not. Resting it the last day of practices had been a good call, but so had playing today. The mild soreness should subside after some icing and a day and a half of rest, especially key given my performance in the scrimmage. I'd shut down my critics. At least on that day. Bouncing around in my seat on that bus, I knew there'd be plenty more critics to silence.

After a sudden stop along the main throughway of the camp, Coach Draveck called to everyone to get off. He led us into the woods, and D yelled, "This is how scary movies start."

"And every one of your ghost stories," Square quipped.

"Don't get him started," Jones muttered.

While D defended his ability to tell a killer ghost story, the creek we'd swum in our first night at camp came into view. The heat of the afternoon fought the breeze and the shade of the canopy of trees. As a senior without any college athletic prospects, the fact I'd never again be back to Camp Sweat and Tears made the sparkling creek twinkle even more. And the green of the trees deeper and yet brighter at the same time.

And the team, more like brothers than strangers. Or maybe it was the week we'd spent together rather than the nostalgia that did that.

Coach Draveck climbed onto a tree stump so everyone could see him. "It's been a hell of a week, team," he said. In the last few days, the coaches had shifted from referring to the group as boys, guys, or men and instead now called us "team."

I liked that.

"You worked hard. You fought through weather, injury, criticism, an intense incident with your coach, and an outright attack on one of our own." He made eye contact with me, his gaze dark, a look that told me he would protect me from anything or anyone. I had to fight a tear. "I'm proud of you. And Coach Vincent's proud of you too."

Draveck pulled his phone from behind his back. On the screen was a paler version of Coach Vincent. He had an Iron Valley shirt over his hospital gown. The team cheered so loud Vincent scrambled to turn his volume down on his phone. A nurse rushed into the background to check his monitors.

"I'm fine," Coach said. "That was my team."

We waved.

"Keep it down," Vincent said. "I don't want them doing any more tests on me."

Everyone laughed.

"I'm honored to be here with you today, even if from a distance. There's lots to say, and trust me, I'll say it as soon as I'm back, but right now, I have a very important task for one of you."

Of course! Filling the Viking Jug.

I wished Vincent were there face-to-face, but if I learned anything about my brothers being far away, video chatting was better than nothing. My teammates' smiling faces communicated they felt the same. Contrary to our last time here when the team doubled over, leaned on trees, or sat on rocks and fallen logs, today they stood tall. Refreshed bodies. More confidence.

Unified.

"Earlier today, after the scrimmage," Coach continued, "you all cast a ballot for a teammate who earned your respect this week. Many players received votes, which shouldn't be any surprise. You all are to be respected. Yet as these things go, there was a clear leader."

Draveck passed his phone to Brighton, who was standing next to him, so he could open his backpack.

"Every year since I became head coach for this team, one player was selected by their peers to fill the Viking Jug!"

Draveck raised the familiar plastic container shaped like our mascot and painted purple and black, and the team cheered. The last time I saw the jug was Jake's sophomore year, when he was selected for the honor. Vincent limited the award to a one-time experience, so the last two years, the jug had been given to graduating seniors.

Which basically meant everyone on the team was eligible for the honor.

Filling the jug with water was no big deal. Your team voting for you to be the one to fill it though? That mattered.

I'd debated my vote. A lot. D elevated the play of everyone around him. He encouraged and cheered, and he led with action too. Square was the strongest linebacker on the team, and his no nonsense attitude kept everyone serious and working hard when they might otherwise goof off.

And Owen. How could I not consider a guy who set aside his own desires for a position and humbly admitted when someone else was better at it than he was. Not to mention, he also earned it with his game.

Brighton stepped up as receiver in a big way, and rather than going into the season with one standout—Owen—we had two incredible targets on the field.

Other players like Drew Peters, who'd really impressed in the slot; Ben Jones, who got over me touching his butt to block for me as if he were auditioning for the Steel Curtain; and even Austin Moody, who played defense like a dog chasing raw meat, were valid contenders.

Ultimately, I'd cast my ballot for Owen.

Maybe a little because my heart told me to. Or because I felt like I'd taken something from his grasp and this was an opportunity to give something else back.

But mostly because he deserved it.

"This week, we saw big hits and big plays," Vincent continued. "You ran and pushed and dug so deep you thought you didn't have anything left. But then you found more in yourselves. Any one of you could have been selected for this, but every player on this team had a voice in this decision, which makes it truly special."

As the announcement approached, I watched Owen, eager to see his reaction if he won the honor. Hoping he did.

"Coach Draveck, can you do the honors?"

Draveck hopped down from the stump and paced around the group. The team called him out for his suspenseful tactics, but he enjoyed the torture too much to stop. He slowed near Square, D, and me, and I wondered which of them it would be. Either would have been a great choice.

But then the jug was in my hands. Hands pounded on my back and arms. They even ruffled my hair and lifted me onto their shoulders. It was the ultimate end zone celebration.

The Iron Valley Viking Jug was in my hands. My teammates had voted to put it there.

They . . . *respected* me.

Back on my feet, I stumbled toward the creek. The rumble of cheers continued with Square and D leading the howling. Owen stepped forward and offered me his arm. This time, I felt confident taking it. Accepting help didn't make me weak. It made me smart.

It made me strong.

I kicked off my shoes and socks.

"Thanks," I said.

He helped me down the hillside to the creek with a proud smile. "Congratulations."

Alone in the water, I looked back at my team. Smiling. Cheering. Hooting. And even D dancing. The coaches clapped too. An image of my first time stepping into the huddle came to me. My offensive line had barely looked at me. Now, they didn't look away. While I might not have gotten his vote, even Moody clapped.

I wondered if I should say something but didn't want to disrupt the celebration. There'd be plenty of time for speeches and pep talks in the next three months—every time I led my team onto the field and in every huddle. I scooped that jug so deep into the water that my sleeve got wet, and I didn't bring it back up until it was full to the brim.

AKNOWLEDGMENTS

FOR A BOOK THAT HAS BEEN MORE THAN FIVE YEARS in the making, I am blessed to have many individuals to thank, and I'm grateful you'll indulge me as I take the time to do so. I always tell my children to find their people in life—the souls with whom they instantly connect, who make them better, and who help them feel at home.

These are my people.

Thank you to my writing friends, teachers, and colleagues at Jacksonville University, the University of St. Andrews, and Indiana University of Pennsylvania. Thank you to my long-time friends from the Mary Roberts Rinehart Chapter of Sisters in Crime, Backspace, and PennWriters. Special thanks to the late Ramona Defelice Long, a wonderful writing teacher and friend with whom I wish I could share this triumph. Attending conferences and workshops with you all taught me about writing and life. Thank you.

I value my writing community more than this acknowledgements page could show. Please accept my deepest gratitude for keeping me positive and willing to push forward. First, huge thanks to the Pitch Wars community, founded by Brenda Drake. Thank you to Molly E. Lee for selecting me as a mentee and to the amazing 2016 class of writers who continue to inspire me every year. Your friendships have far surpassed that of writing colleagues.

Thank you to the readers who have graciously given feedback on early drafts of this book: Jeff Boarts, Jennifer Camiccia, Tara Creel, Annette Dashofy, Kimberly Gabriel, Domenick Girardi, Michael Girardi, Tracy Gold, Jenny Howe, Melissa Nasson, Abigail G. Scheg, Carol Silvis, and Mary Sutton. Thank you especially to my authenticity readers: Libardo Arteaga, Natalia Carpenter, Jamie Beth Cohen, Rachida Essadiq, Valerie Gray, Ashley Pujol, and the amazing Hoover family: Maria, Gordon, Gordy, Grant, and Gianna!

Thank you to the many authors and friends who have offered encouragement, especially in the times I've needed it most: Patrick Bizzaro, Jeff Boarts, Amanda Coffin, Tara Creel, Annette Dashofy, Karen Dionne, Rebecca Drake, Timons Esaias, Tracy Gold, Gennie Gorback, Amy Leskowski, Jonathan Maberry, Nancy Martin, Nova McBee, Susan Meier, Hema Penmetsa, Martha Reed, Sharon Roat, JE Taylor, the Query Warriors, and the Pitch Wars 2016 "AmWriting" Group especially Cass, Elesha, Elliot, Gwynne, Ian, Jen, Meghan, Rosalyn, and Tracie.

To everyone who has kept my kids safe and entertained over the years so I could write: India Awes, Oliva Awes, Barbara Girardi, Lauri Killian, Delaney Lantz, Grace Love, Janet Menhart, Josette Monteleone, Alexis Shirley, and Jessica Stawinski. To my band of work colleagues at HACC—you know who you are! To the librarians at the Community Library of Allegheny Valley, especially Valerie, Bridget, and Casey, who made sure I could still read good books in the midst of lockdown and gave me an unlimited borrowing capacity. To my alma mater, Valley High School, for welcoming me to take my author photos in the stadium where I envisioned Julia playing and to photographer Haley Rosa for taking them with such creativity and style.

To my besties: Janet Menhart, BFF extraordinaire and official Recorder of Names for all my books. I love you! Alicia Giordano for our daily walks and wonderful friendship. Thank you for listening to me talk about writing and helping me laugh about the chaos of life. Heidi Waugaman for always bringing the biggest smile and loving encouragement every time I see her. Abigail G. Scheg for the most hilarious margin comments and your unfailing belief in my work.

To my siblings by blood and by marriage: Roxanne, Wes, Scott, George, Michael, Colleen, David, and Kristen—thank you for your love, support, and encouragement. My deepest gratitude to my parents in heaven, ChrisAnne and Gregory Simpson, and to the grandparents who adopted me and became my parents, the late Anne and Clarence Farneth. You always told me I could do anything, and I believed you. Thank you. I desperately wish you were here to hold this book in your hands.

Thank you also to my found family—the Monteleones who started as neighbors and became so much more. To my mother-in-law, Barbara, and father-in-law, Frank—you have taken me in as your own daughter, and I'm so blessed.

Nova McBee, I owe you more than words can articulate. Thank you for thinking of this book and sending it to your publisher with such a glowing recommendation. Your kindness truly knows no bounds, and kindness is important to me above all else. I'm blessed to know you.

To the team at Wise Wolf Books for loving my writing—there is no better gift for a writer! Thank you to my publisher Rachel Del Grosso for believing in Julia's story and for your kind and patient guidance throughout this experience. Thank you Mandi Andrejka and Sam Towns for your editing prowess, Kristin Yahner for ensuring this book gets into the hands of readers, and Laura Sarrafan for designing the best cover.

Julia's story is about many things, and football is absolutely one of them. Thank you to my friends who played football in high school and college and talked about it all the time! Thank you to the entire Girardi family—the most intense football family I know. Thank you, David, for answering my last minute editing questions about Xs and Os. Thank you to Mike King and the Knoch coaching staff for allowing me to observe football camp. Thank you to Brooke Liebsch for sharing your experiences playing the quarterback position in high school, college, and then professionally.

Publishing a young adult novel has been a goal of mine for the past fifteen years. So many others have supported me along the way. Please know you all have my gratitude.

On one of our first dates in high school, a special person who happened to also be the quarterback of the football team took me to a local park to teach me the proper way to throw a football. Later at dinner, he drew up plays on the back of our restaurant placemats, quizzing me on where I'd throw the ball when the safety moved this way or that. For this book, he taught me the Slugo Seam Route, how to execute three-step and five-step drops, and more. I'm blessed to call him my husband and my partner in life. Thank you, Dom. Love.

And to our four children: Frank, I promised you when you were a baby that by the time you were old enough to read it, I'd publish a book that would make you proud. I hope I've fulfilled that promise. To my girls, Clara and Gabriella, it's my deepest wish that you will read about Julia and know that you can take on any challenge you want in life, even if some small-minded people think otherwise. To Domenick, keep throwing those touchdown passes. I love catching them. You four bring me such joy. My writing journey hasn't been easy or quick, but I hope it's shown you a little about following your dreams with tenacity.

All my love...

ABOUT THE AUTHOR

TAMARA GIRARDI GREW UP PLAYING SPORTS WITH THE neighborhood kids. Often the only girl, she loved nothing more than smashing a home run at the opportune moment or stealing the basketball from one of the guys and scoring two on a breakaway. In high school, she fell in love with the quarterback and played football in the back yard with him and his two quarterback brothers. Watching them play, she wondered, "What would it be like if they'd had a baby sister? Would she play quarterback, too?" And just like that, the idea for Gridiron Girl was born.

Also an academic, Tamara is an Associate Professor of English at HACC, Central Pennsylvania's Community College where she teaches creative writing, technical writing, composition, and literature online. She has a PhD in English from Indiana University of Pennsylvania and studied fiction at the University of St. Andrews in Scotland. Tamara also writes picture books.

She lives in a suburb of Pittsburgh, Pennsylvania with her husband and four adorably rambunctious children.

ABOUT THE AUTHOR